The Steppenwolf

The Steppenwolf

Hermann Hesse

TRANSLATED BY Kurt Beals

W. W. NORTON & COMPANY
Independent Publishers Since 1923

For information about permission to reproduce selections from this
book, write to Permissions, W. W. Norton & Company, Inc.,
500 Fifth Avenue, New York, NY 10110

For information about special discounts for bulk purchases,
please contact W. W. Norton Special Sales at specialsales@wwnorton.com
or 800-233-4830

Manufacturing by Lake Book Manufacturing
Book design by Lovedog Studio
Production manager: Julia Druskin

Library of Congress Control Number: 2022054806

ISBN 978-1-324-10599-2 pbk.

W. W. Norton & Company, Inc., 500 Fifth Avenue, New York, N.Y. 10110
www.wwnorton.com

W. W. Norton & Company Ltd., 15 Carlisle Street, London W1D 3BS

1 2 3 4 5 6 7 8 9 0

INTRODUCTION

BY THE TIME THE CANADIAN AMERICAN ROCK BAND Steppenwolf released their single "Born to Be Wild" in 1968, the German Swiss author Hermann Hesse had been dead for more than five years. There is no way to be sure, then, just what the Nobel Prize–winning novelist would have thought of the seminal heavy metal hit, or of the biker movie *Easy Rider*, which appeared the following year and helped boost the song to even greater popularity. Nevertheless, Hesse's 1927 novel *Der Steppenwolf* (translated as *The Steppenwolf* or just *Steppenwolf*), from which the band took its name, provides some clues. The novel's titular protagonist, Harry Haller, shares more than a few features with Hesse himself: both the novelist and his character have the initials H.H.; both were born in Germany but moved to Switzerland; both were pacifists; both were nearing fifty in the period when the novel unfolds.[1] In the novel, the reclusive intellectual Harry Haller worships Mozart, while initially despising jazz, gramophones, the radio, and movies made to entertain the masses. Such a curmudgeon could hardly be expected to enjoy a rock-anthem-turned-film-soundtrack that became a staple of biker culture. Thus, if this resemblance between author and protagonist is any guide, Hesse would likely have struggled to find any pleasure in "Born to Be Wild."

Yet Haller's misanthropy is only half the story, as readers of the novel will discover—and as the members of the band Steppenwolf apparently discovered only later, having adopted the name at the suggestion of their producer before they took the time to read the novel.[2] While Harry Haller appears at the beginning as a man of uncompromising tastes and judgments—repeatedly expressing his admiration for Mozart and Goethe and his disdain for the intellectual posturing and pretensions of his own contemporaries—he learns over the course of the novel to appreciate the charms and thrills of more worldly amusements. Haller purchases a gramophone, learns the latest jazz dances, and eventually overcomes his strongest inhibitions to test out his newly acquired dance steps in public. But this metamorphosis from a lone wolf into a social butterfly is only an early stage in the transformation that Haller undergoes; in lieu of spoilers, suffice it to say that things get much, much wilder. An indication of just how wild things get for Harry Haller can be seen in the endorsement that *The Steppenwolf* and Hesse's other greatest hit, *Siddhartha*, garnered from Timothy Leary, the prophet of psychedelics: "Before your LSD session, read *Siddhartha* and *Steppenwolf*." Indeed, for all its historical grounding in the Switzerland of the 1920s, there is something very 1960s about some sections of *The Steppenwolf*. Had Harry Haller lived forty years later, he might well have been won over not by 1920s jazz hits like "Yearning" or "Valencia," but by 1960s rock anthems like "Born to Be Wild."

WHILE THE WILDNESS OF *The Steppenwolf* clearly scratched an itch for certain sixties icons, in other respects this novel seems like the unlikeliest candidate among Hesse's works for rediscovery by a generation so strongly associated with youthful rebellion—because what sets Harry Haller apart from Hesse's other notable protagonists is, above all, his age. In general, Hesse's major works (not just *Siddhartha*, but also *Demian*, *Narcissus and Goldmund*, and *The Glass Bead Game*, to name only the most prominent) tend to focus on young men who embark on journeys of self-discovery.

They follow, to a greater or lesser degree, the model of the German bildungsroman, the novel of education or coming-of-age.[3] While the temporal scope of some of these books (such as *Siddhartha*) extends beyond the protagonist's youth, even encompassing old age and death, the youthful drive to self-discovery and self-realization is an essential ingredient in each of these works. As Adam Kirsch wrote in *The New Yorker* in 2018, "The stories [Hesse] tells appeal to young people because they keep faith with the powerful emotions of adolescence, which most adults forget or outgrow—the woundedness, the exaltation, the enormous demands on life."[4]

With all of these tales of youth to choose from, why did young readers in the sixties turn to Hesse's tale of Harry Haller—the Steppenwolf, rapidly approaching fifty, his best days seemingly behind him, whose gout-ridden limbs make it difficult for him to climb the stairs to his garret? (Perhaps I should say "youngish readers"—Leary himself was pushing fifty by the end of the decade.) One possible answer would be that this attraction was the product of a misunderstanding, as Hesse himself suggested in a brief afterword to the book written in 1941 and first published in 1942 in Switzerland, while Germany was under Nazi rule. There Hesse attributed the frequent "misunderstanding" of the book "in part, but only in part, to the fact that this book, written by a fifty-year-old and dealing with problems pertaining to that same age, very frequently fell into the hands of quite young readers." But there are other possibilities as well. Rather than accuse these young readers of misunderstanding the problems of late middle age, perhaps we can read Harry Haller himself, the Steppenwolf, as a figure who "keep[s] faith with the powerful emotions of adolescence."

Or to put it in slightly different terms, perhaps we can see *The Steppenwolf* as a sort of epilogue or sequel to the unwritten bildungsroman of Harry Haller. Although we learn very little about the Steppenwolf's childhood and youth, the hints that the novel provides suggest that he, like many of Hesse's protagonists, set out as a young man to discover himself, to become the person he was destined to be; and he has remained true to that goal, despite the suffering it has caused him. Indeed, his journey seems to have brought him far more pain than glory. The lonely, gouty Harry Haller, particularly as the novel begins, is hardly a figure to be emulated or envied; it would be easier to pity him, if his own stubborn pride did not prohibit us from doing so. But even in his misery, Haller embodies a sort of integrity, refusing to compromise with a world that fails to live up to his standards. Thus for readers coming of age in the sixties—a generation that famously didn't trust anyone over thirty—Haller (and Hesse) might have embodied a perverse sort of hope: the possibility that youthful ideals need not inevitably yield to cynical pragmatism, that the self need not always be corrupted by the obligation to adhere to social norms, to conform, to cut one's hair, join the army, get a job.

But if this is indeed the message that readers in the sixties took from *The Steppenwolf*, they were only getting half the story, and Hesse's earlier accusations of "misunderstanding" did not entirely miss the mark—because Haller's persistent postadolescent alienation is only the starting point, not the end point of the novel. As I have already noted, despite his advancing years, the Harry Haller we meet at the outset has not yet overcome his youthful restlessness and settled into a suitable social niche in which he can spend his adult years; unlike the prototypical protagonist of a bildungsroman, he has not been reconciled and reincorporated into society, though he flirts with such assimilation by leading his nonconformist life in rented rooms of bourgeois apartment buildings, living in the "normie" world without being of it. And yet, even as he persists in living on his own terms, the

Steppenwolf begins to feel what kids today (or yesterday) might call FOMO—or perhaps not so much the fear of missing out as the fear that he has already missed out, that he has let too many chances in life pass him by and has missed the opportunity to become the person he once had the potential to be. And, strikingly, he has missed this opportunity precisely by following the path taken by other Hesse heroes—by setting himself apart from society, from his peers, from the life of the world, and dedicating himself to his own peculiar predilections. In his stubborn insistence on living life on his own terms, Haller has missed out on a great deal of what the world has to offer to less ascetic, less hermetic natures—and this is precisely what the Steppenwolf on the verge of fifty sets out to discover.

HESSE, AS MENTIONED ABOVE, was also nearing fifty as he wrote *The Steppenwolf*, and the author's similarities to his character do not end there—though, to be sure, there are also striking differences. Hermann Hesse was born in 1877 in Calw, Germany, a small town located in the northern Black Forest, roughly halfway between Stuttgart and the Rhine. His mother had been born in India to German Protestant missionaries, though raised in Germany; his father grew up among the German-speaking minority of Estonia, part of the Russian Empire at the time. While this distinctive family background, together with his Pietist religious upbringing, may have helped to make Hermann Hesse a bit of a misfit in his provincial southwestern German surroundings, his family's connections to the outside world also instilled in him an international sensibility, and particularly a curiosity about Eastern religions, which would later play an important role in his literary works. (His maternal grandfather was not only a missionary but also a scholar and linguist who compiled a grammar of Malayalam, a Dravidian language spoken in parts of southern India.) After a youth that included both boarding school and a mental institution, as well as threats of suicide, at the age of eighteen Hesse found work at a bookshop in Tübingen, Germany. Four years later, he took a similar position in Basel, Switzerland, while devoting much of his free time to his own literary work. His first novel, *Peter Camenzind*, published in 1904, became a bestseller, and Hesse resolved henceforth to earn his livelihood as a writer.

That same year, he married Maria Bernoulli, with whom he would have three sons. The family initially lived in southern Germany, but in 1912, following Hesse's return from a long trip to Sri Lanka, Indonesia, and other Far Eastern destinations, they moved to Bern, Switzerland. During the First World War, Hesse spoke out publicly for peace from this neutral ground, drawing criticism from the nationalist German press. Meanwhile, his wife began to suffer from mental illness, which contributed to the dissolution of their marriage—an episode that has echoes in Harry Haller's backstory. After their divorce in 1923, Hesse would marry two more times. The next year, he entered into what would be a three-year marriage to the Swiss singer and painter Ruth Wenger. In 1931 he married the art historian Ninon Dolbin (born Ninon Ausländer in Czernowitz, now Chernivtsi, Ukraine), a union that would endure until the end of his life.

It was in the midst of all this domestic turmoil and transition that Hesse produced his most memorable works of fiction. His novella *Siddhartha*, published in 1922, is set in the world of Gautama Buddha. While drawing on Hesse's explorations of Eastern religions and philosophy and his own travels to South Asia, *Siddhartha* explores many of the same themes of self-discovery and the search for fulfillment that run through the author's works set in European contexts; indeed, his biographer Gunnar Decker has argued that the novella's emphasis on self-discovery and its rejection of discipleship "undoubtedly had more of Nietzsche's Zarathustra about it than of Buddha. 'Don't follow me, follow yourself.' For it was not a question of renouncing the Self but precisely about finding it. This was a very Western line of thought."[5]

A similarly syncretistic, though ultimately Western, impulse can be found in *The Steppenwolf,* which first appeared in print five years after *Siddhartha.* While this novel can be read, from one perspective, as the narrative of Harry Haller's search for fulfillment, from another perspective it is, like most of Hesse's fiction, a meditation on human nature, and as such it draws on an eclectic range of sources. One source for *The Steppenwolf,* as for *Siddhartha,* is the philosophy of Friedrich Nietzsche. Just a few pages into the novel, in the fictional "Editor's Foreword" (ostensibly written by the nephew of the woman from whom Haller rents his room), we read: "I recognized that Haller was a genius of suffering, that he, in the spirit of some of Nietzsche's sayings, had cultivated within himself an ingenious, limitless, terrible capacity for suffering." But Nietzsche is not the only author who influences Haller's view of human nature. Unattributed traces of the Swiss psychiatrist Carl Jung's psychoanalytic theories can be identified throughout the novel, while Haller's self-conception as a creature composed of both wolf and human natures is derived in part from Goethe's *Faust,* with its famous line "Two souls, alas, are housed within my breast!" Yet this notion of a bifurcated human identity is not allowed to stand unchallenged in the novel. In fact, the Faustian view of the self is first made explicit, but then criticized, in an odd pamphlet entitled *Treatise on the Steppenwolf* that Haller receives from a man on the street, in which he finds his own life both described and scrutinized. This treatise invokes Buddhist thought in elaborating a vision of not two, but "countless" souls housed within the human breast.

It is hardly surprising, then, that when Hesse received the Nobel Prize for Literature in 1946, *The Steppenwolf* was praised in the presentation speech as "an inspired account of the split in human nature, the tension between desire and reason in an individual who is outside the social and moral notions of everyday life." However, what exactly it means to live "outside" these "social and moral notions" can surely be a matter of debate. At times, Hesse garnered criticism for his failure to speak out as clearly as many of his contemporaries did against the political developments of his age. There is no question that Hesse was appalled by the Nazis' rise to power, and he had made no secret of his pacifism and his opposition to nationalism and anti-Semitism. His third wife, Ninon Dolbin, was Jewish, and he continued to write reviews of books by Jewish authors after the Nazis came to power, an implicit protest that drew attacks from supporters of the regime. Hesse also opened his home in Switzerland to a number of refugees from Nazi Germany, and lent support of various kinds to fellow writers, including Thomas Mann and Bertolt Brecht, when they went into exile.[6] Nevertheless, he did not adopt as vocal a stance against the Nazis as either of these authors, opting instead for a "politics of detachment" for which he was sometimes condemned.[7] Still, Hesse's literary works—which were ultimately banned by the Nazis in 1943—clearly offer a philosophical and ethical, if not an overtly political, basis for opposition to fascism and other violent, nationalist ideologies. Hesse's failure to more vocally oppose the Nazis was in no way an expression of indifference or neutrality; rather, it was symptomatic of his lifelong tendency to keep his distance from the world. When he was awarded the Nobel Prize, he complained "that the world had decided to 'stone him to death' with letters and messages of congratulation" and responded by retreating to a sanatorium.[8] After receiving the prize, he never wrote another novel.

CERTAINLY HESSE'S OWN UNWORLDLINESS is reflected in the character of the Steppenwolf Harry Haller. That the author should manifest himself in his protagonist is no surprise: Hesse once called art (in his case, writing) "a long, varied, and tortuous route, whose aim is to express the personality of the artist's Self so comprehensively . . . that this Self is ultimately unwrapped and laid bare."[9] Still, as I have suggested above, it would be a mistake to too closely identify the creator with his creation. To begin with, while the two suffer from a number of the same problems—suicidal tendencies, a marriage destroyed by mental illness, the general maladies of advancing age—there are also notable differences. For instance, Hesse, by 1927, had become a much more successful author than Haller seems to be (though Haller is said to have published multiple books, and also writes for newspapers). There is also no indication that Haller has children. Of course, such differences might be dismissed as minor concessions made for the sake of plausible deniability, window dressing to allow the author to make confessions in the guise of fiction that he would not make in a memoir. But there is a more striking reason to avoid assuming such a one-to-one correspondence: namely, the fact that Harry Haller is not the novel's only stand-in for Hermann Hesse.

Particularly notable in this regard is the young woman named Hermine whose acquaintance Harry first makes at a tavern called the Black Eagle. At least, she seems to be named Hermine, and she is called by this name throughout the book; but more skeptical readers might have their doubts. After all, rather than simply tell Harry what her name is, this young woman makes him guess, and in the process draws his attention to the fact that she sometimes has "a boy's face." This prompts Harry to observe: "her face began to speak to me, it reminded me of my own boyhood, and of a friend I had back then whose name was Hermann." He tells her, "If you were a boy . . . your name would have to be Hermann," then tries his luck with the feminine form of the same name, asking, "Is your name Hermine?"—and the putative Hermine nods in affirmation. But is this really her name, or does Hermine allow Harry to believe that it is, to turn her into anyone he wants her to be? To what extent is Hermine a projection of Harry's own psyche, an alter ego? Surely the fact that she resembles Harry's childhood friend, who in turn shares Hermann Hesse's first name, is hardly a coincidence. If the Steppenwolf Harry Haller's breast contains not one, not two, but "countless" souls, as the odd treatise tells him, perhaps *The Steppenwolf*, Hermann Hesse's novel, contains not one, but two, or even countless incarnations of its author.

Such ambiguity and multiplicity is not confined to the blending identities of the novel's characters; rather, throughout the novel, the lines between reality and fantasy are also frequently blurred, transgressed, or rendered irrelevant. When Harry Haller sees letters of light dancing on the gray stone wall that surrounds the yard of an old cloister—letters that then leap off the wall and tumble down onto the ground at his feet—we surely aren't expected to take this literally, are we? And yet, if those letters are not really there, how can we explain the fact that this apparition accurately foretells Harry's later adventures? If those letters are all in his mind, does that go for his later adventures as well? Likewise, the episode in which a stranger presents Harry with the mysterious *Treatise on the Steppenwolf*—in which Harry himself is described—is so improbable as to defy belief, and yet so integral to subsequent developments in the novel that it simply must be true. But true in what sense? Do these fantastical events actually unfold in the reality of the objective world that Harry inhabits, alongside his fellow lodgers and the upright citizens of Switzerland? Or do they represent a parallel reality that exists primarily in Harry's own mind, though at times intersecting with events in the outside world?

Readers who prefer their reality somewhat less wild—readers, that is, who take the latter view—can find support for their position in the aforementioned Editor's Foreword. The narrator of this foreword, while acknowledging the limits of his acquaintance with the Steppenwolf, opines: "It has not been possible for me to determine to what extent the experiences recounted in Haller's manuscript are based in reality. I have no doubt that for the most part they are fiction, not in the sense of arbitrary invention, but in the sense that they attempt to express profound experiences of the soul in the guise of outwardly visible events." But despite his fundamental skepticism, he adds, "I have no doubt that they also have some element of real, external experience at their core." This may indeed be the most reasonable reading, and those readers who feel most comfortable when fiction conforms to the rules of real, external reality can take solace in the editor's perspective. The world, he reassures us, isn't nearly as wild as the Steppenwolf says; the wildest stuff was all inside Haller's head. And yet, this fictional editor, who dutifully pursues his day job when he is not tinkering with his amateur radio set or perusing the papers that the Steppenwolf left behind, is perhaps the least compelling figure we encounter in these pages. Whatever dangers and delusions the Steppenwolf's worldview may entail, there is no question that the tale he tells contains far more excitement than the editor's ever could.

To the editor's assertion of the primacy of objective reality, the Steppenwolf might well respond: "Yes, very well, the world that I describe diverges in countless ways from the world as it appears to you. But even if it lives, in part, inside my head, how much *more* real is that world than the pretty, predictable, bourgeois world that greets you every day?" What is clear, in any case, is that this text, with all its layers, seeks not to lead us to a single, preordained conclusion, but instead to tempt us with a multitude of possible interpretations—much like the multitude of doors that confront Harry in Pablo's magic theater, and the mirrors (a recurrent motif in the novel) in which reality is not only reflected but also multiplied. Should we seek the safety of the editor's worldview? The wildness of Harry's? Should we accept the bifurcated self that Harry initially imagines, or the countless selves as laid out in the *Treatise*? Are all the figures Harry encounters—Hermine, Maria, Pablo, even the "immortals" Goethe and Mozart—merely aspects of Harry's own psyche, expressions of insights already latent in Harry's own mind, or are they guides to take him beyond the boundaries of his own consciousness? The novel's multiple layers of narrative and reality also invite the reader to recognize the holes in Harry's own self-image, undercutting or at least complicating Hesse's allegedly "totally unironic self-seriousness."[10]

PERHAPS THESE GLANCING ENCOUNTERS, if that is what they are, between events in Harry's mind and events in the world around him could be compared to the description that the philosopher Walter Benjamin, a contemporary of Hesse's, offered of the art of translation: "Just as a tangent touches a circle lightly and at but one point, with this touch rather than with the point setting the law according to which it is to continue on its straight path to infinity, a translation touches the original lightly and only at the infinitely small point of the sense."[11] The reality within Harry's mind, we might conclude, likewise touches the reality of the outside world at but one infinitely small point; yet that intersection proves infinitely rich. This richness becomes all the more apparent in the process of translation, in which the subtleties and nuances of Hesse's narrative are brought into relief. *Der Steppenwolf* first appeared in German in 1927, and the first

English-language translation, by Basil Creighton, was published in 1929.[12] Creighton's translation was subsequently reissued in two different revisions in 1963—one in Great Britain (revised by Walter Sorell), the other in the United States (revised by Joseph Mileck and Horst Frenz). In the past twenty years, additional translations have appeared by David Horrocks and Thomas Wayne. Amid this plenitude of translations, what need is there for another?

One answer comes from Gregory Rabassa, the renowned translator of Gabriel García Márquez, among others: "I have always felt that while the original endures and remains eternally young, the translation ages and must be replaced." Certainly some of Creighton's formulations appear more dated today in English than Hesse's do in German. And Creighton (or perhaps the publisher of his translation) made certain concessions to the mores of his age that Hesse apparently deemed unnecessary: Creighton's translation simply omits several mentions of sex between women (though he retains a reference to the "spell of Lesbos"), and in one instance, he magically transforms a prostitute into a "servant." More than these isolated editorial interventions, though, Creighton's translation and, to a lesser extent, more recent translations have failed to reproduce the mood and atmosphere of the book, its stark immediacy, and the characteristic energy of Hesse's prose. If each of those translations, and my own, is only a tangent that lightly touches the original, I like to think that my tangent touches that circle at a significantly different point.

Of course, I do not mean to dismiss the accomplishments of these previous translators, or to deny the merits of their translations; every translation is an interpretation, and two translations may be both different and equally justified. In addition, I have benefited in this new translation from the opportunity to compare my own readings and renderings to those of all of the previous translators, though I did not consult their translations as I worked on my own, instead waiting until I had a complete draft in hand before making comparisons. At times, these comparisons revealed unambiguous errors in the earlier translations, or unconvincing interpretations of the German text. In a handful of other cases, I found the interpretations of earlier translators more plausible than my own, and revised mine accordingly. This is, of course, one benefit of retranslation, both for the new translator and for the reader. In contrast to the legend of the Septuagint, in which seventy translators, working independently, allegedly produced identical Greek translations of the Hebrew Bible, successive retranslations do not aim to be identical or perfect, but they can offer an incremental, asymptotic approximation to the impossible ideal of a single "correct" translation. If my translation corrects some errors of earlier translators, while their translations in turn have helped me to recognize and correct my own, the resulting translation is, hopefully, not only a version of *The Steppenwolf* that will appeal in style and tone to twenty-first-century readers, but also one that comes closer than any previous translation to an accurate rendering of the German text.

Perhaps the most conspicuous departure that I have made from all previous English-language translations is the simple inclusion of the definite article in the title: *The Steppenwolf*. The article is there in Hesse's German—*Der Steppenwolf*—and yet no previous English translator has followed Hesse's lead. The decision makes a difference. Hesse's protagonist, Harry Haller, is not Steppenwolf in the way that Peter Parker is Spider-Man or Clark Kent is Superman; he does not wear the title like a superhero's proper name. Rather, he is The Steppenwolf in the way that, say, Christopher Newman in Henry James's novel is *The American*. That is to say, he is the particular Steppenwolf who concerns us in this particular novel, but that does not mean that there might not be others out there in the world; at times, in fact, Harry himself even refers to "Steppenwolves" in the plural.

Of course, one could go further and translate the word "Steppenwolf" itself, rendering the title into English with a literal equivalent such as *The Steppe Wolf*, *The Wolf of the Steppes*, or *The Caspian Sea Wolf*. But aside from the aesthetic damage that would be done by any of these choices, there is the simple fact that in nearly a century since its first publication, and thanks in part to the rock band, the word "Steppenwolf" has become familiar to the eyes and ears of English-language readers, and it has become just as inseparable from Hesse's novel as, say, *The Metamorphosis* is from Kafka's *Die Verwandlung*, or *Civilization and Its Discontents* from Freud's *Das Unbehagen in der Kultur*.[13] If I had been the first to translate *Der Steppenwolf* into English, I might have considered calling it *The Lone Wolf*, though I would not have done so without hesitation. But like any retranslation, mine is influenced not only by the original work but also by the translations that have formed that work's "afterlife," as Benjamin aptly puts it.[14] Precisely because those earlier translators chose not to translate the term "Steppenwolf," the English language has grown one word richer, and I have gratefully adopted this word for the title of my own translation, enhanced by the addition of my own (and Hesse's) *The*.

As with the title, so too in other instances where I have broken with the precedent set by my translator predecessors, I have done so in order to offer an impression closer to that created by Hesse's original text. Take one particular example, the small tree on a landing in the boardinghouse where Harry Haller lives. Hesse invariably refers to this tree as an *Araukarie*, and all previous translators have opted for a cognate, rendering it into English as an "araucaria." A few good German-English dictionaries seem to support this choice. However, following the trail to the *Oxford English Dictionary*, one finds "araucaria" defined as "A genus of

lofty coniferous trees, native to the southern hemisphere, one species of which (*A. imbricata*, familiarly termed 'puzzle-monkey'
or 'monkey-puzzler'), with the branches in regular whorls, and
closely-imbricated stiff sharp-pointed leaves, has been, since about
1830, cultivated as an ornamental tree in Britain."[15] The name,
and the tree itself, are likely to strike many English-language readers as at least a bit unfamiliar, perhaps even exotic. But there is
another member of the same genus that many will find much
more familiar and mundane: the humble Norfolk Island pine
(*A. heterophylla*). I strongly suspect that this, and not the monkey-
puzzler, is what Hesse had in mind, given that the tree appears in
the novel as a houseplant associated with bland, wholesome bourgeois comfort. Through some searching in periodical databases, I
have confirmed that the Norfolk Island pine was indeed a common sight in Central European bourgeois households in the early
twentieth century—so much so that it was sometimes a subject of
humor—and publications from those decades sometimes referred
to this tree, and not just to the monkey-puzzler, by its genus name,
Araukarie. Having established this, I have rendered Hesse's *Araukarie* as a Norfolk Island pine, which I hope will create, as Hesse's
Araukarie does, an impression of bourgeois familiarity, not a
vision of exotic Chilean vistas.

There are other cases in which closer adherence to Hesse's
model means pulling readers further outside of their comfort zone
than previous translators have ventured to do. My greatest risk
in this regard (and this may say something about what passes for
"risk" among literary translators) is my decision to translate each
one of Hesse's German sentences with a single English sentence,
even when his sentences—as they not infrequently do—twist and
turn for the better part of a page. It is true that German, with its
case system and its wide array of relative pronouns, lends itself
more readily to such sprawling sentences than English does. What

counts as a run-on sentence in English is barely a running start by German standards. But while German does allow such marathon sentences, it does not require them, and not all authors use them in equal measure. Even Hesse can sprint when he wants to. But when his sentences stretch on and on, they do so for a reason. The most circuitous, serpentine sentences in *The Steppenwolf* tend to surface when Harry Haller's mind is at either the heights of inspiration or the depths of desperation, when he is thinking most associatively—or, one could say, when he is thinking musically, for Haller, like Hesse, has a strong musical sensibility, and its influence on his thought is unmistakable; indeed, Hesse once described the structure of *The Steppenwolf* as a sonata.[16] To break these sinuous sentences into bite-sized pieces would be to break up Harry Haller's train of thought, to reorganize his ideas into more compact, more self-contained, more digestible units—and that is precisely what his thoughts, in these moments, are not. By rendering Hesse's sentences at their full length, I hope to offer readers a richer sense of the logic, the alogic, the patterns, the rhythms, and the music of Harry Haller's thought.

I have also, more reluctantly, followed Hesse even when his language leads us into more treacherous territory. Despite his aversion to the most blatantly racist ideologies of his age, Hesse's novel echoes certain stereotypes about non-European, and particularly African, peoples and cultures that were widespread among his European contemporaries, but that appear reductive and offensive in retrospect. On multiple occasions, Hesse invokes the figure of the "primitive" or "savage" or "Negro" as a point of contrast to the refined, sophisticated European. These passages are unpleasant to read, and unpleasant to translate, but they tell us something important about Hesse and the period and culture in which he lived and wrote. (The novel's portrayals of women are also unpleasant at times, though I found that these passages less often turned on a single word choice.) The fact that an author capable of Hesse's most brilliant insights could so easily lapse into these simplistic racist tropes—even in the midst of a text that rails against shallow oversimplification—can, perhaps, offer a valuable lesson. It can remind us not only to read Hesse's text critically—remembering that, at least in its author's mind, the greatest insights contained within these pages were fully compatible with such moments of myopia—but also to ask ourselves which of our own unconscious biases may be just as glaringly obvious one hundred years from now as Hesse's are today. With these principles in mind, I have made no attempt to soften the blow of these passages, either for the reader's sake or for Hesse's. Instead, I offer what I consider to be a faithful rendering of Hesse's words, so that readers of the English translation, like readers of the German original, can draw their own conclusions.

AFTER ALL, *THE STEPPENWOLF* is not a novel that promises moral comfort or certainty. It may ultimately offer us "a positive, joyful world of faith that transcends the personal and the temporal, in contrast to the Steppenwolf's world of suffering," as Hesse argues in his afterword—though surely not all readers will agree. But even this vision of transcendence is not equally accessible to all: "Not for everyone," read the dancing letters on the cloister wall, "only for the insane." There is, of course, something paradoxical about the fact that *The Steppenwolf*—this novel that appeals so strongly to the sense of alienation, the sense of one's own uniqueness, the sense of being misunderstood—has, over the course of nearly a century, reached millions of readers and made so many of them feel personally addressed, personally understood. The same bourgeois conformist who appears from the outside to belong to the undifferentiated "herd" might read Hesse's novel and find himself or herself reflected in its pages as an exceptional and misunderstood individual, a genius with not just two, but countless souls housed within his or her breast. But this, ultimately, may be the best explanation for *The Steppenwolf*'s enduring power: it captures the irreducible and irreconcilable element that persists within each individual, even under the constraints of a life lived in bourgeois society. In this sense, it keeps faith not only "with the powerful emotions of adolescence," but also with the powerful tensions between self and world that are not the sole property of any single age or generation. With this new translation, I hope to have kept faith with *The Steppenwolf* and brought new life into its afterlife.

Kurt Beals
St. Louis, Missouri
January 2022

Notes

1. Hesse completed the final draft of the novel early in 1927, the year he turned fifty; Haller also ruminates on his impending fiftieth birthday. The novel contains no mention of a specific year, but its references to jazz tunes such as the 1926 hit "Valencia" indicate that the period of its action closely coincides with that of its composition. Similarly, while the urban setting of the novel is never identified, it bears a strong resemblance to Basel, where Hesse spent the winters of 1923–24 and 1924–25, though it also incorporates elements of Zurich, where he spent the following two winters and completed the novel.

2. See Regina Bucher and Eva Zimmermann, *Saint Among the Hippies? Hermann Hesse in the USA* (Montagnola, Switz.: Fondazione Hermann Hesse, 2016), 35.

3. See Egon Schwarz, "Zur Erklärung von Hesses 'Steppenwolf,'" *Monatshefte* 53, no. 4 (1961): 191–98; Martin Swales, "*Der Steppenwolf*," in

A Companion to the Works of Hermann Hesse, ed. Ingo Cornils (Rochester, N.Y.: Camden House, 2009), 171–86.

4.   Adam Kirsch, "Hermann Hesse's Arrested Development," *The New Yorker*, November 12, 2018.

5.   Gunnar Decker, *Hesse: The Wanderer and His Shadow*, trans. Peter Lewis (Cambridge, Mass.: Harvard University Press, 2018), 422.

6.   See Decker, *Hesse*, 616–31.

7.   Robert Galbreath, "Hermann Hesse and the Politics of Detachment," *Political Theory* 2, no. 1 (1974): 62–76.

8.   Decker, *Hesse*, 679.

9.   Quoted in Decker, *Hesse*, 486.

10. Kirsch, "Hermann Hesse's Arrested Development."

11. Walter Benjamin, "The Task of the Translator," in *Illuminations: Essays and Reflections*, trans. Harry Zohn (New York: Schocken, 1968), 80.

12. My translation generally follows the German edition of Hesse's complete works: Hermann Hesse, *Sämtliche Werke,* ed. Volker Michels, vol. 4, *Die Romane. Der Steppenwolf. Narziß und Goldmund. Die Morgenlandfahrt* (Frankfurt am Main: Suhrkamp Verlag, 2001), but in a few cases I have returned to the 1927 edition to resolve conflicting variants in later editions.

13. *Die Verwandlung* has been translated into English many times, but almost always as *The Metamorphosis* and only once, to my knowledge, as the equally literal *The Transformation;* for *Das Unbehagen in der Kultur,* Freud himself suggested *Man's Discomfort in Civilization.*

14. Benjamin, "The Task of the Translator," 71.

15. "araucaria, n." *OED Online*. December 2021. Oxford University Press (accessed January 29, 2022).

16. See Theodore Ziolkowski, "Hermann Hesse's *Steppenwolf*: A Sonata in Prose," *Modern Language Quarterly* 19, no. 2 (June 1958): 99.

The Steppenwolf

Editor's Foreword

THIS BOOK CONTAINS THE WRITINGS LEFT TO US by the man whom we, in keeping with his own repeated usage, called the "Steppenwolf." Whether his manuscript requires an introduction may remain an open question; I, in any case, feel compelled to add some pages of my own to those of the Steppenwolf, in which I will attempt to record my recollections of him. I know only a little bit about him, and his entire past and his origins in particular are beyond my ken. But the impression that I have retained of his personality is strong and, as I must say in spite of everything, sympathetic.

The Steppenwolf was a man approaching fifty who presented himself at my aunt's house one day a few years ago, seeking a furnished room. He rented the garret in the attic upstairs, along with the small bedchamber that adjoins it, then returned a few days later with two suitcases and a large crate of books and lived with us for nine or ten months. He lived very quietly and kept to himself, and if the proximity of our sleeping quarters had not led to the occasional chance encounter on the stairs and in the corridor, he and I probably would not have become acquainted with each other at all, for this man was hardly sociable, he was unsociable to a degree that I had never before observed in anyone, he was truly, as he sometimes called himself, a Steppenwolf, a strange, wild, and also shy, indeed, very shy creature from a world unlike my own. How deeply lonely his life had become as a result of his disposition and his fate, and how consciously he recognized this loneliness

as his fate: this, to be sure, I learned only from the notes that he
left behind here; but I had already become acquainted with him
to some extent through our various brief encounters and conversations, and I found the picture of him that I gleaned from his
notes to be fundamentally consistent with the admittedly fainter
and more lacunary one that had emerged from our personal
acquaintance.

As it happened, I was present at the moment when the Steppenwolf first entered our house and rented a room from my aunt.
He came during the lunch hour, the plates were still sitting on
the table, and I still had half an hour of free time left before I had
to return to my office. I have not forgotten the unusual and very
ambivalent impression that he made on me upon our first meeting.
He entered through the glass door after ringing the bell, and in the
half-dark hallway my aunt asked him what he wanted. But he, the
Steppenwolf, had cocked his sharp, closely shorn head in the air as
if to catch a scent, he sniffed about him with his nervous nose and
said, before he even answered or gave his name: "Oh, it smells good
here." He smiled at this, and my good aunt smiled too, but I found
these words of greeting rather odd, which turned me against him.

"Now then," he said, "I've come about the room you have
for rent."

It wasn't until the three of us were climbing the stairs to the
attic together that I had a chance to take a closer look at the man.
He was not very tall, but he walked and carried his head like a tall
man, he wore a comfortable, fashionable winter coat, apart from
that he was decently but carelessly dressed, with a clean-shaven face
and a head of very short hair that shimmered here and there with
a hint of gray. In the beginning, I didn't like the way he walked at
all; there was something labored and indecisive about it that didn't
suit his sharp, intense profile or the tone and temperament of his
speech. Only later did I come to understand that he was ill, and

that walking cost him effort. With a peculiar smile, which I also found unpleasant at the time, he regarded the staircase, the walls and windows, and the tall old cupboards in the stairwell, all of this seemed to please him and yet at the same time seemed somehow ridiculous to him. The whole man made an impression altogether as if he had come to us from a foreign world, perhaps from overseas, and found everything here quite lovely, to be sure, but a bit odd. He was polite, even friendly, I can't deny that, and he immediately approved of the house and the room and the price of the rent and breakfast and everything else with no objections at all, and yet the whole man appeared to be surrounded by a strange and, it seemed to me, unpleasant or hostile atmosphere. He rented the room, and the bedchamber as well, inquired about the heating, water, housekeeping, and house rules, listened to everything with a friendly attentiveness, agreed to everything, even readily offered an advance payment on the rent, and yet he did not quite seem to be present for all of this, he seemed to find his actions strange and not to take them seriously, as if it were curious and novel for him to rent a room and speak German with people, while he was actually, inwardly occupied with different matters altogether. This, in essence, was my impression, and it would not have been a good one had it not been contradicted and corrected by so many little things. It was the man's face, above all, that I liked from the beginning; I liked it in spite of that foreign expression, it was a somewhat peculiar and also a sad face, perhaps, but it was wide awake, very thoughtful, thorough, and imbued with spirit and intellect. And I was further reconciled to him by the fact that his form of courtesy and friendliness, although it seemed to cost him quite some effort, was entirely free of arrogance—on the contrary, there was something almost touching about it, something pleading, for which I found the explanation only later, though it immediately made me a bit more positively disposed toward him.

Even before his inspection of the two rooms and the other negotiations had been completed, my lunch hour was at an end and I had to return to work. I excused myself and left him to my aunt. When I returned that evening, she told me that the stranger had rented the room and would be moving in any day now; he had only asked that we not register his arrival with the police, since he, a sickly man, could not bear those formalities, all the standing around in the police station and so on. I remember very well how disconcerted that made me, and how I warned my aunt not to agree to this stipulation. This man's wariness of the police, it seemed to me, fit all too well with his strange and unfamiliar manner, so that it could not fail to be seen as suspicious. I explained to my aunt that she was not under any circumstances to grant this request to a complete stranger, a request that was somewhat peculiar in itself, and which, if granted, could under certain circumstances have quite horrible consequences for her. But then it transpired that my aunt had already acceded to his wish, and had allowed herself to be quite thoroughly captivated and charmed by this stranger; for she has never taken in lodgers with whom she could not establish some sort of personal, friendly and aunty or even motherly rapport, a fact that has been amply exploited by some of her previous lodgers. And in the first few weeks it continued in this fashion, I found many faults with the new lodger, while my aunt always warmly stood up for him.

Since I was not pleased about this neglect to inform the police, I wanted at least to find out what my aunt knew about the stranger, about his background and intentions. And she did in fact know this and that, although he had only stayed for a very short time after I departed around noon. He had told her that he intended to spend several months in our city, to use the libraries and see the city's antiquities. In fact, it did not suit my aunt that he wanted to rent the room for such a short time, but he had clearly won her over already, despite his somewhat unusual demeanor. In short, the rooms were rented, and my objections came too late.

"Why do you think he said that it smelled so good here?" I asked.

To that, my aunt, who sometimes has quite good hunches, said: "I know very well. Our house smells of cleanliness and order and a friendly and decent life, and that's why he liked it. He looks like he isn't used to that anymore, and he's been missing it."

Well yes, I thought, I'll grant you that. "But," I said, "if he isn't used to an orderly and decent life, then how is all of this going to work out? What are you going to do if he's dirty and makes a mess of everything, or if he comes home drunk at all hours of the night?"

"We'll see about that," she said with a laugh, and I let the matter rest.

As it turned out, my fears were unfounded. The lodger, although he by no means led an orderly and reasonable life, neither bothered us nor did us any harm, and we still think of him fondly to this day. But inwardly, in our souls, this man disturbed and troubled both of us a great deal, my aunt and me, and to be frank, I am far from getting over him. Sometimes at night I dream of him and find myself deeply disturbed and unsettled by him, by the mere existence of such a being, although over time he became quite dear to me.

TWO DAYS LATER, a coachman brought the belongings of this stranger, whose name was Harry Haller. There was a very fine leather suitcase that made a good impression on me, and a large, flat cabin trunk that seemed to hint at long journeys past, at least it was covered with yellowed stickers from hotels and transport companies in various countries, some of them overseas.

Then he himself appeared, and thus began the period of time

during which I gradually made the acquaintance of this unusual man. In the beginning, I made no efforts of my own in this regard. Although I had been interested in Haller since the first moment I saw him, I took no steps in the first few weeks to encounter him or engage him in conversation. On the other hand, I must confess that I did observe the man a bit from the very beginning, sometimes entering his room while he was out, and on the whole, out of curiosity, undertaking a bit of espionage.

I have already provided some details about the Steppenwolf's outward appearance. From the very first glance, he made the distinct impression of an important, rare, and unusually gifted person, his face was full of spirit and intellect, and the extraordinarily delicate and active play of his features was indicative of an interesting, highly animated, uncommonly delicate and sensitive life of the soul. When one spoke with him and he went beyond pleasantries (which he did not always do) and spoke his own, personal words, giving voice to his own strange perspective, then a man such as myself had to defer to him without further ado, for he had thought more than other people, and in intellectual matters he had that almost cool objectivity, that surety of thought and knowledge, which only truly intellectual people have, those who lack any ambition, who have no wish to stand out or to persuade others or to prove themselves right.

I remember one such remark, which was not even a remark but merely a look, from near the end of his time here. A famous philosopher of history and cultural critic, a man whose name is known throughout Europe, had announced that he would give a lecture in the university auditorium, and I had succeeded in persuading the Steppenwolf, who initially had no desire to attend the lecture, to come along with me. We went together and sat side by side in the lecture hall. When the speaker mounted the rostrum and began his address, some listeners who had imagined

him to be a sort of prophet were disappointed by his rather preen-
ing and vain demeanor. When he began to speak, starting with
a few words of flattery for the audience and thanking them for
attending in such great numbers, the Steppenwolf cast a very brief
glance in my direction, a glance that was critical of these words
and of the speaker's whole person, oh, an unforgettable and terrible glance, a whole book could be written about its meaning!
His glance did not merely criticize the speaker and annihilate
that famous man with its compelling, though gentle irony—that
was the least of it. His glance was much more sad than ironic, it
was even abysmally, hopelessly sad; this glance contained within
it a silent despair that had already become certainty, become a
habit and a form, so to speak. It not only penetrated the vain
speaker with its light, revealing him with despairing clarity, not
only ironized and dismissed the situation of that moment, the
expectation and the mood of the audience, the somewhat preten-
tious title of the promised speech—no, the Steppenwolf's glance
pierced through our entire age, all the bustling fuss, all the striving, all the vanity, the whole superficial display of imaginary,
shallow intellectualism—ah, and sadly, the glance went even
deeper, went much further, than merely to the shortcomings and
hopelessness of our time, of our intellectual life, of our culture.
It went to the heart of all humanity, it eloquently expressed in a
single second all the doubts of a thinker, perhaps a knower, about
the dignity, the meaning of human life as such. That glance said,
"Look, this is the kind of monkey we are! Look, this is what
man is like!" and all fame, all cleverness, all feats of intellect, all
human attempts at sublimity, greatness, and perseverance fell flat
and were nothing but a monkey's game!

In saying this, I have gotten far ahead of myself and, contrary to
my own plan and intention, I have already fundamentally said the
most essential things about Haller, whereas originally I meant to

reveal his image only gradually, by recounting step by step how I made his acquaintance.

But now that I have gotten ahead of myself in this way, there is no need to speak any further about Haller's mysterious "strangeness," or to report in detail how I slowly began to sense and recognize the sources and meanings of this strangeness, of this extraordinary and terrible loneliness. It is better that way, since I prefer to leave myself in the background if at all possible. I do not wish to give my confessions or tell stories or practice psychology, but merely to add my own eyewitness account to the depiction of the peculiar man who left these Steppenwolf manuscripts behind.

From the first moment I saw him, when he entered through my aunt's glass door, cocked his head like a bird, and praised the good smell of the house, I had somehow noticed something special about this man, and my first naïve reaction to this had been aversion. I felt (and my aunt, who unlike me is not an intellectual person at all, felt almost exactly the same thing)—I felt that the man was sick, somehow sick in mind or spirit or character, and I defended myself against this with the instinct of a healthy man. In the course of time, this resistance was replaced by a sympathy founded on my great compassion for this deeply and perpetually suffering man, to whose loneliness and inner death I bore witness. During this period, I became more and more aware that this suffering man's illness was due not to any shortcomings in his nature, but on the contrary only to his great wealth of gifts and powers which had not been brought into harmony. I recognized that Haller was a genius of suffering, that he, in the spirit of some of Nietzsche's sayings, had cultivated within himself an ingenious, limitless, terrible capacity for suffering. At the same time, I realized that the basis of his pessimism was not contempt for the world, but contempt for himself, for however unsparingly and devastatingly he could speak of institutions or persons, he never excluded himself, he himself was always the first target of his own arrows, he himself was the first person he hated and rejected. . . .

Here I must add a psychological observation. Although I know very little about the life of the Steppenwolf, I have every reason to suspect that he was brought up by loving but strict and very pious parents and teachers who believed that the "breaking of the will" is the cornerstone of education. Now, in this case they had not succeeded in crushing the student's personality and breaking his will; he was much too strong and hard, much too proud and firm of spirit for that. Instead of crushing his personality, they had only succeeded in teaching him to hate himself. And so, for the rest of his life, he directed all the genius of his imagination, all his power of thought, against himself, against this innocent and noble object. For in this respect, in spite of everything, he was a Christian through and through, a martyr through and through: he unleashed all the severity, all the criticism, all the malice, all the hatred he could muster upon himself first and foremost. As far as others were concerned, and the world around him, he constantly made the most heroic and earnest attempts to love them, to do them justice, not to hurt them, for "love thy neighbor" was as deeply drilled into him as hatred of himself, and so his entire life was an example of the fact that without love of self, love of neighbor, too, is impossible, that self-hatred is exactly the same thing—and, in the end, leads to exactly the same dreadful isolation and despair—as glaring egoism.

But it is time now that I put my thoughts aside and speak of realities. Thus the first thing that I learned about Mr. Haller, partly through my espionage and partly from my aunt's remarks, related to the way he lived his life. It was soon apparent that he was a man of thoughts and books, and that he did not ply any practical trade. He always lay in bed for hours, often it was nearly noon before he got up, put on his robe, and walked the few steps from his bedchamber to his living room. After just a few days, this living room, a large and welcoming garret with two windows, looked different than it had when it was occupied by other lodgers. It began to fill up, and over time it grew more and more crowded. Pictures were hung on the walls, drawings were pinned up, sometimes pictures cut out of magazines, which were frequently replaced by others. There was a landscape somewhere in the south, there were some photographs of a small German country village, evidently Haller's hometown, with colorful, luminous watercolors hung between them, only later did we learn that he had painted these himself. Then a photograph of a pretty young woman or girl. For a while there was a Siamese Buddha hanging on the wall, it was replaced by a reproduction of Michelangelo's *Night*, then by a portrait of Mahatma Gandhi. Books not only filled the large bookcase but also lay strewn all over the tables, the pretty old writing desk, the divan, the chairs, and the floor, with paper bookmarks inserted between their pages that were constantly changing places. The number of books was constantly increasing, because he not only brought whole piles of them home from the libraries but also very frequently received parcels by mail. The occupant of this room could very well have been a scholar. That impression was reinforced by the cigar smoke that enveloped everything, and the cigar stubs and ashes that lay around everywhere. However, a significant number of the books were not of a scholarly nature; the vast majority were the works of literary writers of all eras and nationalities. For a while, all six thick volumes of a late-eighteenth-century work entitled *Sophie's Journey from Memel to Saxony* were spread out on the divan, where he often spent entire days. A complete edition of Goethe and one of Jean Paul appeared to see a great deal of use, as did Novalis, but also Lessing, Jacobi, and Lichtenberg. Some volumes of Dostoevsky were filled with handwritten notes on slips of paper. There was often a bouquet of flowers on the large table among the many books and papers, and there was also a watercolor case floating around, but it was always full of dust, alongside these were the ashtrays and—let this not be a secret, either—all sorts of bottles full of drink. One bottle, wrapped in woven straw, was usually filled with Italian red wine that he bought at a small shop nearby, a bottle of Burgundy sometimes appeared, as well as Malaga, and I saw a squat bottle of cherry brandy go from full to nearly empty in just a short time, but then it disappeared into a corner of the room, where it gathered dust while the rest of its contents remained untouched. I have no intention of justifying the espionage that I engaged in, and I openly confess that in the early days I was filled with disgust and mistrust by all these indications of a life that, despite being rich in intellectual interests, was nevertheless quite idle and lacking in discipline. I am not only a bourgeois person with a routine way of life, accustomed to work and precise time management, I am also a teetotaler and nonsmoker, and those bottles in Haller's room appealed to me even less than the rest of the painterly disorder.

Just as in his sleep and work, so too in matters of food and drink the stranger led a very inconsistent and erratic life. Some days he didn't leave the house at all, consuming absolutely nothing but his morning coffee; at times my aunt would find no remnant of his meal but a banana peel; but on other days he dined in restaurants, sometimes in fine and elegant ones, sometimes in small neighborhood drinking houses. He didn't seem to be in good health; aside from the stiffness in his legs, which often made it quite difficult for him to climb the stairs, he also seemed to be plagued by other disorders, and he once said in passing that he had not enjoyed proper digestion or sleep in years. I attributed this above all to his drinking. Later, when I occasionally accompanied him to one of his taverns, I sometimes witnessed how quickly he gulped down the wines when the mood overcame him, but neither I nor anyone else ever saw him really drunk.

I will never forget our first more personal encounter. We knew each other only as next-door neighbors in an apartment building do. Then one evening, as I was returning home from work, I was astonished to find Mr. Haller seated on the stairs, at the landing between the second and third floors. He had sat down on the top step, and he moved aside to let me pass. I asked him if he was unwell and offered to accompany him all the way upstairs.

Haller looked at me, and I realized that I had awakened him from a sort of trance. Slowly he began to smile, his handsome and miserable smile that would so often weigh upon my heart, then he invited me to sit down beside him. I thanked him and said that it was not my habit to sit on the stairs in front of other people's apartments.

"Oh yes," he said, smiling more broadly, "you're right. But wait a moment, I must show you why I had to stop and sit here for a bit."

As he said this, he gestured to the vestibule of the second-floor apartment, where a widow lived. On the small square of parquet floor that lay between the stairs, the window, and the glass door, a tall mahogany cupboard stood against the wall, complete with old pewter hardware, and on the floor in front of the cupboard, on two small, low pedestals, were two plants in large pots: an azalea and a Norfolk Island pine. The plants looked pretty, and they were always kept very clean and tidy, as I myself had also noted with pleasure.

"You see," Haller continued, "this little vestibule with the Norfolk Island pine, it smells so fabulous, I often can't even pass by without stopping here for a while. Of course your aunt's apartment smells good, too, she keeps it neat and very clean, but the landing here with the Norfolk Island pine is so radiantly pure, so thoroughly dusted and wiped and washed, so impeccably immaculate, that it positively gleams. I always have to draw a deep breath through my nose there—don't you smell it, too? The way the scent of floor wax and a faint echo of turpentine come together there with the mahogany, the well-washed leaves of the plants, and everything else to produce a fragrance, a superlative odor of bourgeois purity, of care and precision, of dutifulness and loyalty writ small. I don't know who lives there, but behind that glass door there must be a paradise of cleanliness and dust-free bourgeois life, of order and an anxious, touching devotion to petty habits and duties."

As I remained silent, he continued: "Please don't think that I'm speaking ironically! Dear sir, nothing could be further from my intention than to ridicule this bourgeois, orderly way of life. Of course, it's true that I myself live in a different world, not in this one, and perhaps I would not be capable of enduring even a single day in an apartment with those Norfolk Island pines. But even though I may be a sort of gruff old Steppenwolf, I'm the son of a mother all the same, and my mother was also a bourgeois housewife who grew flowers and minded the parlor and the stairs, the furniture and the curtains, and she did her best to make her home and her life as clean, pure, and orderly as she could. That's what the whiff of turpentine reminds me of, and the Norfolk Island pine, and that's why I sit here now and then, looking into that quiet little garden of order, and rejoicing that it still exists."

He started to stand up, but he was having trouble, and he did not refuse my offer of assistance. I remained silent, but I was now under the sort of spell that this curious man could sometimes cast, just as my aunt had been before. We slowly climbed the stairs together, and when we reached his door, with his keys already in hand, he looked me squarely in the face again, a very friendly look, and said: "You were just getting home from work? Well, I don't know anything about that, I live a bit off the beaten path, a bit on the edge, you know. But I think you're also interested in books and

such, your aunt once told me that you graduated from a grammar
school and you did well in Greek. Well, this morning I found a
sentence in Novalis, may I show it to you? You'll enjoy it, too."

He led me into his room, which smelled strongly of tobacco,
pulled a book from a pile, and leafed through it, looking
for something—

"That's good, too, very good," he said, "just listen to this sentence: 'One should be proud of pain—all pain is a remembrance
of our lofty rank.' Excellent! Eighty years before Nietzsche! But
that's not the saying I was thinking of—wait—there I have it. So:
'The majority of people do not want to swim, until they are already
able to.' Isn't that funny? Of course they don't want to swim! They
were born for the land, not for the water. And of course they don't
want to think; they were made for living, not for thinking! Yes,
and whoever thinks, whoever makes thinking his primary aim,
can make great progress in it, but he's just exchanged the land for
the water, and one day he will drown."

Now he had drawn me in and piqued my interest, and I stayed
there with him for a little while, and from then on we not infrequently spoke a bit when we encountered each other on the stairs
or in the street. At first I always had the same feeling I'd had at
the Norfolk Island pine, the sense that he was treating me ironically. But that was not the case. He honestly respected me, as
he did the Norfolk Island pine; he was so fully convinced of his
loneliness, his swimming in the water, his uprootedness, that the
sight of some everyday bourgeois behavior such as my punctual
departure for the office, or the utterance of a servant or a streetcar
conductor, could truly delight him, without the slightest hint of
mockery. Initially, this all seemed quite ridiculous and overdone
to me, such a genteel and idle attitude, a foolish sentimentality.
But more and more I had to see that from where he stood within
his airless space, within all his alienation and Steppenwolfishness,

he honestly admired and loved our little bourgeois world, he saw it as a place both solid and secure, both distant and inaccessible to him, as the homeland and the peace to which no road could lead him. He always tipped his hat with true reverence to our house-keeper, a decent woman, and any time my aunt would chat with him a bit or point out something in his laundry that needed to be mended or a loose button on his coat, he would listen with pecu-liar attentiveness and seriousness, as if he were making an immense and hopeless effort to find some crack through which he could slip into this small, peaceful world and make himself at home there, if only for an hour.

He called himself the Steppenwolf even during that first conver-sation by the Norfolk Island pine, and this, too, alienated and dis-turbed me a bit. What sort of expressions were these?! But not only did I learn through repeated exposure to accept the expression, soon I had stopped calling the man anything other than the Steppenwolf in my own thoughts, and even today I can think of no more fitting word for that figure. A lone wolf who had strayed from the steppes and made his way to our cities, to this herd life—no other image could show him more strikingly, his wary loneliness, his wildness, his restlessness, his homesickness and his homelessness.

Once I had a chance to observe him for a whole evening at a symphony concert where, to my surprise, I saw him sitting near me without noticing me. The first piece was Handel, a refined and beautiful piece of music, but the Steppenwolf just sat there absorbed in himself, with no connection to the music or to his surroundings. He sat there lonely and remote, as if he did not belong, with downcast eyes and a cool but worried face. Another piece followed, a little symphony by Friedemann Bach, and I was quite astonished to see how after just a few bars, my strange friend began to smile and surrender himself to the music, he turned fully inward, and for about ten minutes he looked so happily absorbed and lost in good dreams that I paid more attention to him than to the music. When the piece was over, he came to, sat up straighter, and appeared to be on the verge of getting up and leaving, but then he remained seated after all and listened to the final piece as well, some variations by Reger, which many people found to be somewhat long and tedious. And the Steppenwolf, too, who had initially given the music his attention and goodwill, lost interest again, he put his hands into his pockets and sank back into himself, only this time not happily and dreamily, but sadly and in the end even angrily, his face was once again distant, gray, and sunken, he looked old and ill and dissatisfied.

After the concert I saw him again on the street and followed him; bundled up in his coat, he was plodding wearily and listlessly in the direction of our neighborhood, but he stopped in front of a small old-fashioned tavern, indecisively checked the time, and went inside. Acting on an impulse, I followed him. He was sitting at the sort of common table typically found in petit bourgeois taverns of that kind, the two women behind the bar—the tavern-keeper and the barmaid—greeted him as a regular guest, and I gave my greeting and sat down with him. We sat there for an hour, and while I drank two glasses of mineral water, he ordered half a liter and then another quarter liter of red wine. I said that I had been at the concert, but he did not engage me on the topic. He read the label on my water bottle and asked if I didn't want to drink wine, it would be his treat. When he heard that I never drink wine, he made another helpless face and said: "Yes, you're right. I abstained for years, too, and even fasted for long periods, but right now I'm in the sign of Aquarius again, a dark, damp sign."

And when I jokingly picked up on this allusion and remarked on how improbable I found it that he of all people would believe in astrology, he reverted to the polite tone that often aggrieved me and said: "Quite right, unfortunately I do not believe in this science, either."

I excused myself and took my leave, and he did not come home until very late that night, but his footsteps sounded as they always did, and as usual he did not go straight to bed (I could hear that very clearly from my adjoining room), but probably stayed up for another hour in his living room with the lights on.

And there was another evening that I have not forgotten. I was at home alone, my aunt was not there, the doorbell rang, and when I answered the door, a young, very pretty lady was standing there, and when she asked for Mr. Haller, I recognized her: she was the woman from the photograph in his room. I showed her to his door and withdrew, she stayed upstairs for a while, but soon I heard them going down the stairs and leaving the house together, in a lively and cheerful mood and engaged in a playful conversation. I was very surprised that the hermit had a girlfriend, particularly such a young, pretty, and elegant one, and I began to question all of my assumptions about him and his life. But just one short hour later he came home, alone, walking with heavy, sad steps, struggled up the stairs, and then quietly paced to and fro in his living room for hours, just as a wolf prowls in its cage, and the light in his room was on all night until almost morning.

I don't know anything about that relationship and only want to add: I saw him with that same woman on one other occasion, on one of the streets of the city. They were walking arm in arm, he looked happy, and I marveled again at how much grace, even child-ishness, his careworn, lonely face could sometimes have, and then I understood the woman, and also understood the sympathy that my aunt had for this man. But that day, too, he came home in the evening sad and miserable; I met him at the front door, he had the bottle of Italian wine under his coat, as he so often did, and he sat up with it for half the night in his upstairs lair. I felt sorry for him, but what a bleak, lost, and helpless life he led!

Well, enough of this gossip. No further reports or descriptions are necessary to show that the Steppenwolf led a suicidal life. Still, I do not believe that he took his own life when he left our city one day—without warning and without saying goodbye, but after paying all of his outstanding debts—and disappeared. We never heard from him again, and we are still holding on to some letters that arrived for him after his departure. He left nothing behind but the manuscript he had written during his stay here, which he dedicated to me with a few brief lines, saying that I could do with it as I pleased.

It has not been possible for me to determine to what extent the experiences recounted in Haller's manuscript are based in reality. I have no doubt that for the most part they are fiction, not in the sense of arbitrary invention, but in the sense that they attempt to express profound experiences of the soul in the guise of out-wardly visible events. The episodes in Haller's writing, some of which are fantastical, presumably date from the final period of his stay here, and I have no doubt that they also have some element of real, external experience at their core. During that time, our guest did indeed exhibit a rather transformed demeanor and appear-ance, he spent a great deal of time—sometimes entire nights—out of the house, and his books lay untouched. The few times that I encountered him during that period, he seemed strikingly alive and rejuvenated, occasionally downright cheerful. However, this was immediately followed by a renewed, severe depression, he lay in bed for days with no desire for food, and during that time he also had an extraordinarily heated, even brutal quarrel with his girlfriend who had turned up again, a quarrel that brought the whole house into an uproar, for which Haller apologized to my aunt the next day.

No, I am convinced that he did not take his own life. He is still alive somewhere, walking up and down the stairs of unfamiliar houses on his weary legs, staring at shiny parquet floors and neatly tended Norfolk Island pines, sitting in libraries by day and taverns by night or lying on the sofa of a rented room, listening to the world and the people going about their lives outside the windows, and knowing that he is excluded, but not killing himself, because some residue of faith tells him that he must savor this suffering, this evil suffering, in his heart to the end, and that it is this suffering itself that must one day kill him. I think of him often, he did not make my life any easier, he was unable to support and encourage the strong and joyful aspects of my personality, oh, quite the opposite! But then I am not the person he is, I do not lead his kind of life, but rather my own, a small, bourgeois life, but one that comes with security and a wealth of duties. And so we can think of him in peace and friendship, my aunt and I, she would be able to say more about him than I can, but it all remains concealed within her kind heart.

AS FOR HALLER'S WRITINGS, these bizarre, sometimes sick, sometimes beautiful and thoughtful fantasies, I must say that had these pages fallen into my hands by chance and their author not been known to me, I certainly would have thrown them away in disgust. But my acquaintance with Haller has made it possible for me, at least in part, to understand them, even to approve of them. I would hesitate to share them with others if I saw in them merely the pathological fantasies of an individual, an unfortunate, mentally ill man. But what I see in them is more than that, it is a document of the times, for the sickness that plagues Haller's soul—as I see today—is not the idiosyncrasy of one individual, but rather the sickness of the times themselves, the neurosis of Haller's entire generation, which seems to afflict by no means only weak and inferior individuals, but rather the strong, the most intellectual, the most gifted.

These writings—regardless of how much or how little foundation they may have in actual experience—are an attempt to overcome the great sickness of the time not by evading and glossing over it, but rather by making that sickness itself the object of representation. They represent, quite literally, a passage through hell—a passage, now fearful, now bold, through the chaos of a darkened world of the soul, undertaken with the will to cross through hell, to confront chaos, to suffer evil to the end.

Something Haller once said gave me the key to understanding this. He said to me, when we had been talking about the so-called barbarities of the Middle Ages: "In reality, these are not barbarities at all. A man of the Middle Ages would find the entire lifestyle of our present day cruel, horrible, and barbaric in a completely different way! Every epoch, every culture, every custom and tradition has its style, has its own characteristic forms of tenderness and cruelty, beauty and barbarity, takes certain forms of suffering for granted, patiently tolerates certain evils. Human life only becomes true suffering, true hell, where two epochs, two cultures and religions overlap. A man of classical antiquity who had to live in the Middle Ages would have been miserably suffocated by it, just as a savage would suffocate in the midst of our civilization. There are times when a whole generation is caught between two epochs, between two lifestyles, in such a way that it loses all of its self-evidence, all of its customs, its sense of security and innocence. Of course, not everyone experiences this equally strongly. Nietzsche's nature was such that he had to suffer the misery of our day more than a generation ahead of time—and what he had to endure, alone and misunderstood, is suffered today by thousands."

I had to think of these words often while reading Haller's writings. Haller is one of those who are caught between two epochs, who have fallen from the state of security and innocence, one of those whose fate it is to experience all the dubiousness of human life intensified into a personal torment and hell.

In this, it seems to me, lies the meaning that his writings can have for us, and that is why I have decided to share them. Beyond that, I have no desire to defend them, nor to judge them—let each reader do so according to his conscience!

Harry Haller's
Notebooks

▼▼▼▼▼▼

Only for the Insane

T HE DAY HAD PASSED THE WAY DAYS TEND TO
pass; I'd killed the time, killed it softly, with my primitive
and timid art of living; I'd spent a few hours working, poring
over old books, I'd suffered through two hours of pain, the kind
old people tend to have, I'd taken a powder and found to my delight that the pain was no match for it, I'd reclined in a hot bath,
soaking up the warmth, received the mail three times and sorted
through all the unnecessary letters and brochures, I'd done my
breathing exercises, but skipped the mental exercises today out
of sheer laziness, I'd taken an hour-long walk and found pretty,
delicate, precious patterns of feathery clouds traced out across the
sky. That was quite lovely, just as it was to read the old books, to
recline in the warm bath, but—all in all—it wasn't exactly a rapturous, resplendent day of happiness and joy, instead it was just one
of those sorts of days that ought to be normal and familiar to me
by now: the moderately pleasant, thoroughly endurable, bearable,
lukewarm days of an older, discontented gentleman, days without
any particular pains, without any particular worries, without real
sorrow, without despair, days when even the question of whether it
might not be time to follow Adalbert Stifter's example and suffer
an unfortunate accident while shaving can be considered calmly
and objectively, without a trace of agitation or fear.

Anyone who has tasted of those other days—the terrible days
when gout attacks, or the days when such horrible headaches take
root behind the eyeballs and cast their wicked spell on any actions

of the eye and ear simply for the pleasure of causing pain, or the days when the soul itself dies, those awful days of inner emptiness and despair, when, in the midst of this ravaged earth sucked dry by corporations, we are suddenly confronted by the grinning face of the world of men and their so-called culture, leering at us nauseatingly at every turn with its lying, nasty, tinny carnival veneer, until that nausea is concentrated and pushed to an unbearable extreme within our own sick selves—anyone who has tasted of those hellish days is very satisfied with normal, half-and-half days like today, he sits gratefully beside the warm heating stove, he notes gratefully as he reads the morning paper that no new war has broken out today, no new dictatorship has been installed, no particularly flagrant cases of corruption have been revealed in politics and business, he gratefully tunes the strings of his rusty lyre to a moderate, passably happy, nearly cheerful psalm of thanksgiving, with which he lulls his half-and-half god of contentment into boredom, that silent, soft, and somewhat bromide-benumbed deity, and in the balmy air of this contented boredom, in this painlessness for which such thanks are due, the two—the wearily nodding half-and-half god and the lightly graying half-and-half man who sings his subdued psalm—appear as alike as twins.

It's a fine thing, this contentment, this painlessness, these endurable, hunched-over days, when neither pain nor pleasure dares to cry out, when they only whisper and tiptoe around. But unfortunately in my case this contentment doesn't sit well with me at all, after only a short time it becomes insufferably abhorrent and repugnant, and I have to desperately seek out other climes, following the path of pleasure if possible, but the path of pain if necessary. When I have gone a while without pleasure and without pain, breathing the lukewarm, stuffy endurability of so-called good days, then my childish soul grows full of so much windy woe and wretchedness that I take the rusty lyre of gratitude and smash it into the contented countenance of that sleepy god of contentment, and I would rather feel a truly diabolical pain burning inside me than this salubrious room temperature. Then a wild desire begins to burn within me, a desire for powerful feelings, for sensations, a rage against this tempered, flat, normalized, and sterilized life, and a furious drive to smash something to pieces, maybe a department store or a cathedral or myself, to recklessly commit foolish deeds, to rip the wigs from a couple of venerated idols, to provide a couple of rebellious schoolboys with a coveted train ticket to Hamburg, to seduce a young girl, or to twist the faces of a few representatives of the bourgeois world order back into their necks. Because that is really what I hated, detested, and cursed most of all, most profoundly: that contentment, that health, comfort, that well-groomed bourgeois optimism, that fat and thriving cultivation of the mediocre, the normal, the average.

That, then, was the mood in which I concluded this bearable, dime-a-dozen day as dusk fell. I did not conclude the day in the normal and salubrious way befitting a somewhat suffering man, by allowing myself to be ensnared by my bed, which stood prepared and even outfitted with a hot-water bottle as bait, but rather, feeling unsatisfied and disgusted by my modest daily labor and filled with discontent, I pulled on my shoes, slipped into my coat, and set out into the dark and fog-cloaked city, heading to the Steel Helmet Tavern to drink what drinking men have made it their custom to call "a little glass of wine."

So I descended the stairs from my garret, these foreign stairs so difficult to climb, the thoroughly bourgeois, clean-scrubbed, spotless stairs of a highly respectable three-family apartment building, where I have found my sanctuary in the attic. I don't know how it happens, but I, the homeless Steppenwolf and solitary despiser of the petit bourgeois world, always live in proper bourgeois houses, that is an old weakness of mine. I live not in palaces or proletarian

houses, but rather, of all places, in these highly respectable, highly
boring, impeccably maintained redoubts of the petite bourgeoisie
where it smells of a bit of turpentine and a bit of soap and where it
is cause for alarm if you close the front door too loudly or step into
the house wearing dirty shoes. My love of this atmosphere surely
has its roots in my childhood days, and my secret longing for something like home leads me hopelessly down these stupid old paths,
time and again. And, well, I also like the contrast in which my
life, my lonely, loveless, harried, thoroughly disordered life, stands
to this milieu of families and the bourgeoisie. I like to breathe
this scent of silence, order, cleanliness, decency, and domesticity
in the stairwell, this scent that retains a touching quality for me
despite my hatred of the bourgeoisie, and then I like to step across
the threshold of my own room, where all of that comes to an end,
where cigar stubs lie about and wine bottles stand between the
piles of books, where everything is disorderly, inhospitable, and
unkempt, and where everything, books, manuscripts, thoughts,
is stamped and saturated with the misery of the lonely, with the
problematic of being human, with the longing for a new source of
meaning for human life, which has become meaningless.

And now I had come to the Norfolk Island pine. You see, on
the second floor of the house the stairs lead past the small vestibule of an apartment, one that is doubtlessly even more impecca-
ble, more spotless, more cleanly scrubbed than the others, because
this small vestibule gleams with superhuman tidiness, it is a small,
shining temple of order. There, on a parquet floor on which one
barely dares to tread, stand two graceful stools, and on each stool
a large pot, one holding an azalea, the other a quite stately Norfolk Island pine, a healthy, strapping young tree, a paragon of perfection, and even the last needle on the last branch gleams with a
freshly washed sparkle. From time to time, when I know that I am
not being observed, I use this spot as a temple, I sit down on a step

above the Norfolk Island pine, rest a bit, fold my hands, and gaze reverently down into this small garden of order, its touching countenance and its lonely absurdity somehow take hold of my soul. Behind this vestibule, in the sacred shadow of the Norfolk Island pine, so to speak, I imagine an apartment full of gleaming mahogany and a life full of health and decency, marked by early rising, the fulfillment of duty, moderately lively family gatherings, Sunday church services, and an early bedtime.

Affecting high spirits, I trotted along the damp, foggy asphalt of the narrow streets, the lanterns cast their tearful, misty gaze down through the cool, damp gloom, drawing sluggish reflections from the sodden ground. The forgotten years of my youth flooded back to me—how I used to love such dark and gloomy evenings in the late fall and winter, with what eager intoxication I used to soak up the moods of loneliness and melancholy, when I would spend half the night trudging through hostile, leafless nature, through rain and storms, wrapped in my coat, already lonely even then, but filled with a deep satisfaction, and filled with verses that I would later write down by candlelight in my room, perched on the edge of my bed! Now that was all in the past, I had drained that cup and it would not be filled again. Was that a shame? No, it was not a shame. What lay behind was not a shame at all. What was a shame was in the here and now, these countless hours and days that I lost, that I merely suffered through, that brought me neither gifts nor shocks of any kind. But thank God there were also exceptions—sometimes, rarely, there were those other hours, hours that brought shocks, brought gifts, broke down walls and brought me, errant that I am, back again to the living heart of the world. Sad and yet profoundly agitated, I sought to remember my most recent experience of that sort. It had happened at a concert, it was a program of magnificent old music, and just as the woodwinds were playing a quiet passage, suddenly, between two beats, the door to the beyond had swung open to me again, I had flown through the heavens and seen God at work, I had suffered blissful pains and ceased to defend myself against anything in the world, ceased to fear anything in the world, I had affirmed everything, had given my heart to everything. It had not lasted long, perhaps a quarter of an hour, but it returned to me that night in a dream, and since then, throughout all the bleak days, it had secretly shone for me from time to time, sometimes I saw it clearly for minutes on end, leading like a golden, godly path through my life, almost always deeply buried beneath dung and dust, but then shining forth again in golden sparks, seeming as if it could never be lost again, and yet soon it was deeply lost indeed. On one occasion, when I was lying awake at night, I suddenly began reciting verses, verses so beautiful and so bizarre that it never could have occurred to me to write them down, by morning I had forgotten them, and yet they lay concealed within me like a heavy nut in an old and fragile shell. On other occasions it happened when I was reading a poet, when I was reflecting on an idea from Descartes, from Pascal, or again it shone forth and led me onward along the golden path into the heavens when I was with my lover. Oh, it is hard to find that godly path in the midst of this life that we lead, in the midst of such a very contented, very bourgeois, very mindless age, when we are confronted with this architecture, these businesses, these politics, these people! How could I be anything but a Steppenwolf and a surly hermit in the midst of a world full of goals none of which I share, and pleasures none of which I desire! I can't bear to sit too long in a theater or cinema, I can barely read a newspaper, rarely a modern book, I can't understand what pleasure and joy it is that people seek in the overfilled trains and hotels, in the overfilled cafés with their oppressive, overbearing music, in the bars and cabarets of the elegant cities of luxury, in the world's fairs, on the promenades, in the lectures for the intellectually curious, at the great athletic fields—I cannot understand all of these joys, I cannot share them, though surely they would be within my reach, while thousands of others must toil and push to attain them. And, on the other hand, those things that bring me my few hours of joy, that bring me bliss, adventure, ecstasy, and exaltation, those are things that the world knows and seeks and loves only in literature, if at all, in life the world considers them insane. And indeed, if the world is right—if all this music in the cafés, all these mass entertainments, all these Americanized people who are content with so little, if all of them are right—then I really am the Steppenwolf that I have often called myself, an animal that has strayed into a foreign world it does not understand, where it no longer finds its home, its air, its nourishment.

Thinking these familiar thoughts, I continued walking along the damp street, through one of the quietest and oldest quarters of the city. There, in the darkness on the other side of the narrow street, stood an old gray stone wall that I was always glad to see, it was always standing there, so old and unconcerned, between a small church and an old hospital, during the day I often let my eyes rest on its rough surface, there were not many surfaces that were so calm, so good, so silent in the center of the city, where otherwise every half a square meter was occupied by some shop, some lawyer, some inventor, some doctor, some barber, or some miracle worker with a cure for corns who shouted out his name in your direction. And once again I saw the old wall standing there, peaceful and still, yet something about it had changed, I saw a pretty little portal with a pointed arch in the middle of the wall and I was plunged into doubt, because I truly did not know anymore whether the portal had always been there, or whether it had only just been added. It certainly looked old, ancient; presumably the little closed entryway with its dark wooden door had been there for centuries, leading into the sleepy courtyard of some cloister, and still did so today, even if the cloister was no longer standing, and I had probably seen the gate a hundred times and simply never taken any notice of it, perhaps it had been freshly painted and that was what drew my attention. All the same, I stood still and looked attentively across the street, but without crossing, since the street that lay between was so unfathomably marshy and wet; I stayed on the sidewalk just looking across, the night was already quite dark, and it seemed to me that a wreath or some other colorful decoration was twined around the archway. And now that I was pushing myself to look more closely, I saw a bright sign above the portal, on which it appeared to me that something was written. I strained my eyes, and finally I crossed the street despite the dirt and puddles. There, above the portal, I saw that one spot on the old gray-green of the wall was illuminated by a dim light, and colorful moving letters were appearing on this spot and quickly disappearing again, returning and vanishing. So, I thought, now they've even gone and exploited this good old wall for a neon sign! Meanwhile I was deciphering some of the words as they flitted by, they were hard to read so I had to guess half of them, the let-ters appeared so pale and frail, with uneven spacing in between, and they faded again so quickly. Whoever had hoped to make money that way was not a shrewd man, he was a Steppenwolf, the poor wretch; why was he sending his letters out to play here on this wall, in the darkest street in the old city, at this time of day, in rainy weather, where no one was about, and why were they so fleeting, so windblown, so skittish and illegible? But wait, now I was getting it, I was able to catch a glimpse of several words in a row, they spelled:

Magic Theater
Admission not for everyone
—not for everyone

I tried to open the door, the heavy old latch would not yield to any force. The letters' game had come to an end, it had stopped suddenly, sadly, having become aware of its own futility. I took a few steps back, stepped deep into the mud, no more letters appeared, the game had faded away, I remained standing in the mud for a long time, waiting in vain.

Then, just as I was giving up, when I had already returned to the sidewalk, a few colorful, glowing letters sprinkled down across the reflective asphalt in front of me.

I read:

Only——for——the in——sane!

My feet had gotten wet and I was freezing, but still I stood there quite a while longer, waiting. No more. As I stood there, thinking how prettily the delicate, colorful will-o'-the-wisp letters had flickered across the damp wall and the shiny black asphalt, suddenly a fragment of my earlier reflections came back to me: the parable of the golden path that all at once grows distant and elusive again.

I was freezing, so I walked on, dreaming my way along that path, yearning for the entrance to a magic theater, only for the insane. By now I had reached the market district, where there was no shortage of evening entertainment, every few steps I saw another poster or signboard advertising: Ladies' dance band—vaudeville—cinema—dance night—but all that was not for me, it was for "everyone," for normal people, the people I saw everywhere in droves, thronging the entrances. Nevertheless, my sadness had lifted a bit, I had been brushed by a greeting from the other world, a few colorful letters had danced and played upon my soul and struck hidden chords, a glimmer of the golden path had grown visible again.

I went to the little old-fashioned drinking house where nothing has changed since the first time I stayed in this city, roughly twenty-five years ago, even the tavernkeeper is the same woman as back then, and some of the guests who sit here today were already sitting here back then, in the same seats, in front of the same glasses. I entered the modest tavern, now this was a refuge. True, it was only a refuge like the one in the stairwell by the Norfolk Island pine, even here I could not find a home or a community, I could only find a spot for a quiet spectator, in front of a stage on which strange people performed strange plays, but even this quiet place was good for something: there was no crowd, no shouting, no music, just a few quiet townspeople at bare wooden tables (no marble, no enameled metal, no plush, no brass!), each of them with an evening drink in front of him, a good hearty wine. Perhaps these few regulars, all of whom I knew by sight, were true philistines, perhaps they had dreary altars to stupid household gods of contentment at home in their philistine apartments, or perhaps they were lonely fellows like me who had run off the rails, quietly and thoughtfully drinking away their bankrupt ideals, perhaps they, too, were Steppenwolves and poor devils; I didn't know. Each of them was drawn here by some homesickness, some disappointment, some need to compensate; here the married man sought the ambience of his bachelor days, the old civil servant the echoes of his student years; they were all rather quiet, they were all drinkers and, like me, they would rather sit in front of a half liter of Alsatian wine than in front of a ladies' dance band. Here I cast my anchor, I could bear it here for an hour, even two. I had hardly taken a sip of the Alsatian wine when I realized that I hadn't eaten anything all day except my breakfast bread.

It's incredible what all a person can swallow! For about ten minutes I read a newspaper, letting the spirit of an irresponsible man enter me through my eyes, the spirit of someone who chews the words of others in his mouth and then spits them out again, saliva-drenched but undigested. I devoured it, a whole column of it. And then I ate a big piece of liver that someone had cut from the body of a calf after it was clubbed to death. Incredible! The best part was the Alsatian wine. I don't like wild, intense wines, at least not every day, the ones that make a show of their powerful charms and enjoy a reputation for their special flavors. What I love most of all are very pure, light, modest country wines that don't have any special names, you can down quite a bit of those wines, and they taste nice and friendly, like land and earth and sky and woods. A cup of Alsatian wine and a piece of good bread, that's the best meal of all. But I already had a portion of liver in me, an unusual pleasure for me since I rarely eat meat, and the second cup was sitting in front of me. That was incredible, too: the fact that somewhere, in green valleys, wholesome, healthy people were cultivating vines and pressing grapes, so that here and there in the world, far away from them, disappointed townspeople and clueless Steppenwolves could quietly sip a bit of courage and good humor from their cups.

Very well then, let it be incredible! It was good, it was helping, the good humor was coming. I let out a burst of belated laughter at the mishmash of words in the newspaper article, and suddenly I remembered the forgotten melody of that soft passage that the woodwinds had played, it rose up in me like a small, reflective soap bubble, it shone, it reflected the whole world, colorful and small, and then it softly disappeared again. If this heavenly little melody had been able to secretly take root in my soul, and one day to raise its fair flower in me again with all its lovely colors, could I be completely lost? Even if I was a stray animal that could not understand its surroundings, still there was some meaning in my foolish life, something in me responded, answered calls from distant worlds on high, there were a thousand images piled up in my brain:

Giotto's companies of angels from the blue vaulted ceiling of a small church in Padua, accompanied by Hamlet and Ophelia with her garland, beautiful parables of all the sorrow and misunderstanding in the world, and there in the burning balloon stood the aeronaut Giannozzo, blowing his horn, Attila Schmelzle held his new hat in his hand, the sculpted mountain Borobudur towered up into the air. And even if all of these beautiful figures lived in a thousand other hearts as well, there were still ten thousand other, unknown images and sounds, whose homes and seeing eyes and hearing ears lived only within me. The old hospital wall with its old, weathered, dappled gray-green, in whose cracks and wear a thousand frescoes could be discerned—who answered its call, who let it into his soul, who loved it, who felt the magic of its delicate, dying colors? The old books of the monks, with their softly glowing miniatures, and the books of German authors from two hundred years, one hundred years ago, forgotten by their people, all the worn and mildewed volumes, and the prints and manuscripts of the old musicians, the sturdy, yellowed sheets of music with their frozen dreams of sound—who heard their spirited, mischievous, and yearning voices, who bore a heart filled with their spirit and magic through another age, one alien to them? Who still remembered that small, tenacious cypress tree high on the mountain above Gubbio, bowed and split by a rockslide and yet clinging to life, even sprouting a scraggly new tip in its distress? Who did justice to the diligent lady of the house on the second floor and her gleaming Norfolk Island pine? Who read the cloud writing in the mists that drift over the Rhine at night? It was the Steppenwolf. And who sought out the meaning that fluttered over the ruins of his life, suffered the seemingly meaningless, experienced the seemingly insane, secretly hoped that in this last mad chaos he might yet find revelation and nearness to God?

I held on tightly to my cup, which the tavernkeeper was preparing to fill for me again, and stood up. I didn't need any more wine. The golden path had flashed up before me, reminding me of the eternal, of Mozart, of the stars. For an hour I could breathe again, could live, could exist, I did not have to suffer agonies, to be afraid, to be ashamed.

A light drizzle, tousled by the cold wind, was rattling around the lanterns and sparkling with a glassy glimmer as I stepped out into the quiet street. Where to now? If I had had the power at that moment to grant my own wishes, I would have been presented at once with a small, pretty salon in the style of Louis XVI, where a few good musicians would have played me two or three pieces by Handel and Mozart. That would have been just what I wanted right now, I would have sipped the cool, exquisite music as the gods sip nectar. Oh, if I had had a friend now, a friend in some garret, brooding by candlelight with a violin lying next to him! How I would have crept up on him in the still of night, silently climbing the winding staircase to surprise him, and we would have savored a few unearthly hours of the night with conversation and music! I had often tasted of this happiness long ago, in years gone by, but this, too, had come unmoored and drifted away from me with the passage of time, withered years lay between here and there.

I reluctantly headed home, turning up the collar of my coat and striking the wet pavement with my cane. But no matter how slowly I might make my way home, all too soon I would be sitting in my garret again, in my little imitation of a home, which I did not love and yet could not do without, for the days when I could spend a rainy winter's night wandering outdoors were past for me. Well, in God's name, I didn't want to let anything spoil my good mood this evening, not the rain, not the gout, not the Norfolk Island pine, and even if there was no chamber orchestra to be had, and no lonely friend with a violin to be found, still that precious melody was sounding within me, and I could play at least a hint of it to myself, humming softly as I rhythmically drew my breath. I continued on my way, lost in thought. No, it was possible even without the chamber music and without the friend, and it was ridiculous to let myself be consumed by an impotent desire for warmth. Solitude is independence, it is what I had wished for and finally attained over all these long years. It was cold, oh yes, but it was also quiet, wonderfully quiet and vast, like the cold, silent space in which the stars revolve.

As I passed a dance hall, boisterous jazz music blared out at me, as hot and raw as the steam that rises from raw meat. I stopped for a moment; as much as I detested this kind of music, it always held a secret allure for me. Jazz was repugnant to me, but still I found it ten times better than all of today's academic music; even for me its joyful, raw wildness reached deep into the world of instinctual drives, and it breathed a naïve, honest sensuality.

I stood there for a moment with my nose in the air, catching the scent of that bloody, jarring music, wickedly and lasciviously sniffing the atmosphere of those halls. One half of the music, the lyrics, was schmaltzy, sugarcoated, and dripping with sentimentality, the other half was wild, moody, and powerful, and yet the two halves came together, naïvely and peacefully, to form a whole. It was decadent music, there must have been similar music in Rome in the days of the last emperors. Of course, it was a disgrace compared to Bach and Mozart and real music—but then so was all of our art, all of our thought, all of our pseudo-culture, as soon as it was compared to real culture. And this music had the merit of its great sincerity, its endearing, unrepentant blackness, and its joyful, childlike whimsy. It had something of the Negro and something of the American, who, in all his strength, seems so boyishly fresh and childlike to us Europeans. Would Europe turn out like that, too? Was it already on its way there? And as for us, the old connoisseurs and admirers of a bygone Europe, of its bygone authentic music, of its erstwhile authentic poetry, were we just a small, stupid minority of complicated neurotics who would be forgotten and mocked tomorrow? What we called "culture," what we called spirit, what we called soul, what we called beautiful, what we called sacred—was all of that merely a specter, something long dead, that appeared authentic and alive only to us few fools? Perhaps it had never been authentic and alive to begin with? Perhaps the thing we fools were striving for had never been anything more than a phantom?

The old town quarter welcomed me, the little church stood there faded and unreal in the midst of all that gray. Suddenly my experience from earlier that evening came back to me, the mysterious door with its pointed arch, the mysterious plaque above it, those taunting, dancing letters of light. What had they spelled out with their inscription? "Admission not for everyone." And: "Only for the insane." I glanced over at the old wall, examining it, secretly wishing that the magic would begin again, that the inscription would invite me in, insane as I am, that the little gate would open for me. Perhaps what I desired was there, perhaps my music would be playing there?

The dark stone wall gazed at me serenely in the deep twilight, closed off, deeply immersed in its dream. And there was no gate to be seen, no pointed arch, just a dark, silent wall without an opening. I walked on, smiling, nodding kindly to the stonework. "Sleep well, wall, I won't wake you. The time will come when they'll tear you down or plaster you with their greedy advertising signs, but for now you're still here, you're still beautiful and quiet and dear to me."

I was startled by a man who was spat out of the dark gorge of an alleyway just in front of me, a lonely man returning home late at night with weary steps, a cap perched on his head, dressed in a blue shirt and carrying a sign on a pole slung over his shoulder, with a strap around his waist supporting an open tray, like the ones that vendors wear at fairs. He walked wearily in front

of me without looking back in my direction, otherwise I would
have greeted him and given him a cigar. I tried to read his placard
in the light of the nearest streetlamp, the red placard on his pole,
but it was swaying back and forth, and I could not decipher anything. So I called out to him, asking him to show me the sign. He
stopped and held his pole a little straighter, and I could read the
dancing, tumbling letters:

> *Anarchistic evening entertainment!*
> *Magic theater!*
> *Admission not for ev . . .*

"You're just the man I've been looking for," I joyfully exclaimed.
"What is this about evening entertainment? Where is it? When?"
He had already started walking again.

"Not for everyone," he said indifferently, in a sleepy voice, and
kept on walking. He had had enough, he wanted to go home.

"Stop," I called out, running after him. "What do you have in
your box there? I want to buy something from you."

Without stopping, the man mechanically reached into his box,
pulled out a small booklet, and held it out to me. I quickly took it
and stuck it into my pocket. While I was fumbling with the but-
tons of my coat and looking for money, he turned off to the side at
a doorway, pulled the door closed behind him, and disappeared.
His heavy footsteps sounded in the courtyard, first on the paving
stones, then on a wooden staircase, and then I heard no more. And
suddenly I, too, was very tired, I had the feeling it was very late and
it would be good to be home now. I started walking faster, and soon
I had emerged from the sleepy alley of the outlying district into my
own neighborhood within the city walls, where the civil servants
and small pensioners live in small, tidy apartment houses behind
a bit of lawn and ivy. Passing by the ivy, the lawn, the little fir tree,

I came to the front door, found the keyhole, found the button for the light, crept past the glass doors, the polished cupboards, and the potted plants, and unlocked the door to my living room, my little imitation of a home, where the armchair and the stove, the inkwell and the paint box, the Novalis and the Dostoevsky were all waiting for me, just as when other people, real people, come home they find their mother or wife, their children, their maids, their dogs, their cats waiting for them.

As I took off my wet coat, my hand fell on that little book again. I pulled it out, it was slim and poorly printed, on low-quality paper, the kind of booklet you might find at a fair: "January's Child" or "How to Look Twenty Years Younger in Eight Days."

But when I had nestled into my armchair and put on my reading glasses, I looked at the cover of this little carnival booklet with astonishment and a sudden sense of fate as I read the title: *Treatise on the Steppenwolf. Not for Everyone.*

And the content of this text, which I read in a single sitting with ever-increasing excitement, was as follows:

Treatise on the Steppenwolf

Only for the Insane

Once upon a time there was a man named Harry, who was known as the Steppenwolf. He walked on two legs, he wore clothes, and he was a human being, but in fact he was really a Steppenwolf. He had learned many of the things that people with good sense can learn, and he was quite an intelligent man. But what he had not learned was this: how to be satisfied with himself and his life. This he could not do, he was a dissatisfied man. That was probably due to the fact that deep in his heart, he always knew (or thought he knew) that he actually was not a man at all, but a wolf from the steppes. Intelligent people may disagree about whether he was really a wolf, whether he had been enchanted at some point, perhaps even before he was born, and turned from a wolf into a human being, or whether he was born as a human but endowed with the soul of a Steppenwolf and possessed by it, or whether perhaps this belief that he was actually a wolf was merely a figment of his imagination or his illness. For example, it would be possible that this man was a wild, unruly, and disorderly child, that his educators had tried to kill the beast within him, and that by doing so they had instilled in him the notion and belief that he was, in fact, a beast, with only a thin veneer of education and humanity to conceal it. People could have long and engaging conversations about this question and even write books about it; but none of that would do the Steppenwolf any good, because for him it was all the same whether the wolf had been enchanted or beaten into him or whether it was only an illusion of his soul. What other people might think about it, and even what he himself might think about it, was a matter of indifference to him, because it would never get the wolf out of him.

Thus the Steppenwolf had two natures, one human and one wolfish, this was his fate, and it may well be that this fate was not so rare or unusual. It is said that many people have been seen who had a lot of the dog or the fox, the fish or the snake in them, but they have not experienced any particular difficulties on that account. In those people, the man and the fox, the man and the fish lived cheek by jowl, and neither did the other any harm, one even helped the other, and in many a man who has made it far in life and earned the envy of others, it was more the fox or the monkey than the man who made his fortune. This much is common knowledge. With Harry, however, it was different; in him the man and the wolf ran side by side, and far from helping one another, they were locked in constant mortal enmity, each lived only to do the other harm, and when two beings who share a single blood and a single soul are mortal enemies, then that is an abominable life. Well, each man has his lot, and not one of them is easy.

In the case of our Steppenwolf, he felt that he lived as a wolf sometimes and a man at others, as all crossbreeds do, but that when he was a wolf, the man in him was always watching, criticizing and passing judgment—and when he was a man, the wolf did the same. For example, when Harry the man had a beautiful thought, felt a fine, noble sentiment, or performed a so-called good deed, then the wolf in him bared its teeth and laughed, showing him with its bloody scorn how ridiculous all this noble theater appeared to an animal of the steppes, a wolf, who knew in his heart exactly what he desired, namely to trot

*in solitude through the steppes, occasionally to drink blood or
to pursue a she-wolf—and, from the wolf's point of view, this
meant that every human action was horribly strange and awkward, stupid and vain. But it was quite the same when Harry
felt and behaved like a wolf, when he bared his teeth at others,
when he felt hatred and mortal enmity toward all men and
their lying and degenerate manners and customs. For then the
human part of him lay in wait, observing the wolf, calling him
a brute and a beast, ruining and spoiling all of his joy in his
simple, healthy, wild wolf nature.*

*This is how it was with the Steppenwolf, and one can imag-
ine that Harry did not exactly lead a pleasant and happy life.
But that is not to say that he was unusually unhappy (although
it certainly seemed that way to him, just as every man considers the sufferings that afflict him to be the greatest). That much
should not be said of any man. Even someone who has no wolf
at all within him need not be happy just on that account. And
even the most unhappy life has its hours of sunshine and its
little flowers of happiness that bloom among the sand and the
stones. So it was with the Steppenwolf as well. He was usually
very unhappy, that can hardly be denied, and he could also
make others unhappy, namely when he loved them and they
loved him. For those who grew fond of him always saw only
one side of him. Some loved him as a fine, clever, and singular
person and were horrified and disappointed when they were
suddenly forced to discover the wolf within him. And that they
did, because Harry, like every creature, wanted to be loved as
a whole, and therefore he could not conceal the wolf within
him or deny it to those whose love was so important to him.
But there were also those who loved precisely the wolf within
him, precisely that part of him that was free, wild, untam-
able, dangerous, and strong, and to those people in turn it was*

extraordinarily disappointing and despicable when suddenly the wild, wicked wolf turned out to be a human being as well, when he also contained within him a longing for goodness and tenderness, a desire to listen to Mozart, read poetry, and entertain ideals of humanity. And these were the very people who were usually most disappointed and angriest of all, and so the Steppenwolf's double, equivocal nature always gave something of its own shape to the fates of those upon whose lives he made his mark.

But anyone who thinks that he knows the Steppenwolf and can imagine his miserable, tattered life is still mistaken, for he is still far from knowing everything. He does not know that (just as there is no rule without an exception, and just as one sinner is dearer to God under certain circumstances than ninety-nine righteous persons)—that Harry, too, was not immune to exceptions and strokes of luck, that there were times when he could feel just the wolf, or just the man, breathing, thinking, and feeling within him, alone and undisturbed, that sometimes, in very rare hours, the two even made their peace and lived for each other's sake, so that the one did not merely sleep while the other kept watch, but the two strengthened one another and each one was the other's double. Even in this man's life, as everywhere else in the world, it sometimes seemed that everything familiar, everyday, well known, and ordinary existed for no other purpose than to be interrupted now and then for just a few seconds, to make room for the extraordinary, for the miracle, for grace. Now, whether these short, rare hours of happiness compensated for the awful plight of the Steppenwolf and ameliorated it, so that happiness and suffering finally stood in balance, or whether perhaps even the short but intense happiness of those few hours absorbed all suffering and produced a surplus, that is another question over which the idle may brood at will. The wolf, too, often brooded over it, and those were his idle and useless days.

One thing remains to be said about this matter. There are quite a few people similar in kind to Harry, many artists in particular are people of this sort. All of these people have two souls, two natures within them, they contain both the divine and the diabolical, maternal and paternal blood, the capacity for happiness and for suffering, and these two elements appear both side by side and within each other, as hostile and entangled as wolf and man in Harry. And these people, who live very uneasy lives, occasionally experience such powerful and indescribably beautiful things in their rare moments of happiness—the foam in that moment of happiness occasionally sprays up so high and blindingly above the sea of suffering—that this brief flash of happiness radiates outward, touching and enchanting others. This precious, fleeting foam of happiness above the sea of suffering is the origin of all those works of art in which a single, suffering man raises himself above his own fate for an hour, so high that his happiness shines like a star, and all who see it take it for something eternal, for their own dream of happiness. All of these people, whatever their deeds and works may be, actually have no life at all, that is, their life is not an existence, it has no form, they are not heroes or artists or thinkers in the way that others are judges, doctors, shoemakers, or teachers, rather the life of each is one eternal movement and surging tide of suffering, it is unhappy and painfully riven and dreadful and meaningless, unless one is prepared to find meaning in just those rare experiences, deeds, thoughts, and works that shine above the chaos of such a life. These people are the source of the dangerous and terrible idea that human life as such might be no more than an awful mistake, a disastrous miscarriage of the primal mother, an experiment of nature gone wildly and horribly awry. But they are also the source of another idea, that man might be not only a halfway rational animal, but also a child of the gods, destined for immortality.

Every species of man has its distinguishing characteristics, its signatures, its virtues and vices, its deadly sins. One such characteristic of the Steppenwolf was that he was an evening person. The morning was a bad time of day for him, one that he feared and that had never brought him good fortune. Never on any morning of his life was he truly happy, never in the hours before noon did he himself do any good, have any good inspirations, bring any joy to himself or to others. Only in the course of the afternoon did he slowly grow warm and lively, and only toward evening, on his good days, did he become productive, active, sometimes even radiant and joyful. This was also tied to his need for solitude and independence. Never has a man had a deeper, more passionate need for independence than he had. In his youth, when he was still poor and struggling to earn his bread, he preferred to starve and go about in ragged clothing, if that meant that he could salvage a bit of independence. He never sold himself for money or for luxury, to women or to the powerful, and a hundred times over he cast aside and rejected those things that clearly promised him advantage and good fortune in the eyes of the world, just in order to retain his freedom. He could imagine nothing more abhorrent and atrocious than the obligation to carry out official duties, adhere to a regular daily and yearly schedule, obey the orders of others. An office, a law chamber, the halls of bureaucracy were as abhorrent to him as death, and the most horrible thing he could experience in a dream was to be confined to an army barracks. He knew how to extricate himself from all of these circumstances, often at great cost to himself.

THE STEPPENWOLF

Herein lay his strength and virtue, in this he was unshakable and incorruptible, in this his character was firm and straight. But this virtue, in turn, was very closely tied to his suffering and his fate. He fared as everyone fares: he obtained what he most stubbornly sought and strove for, compelled by his own innermost drives, but he obtained more than is good for any man. At first it was his dream and his delight, but later it became his bitter fate. Men of power are brought low by power, men of money by money, the subservient by serving, the slave to passion by passion. And so it was that the Steppenwolf was brought low by his independence. He attained his goal, he became ever more independent, no one could give him orders, no one could compel him to conform, and he could decide, freely and alone, what to do and what to leave undone. For every strong man unfailingly achieves any goal that he is truly driven to seek. But in the midst of this freedom that he had attained, Harry suddenly realized that his freedom was a kind of death, that he stood alone, that the world had left him in peace of a very uncanny sort, that men no longer meant anything to him, nor, indeed, did he to himself, that he was slowly suffocating in the more and more rarefied air of social isolation and loneliness. For now it was no longer his wish and goal to be alone and independent, instead it was his lot, his sentence; his magic wish had been granted and could not be undone, nor would it help if he reached out his arms, full of yearning and goodwill, to seek new bonds of fellowship: now people left him alone. Yet it was not as if they found him abhorrent and detestable. On the contrary, he had very many friends. Many people liked him. But it was always just sympathy and friendliness that he found, people sent him invitations, gave him gifts, wrote him nice letters, but no one came close to him, no bonds were formed, no one was willing and able to

share his life. He was surrounded by the air of loneliness, a quiet atmosphere, the world around him was slipping away, he was incapable of any relationships, and there was nothing that any will or desire could do about it. This was one of the important hallmarks of his life.

Another was his status as a suicide. It must be said here that it is incorrect to apply the term "suicide" only to those who actually kill themselves. In fact, the latter group includes many people who only become suicides incidentally, so to speak, who are not suicides of necessity, in their very nature. Among those without a personality, without a strong stamp, without a strong fate, among the dime-a-dozen men of the herd, there are many who die by suicide, though they are not suicides through and through, it is not their whole signature and stamp, while on the other hand, among those who are suicides in their very nature, there are very many, perhaps the majority, who never actually lay hands upon themselves. The "suicide"—and Harry was one—does not necessarily need to live in a particularly close relationship to death—and one can also do that without being a suicide. But it is a peculiar trait of the suicide that he, rightly or wrongly, experiences his own self as a particularly dangerous, dubious, and endangered spawn of nature, that he always perceives himself as extraordinarily exposed and imperiled, as if he were standing on the narrowest ledge of a precipice, where a little push from without or the slightest weakness from within would suffice to send him plunging into the abyss. People of this sort are distinguished in their lines of fate by the fact that suicide is the most likely cause of death for them, at least in their own imagination. The precondition of this disposition, which almost always manifests itself by early youth and accompanies these men throughout their lives, is by no means a particular lack of vitality, on the contrary, some extraordinarily tenacious, passionate, and bold constitutions can be found among the "suicides." But just as there are certain constitutions that tend toward fever at the slightest sign of illness, these constitutions, whom we dub "suicides," and who are always very delicate and sensitive, begin intensely to dwell upon the prospect of suicide at the slightest shock. If we had a science with the courage to assume the great responsibility of studying human beings as such, rather than only the mechanisms of living organisms—if we had something like an anthropology, a psychology—these facts would be known to everyone.

Of course, what we have said here about suicides is merely superficial, a matter of appearances—it is psychology, that is, a part of physics. From a metaphysical standpoint, the situation looks very different and much clearer, because from that perspective the "suicides" appear to us as those who suffer from the guilt of individuation, those souls who no longer see their goal in life as the perfection and organization of the self, but rather as its dissolution, a return to the mother, a return to God, a return to the universe. Among these sorts of people, there are many who are fully incapable of ever actually committing suicide, because they are deeply aware of its sinfulness. Nevertheless, for us they are suicides, because they see redemption in death, not in life, they are prepared to cast themselves aside, to sacrifice and extinguish themselves and return to the beginning.

Just as every strength can also become a weakness (indeed, under certain circumstances it must become one), so, conversely, the typical suicide can often make of his apparent weakness a form of strength and support, indeed, he does this extraordinarily often. This was likewise the case for Harry, the Steppenwolf. Like thousands of his kind, he did not use the notion that the path to death stood open to him at every moment merely as the basis for a youthful, melancholy play of fantasy; rather, he made of this very thought a source of consolation and support. True, every shock, every pain, every bitter circumstance in life immediately awakened in him the wish to take refuge in death, as is the case for every man of his ilk. But he gradually transformed this inclination into a philosophy that was positively conducive to life. His intimate acquaintance with the thought that that emergency exit perpetually stood open to him gave him strength, made him curious to savor pains and bitter circumstances, and when he was particularly miserable, he could at times feel with a grim joy, with a sort of schadenfreude: "I'm curious to see how much a man can really endure after all! Whenever I reach the limits of what is bearable, I need only open the door, and I can escape." There are many suicides who derive unusual strength from this thought.

On the other hand, all suicides also know the struggle against the temptation to end their own lives. Every one of them knows very well, in some corner of his soul, that suicide is a way out, but really just a slightly shabby, illegitimate emergency exit, and that ultimately it is more noble and beautiful to allow oneself to be vanquished and laid low by life itself than to perform this deed with one's own hand. This knowledge, this bad conscience, which shares a common source with the bad conscience of so-called self-pleasurers, for instance, spurs most "suicides" to engage in a protracted struggle against their temptation. They struggle as the kleptomaniac struggles against his vice. The Steppenwolf, too, was a veteran of this struggle, he had waged it with many weapons in turn. Finally, at the age of roughly forty-seven years, he chanced upon a clever idea that was by no means without its

humor, and that often brought him joy. He designated his fif-
tieth birthday as the day on which he would allow himself to
commit suicide. On that day, he told himself, it would be up to
him to use the emergency exit or not, depending on his mood.
Whatever might happen to him now—if he should become
sick, impoverished, endure suffering and bitterness—was only
temporary, at the very most it could only last those few years,
months, and days, and their number was growing smaller by
the day! And indeed, he now bore many an adversity much
more lightly, even those that would once have tormented him
longer and more deeply, that would perhaps even have shaken
him to the core. When for one reason or another he was doing
particularly badly, when the barrenness, loneliness, and wild-
ness of his life were exacerbated by particular pains or losses,
then he could say to those pains: "Just you wait, just two more
years, then I will be your master!" And then he loved to lose
himself in the thought of how on the morning of his fiftieth
birthday the letters and congratulations would arrive, even as
he, firmly grasping his straight razor, took leave of all of his
pains and pulled the door shut behind him. Then the gout in
his bones, his melancholy, his headaches and stomachaches,
would just have to fend for themselves.

It remains for us to explain the exceptional case of the Step-
penwolf, and particularly his unusual relationship to the
bourgeoisie, by tracing these phenomena back to their first
principles. Let us take his relationship to the "bourgeois" as
our starting point, since it lends itself to the purpose!

The Steppenwolf, by his own estimation, stood wholly out-
side the bourgeois world, since he knew neither family life nor
social ambition. He felt that he was very much on his own, at

times as an eccentric and a pathological hermit, at other times as an exceptional individual with an inclination to genius, elevated above the petty norms of ordinary life. He consciously disdained bourgeois men and was proud not to be one. Nevertheless, in certain respects he led a fully bourgeois life, he had money in the bank and supported poor relatives, in his manner of dress he was careless but respectable and inconspicuous, and he strove to live in peace with the police, the tax collectors, and similar authorities. But even apart from that, he was constantly drawn by a strong, secret desire to the little world of the bourgeoisie, to the quiet, respectable family homes with small manicured gardens, a stairwell polished to a shine, and the whole unassuming atmosphere of order and respectability. He liked to have his little vices and extravagances, to feel that he was outside of the bourgeoisie, an eccentric or a genius, yet he never made his home or dwelt in those provinces of life, so to speak, that lay beyond the boundaries of the bourgeoisie. He was not at home in the company of violent or deviant individuals, nor among the criminals or those who had forfeited their legal rights; rather, he always lived in the province of the bourgeoisie, defining himself in relation to their habits, norms, and atmosphere, even if this relationship was always one of opposition and revolt. Besides, he had experienced a petit bourgeois upbringing, and quite a few of those concepts and patterns remained ingrained in him. In theory he had nothing at all against prostitution, but he personally would have been incapable of taking a prostitute seriously and truly viewing her as his equal. He could love the political criminal, the revolutionary, or the intellectual firebrand as his brother, these men ostracized by state and society, but he would not have known what to do with a thief, a burglar, or a sex killer, except to pity them in a quite bourgeois fashion.

In this way, he unfailingly respected and affirmed the same things with one half of his nature and his deeds that he fought and opposed with the other. Having grown up in a refined, bourgeois household, with its established forms and customs, he had remained attached to the order of this world with one part of his soul, even after he had long since attained a degree of individuation far exceeding what was possible by bourgeois standards and liberated himself from the content of bourgeois ideals and beliefs.

Now the "bourgeois" life, considered as a perennial condition of humanity, is nothing more than an attempt at balance, a striving for a balanced middle ground between the countless extremes and oppositions of human behavior. If we take one of these pairs of opposites as an example—for instance, the saint and the libertine—our analogy will soon be understood. A man has the option of devoting himself fully to the spiritual, to the pursuit of the divine, to the ideal of the sacred. On the other hand, he has the option of devoting himself fully to his urges, to his sensual appetites, and of directing all of his striving toward the pursuit of a moment's pleasure. The former path leads to sainthood, martyrdom to the spirit, the surrender of the self to God. The latter path leads to libertinage, martyrdom to the drives, the surrender of the self to corruption. Now the bourgeois man attempts to live in the happy medium between the two. He will never surrender himself, never devote himself fully to either intoxication or asceticism, he will never be a martyr, never consent to his own annihilation—to the contrary, his ideal is not the abandonment, but rather the preservation of the self, he strives for neither sainthood nor its opposite, he cannot bear such unconditional commitments; he does want to serve God, but he wants intoxication, too; he wants to be virtuous, but he also wants to have a little pleasure and comfort during his time on earth. In short, he attempts to

*place himself in the middle between the extremes, in a temper-
ate and salubrious zone free of all violent storms or tempests;
and he succeeds, too, but only at the cost of that intensity of
life and feeling that is experienced by those who pursue the
unconditional and the extreme. One can only live intensely at
the expense of the self. Now the bourgeois man values nothing
more highly than the self (albeit a quite rudimentary self).
And so, by surrendering intensity, he gains stability and security; in place of zealotry, he gains a clear conscience; in place
of passion, pleasure; in place of freedom, comfort; in place of
deadly fervor, an agreeable temperature. Hence the bourgeois
man is by nature a creature whose vital drive is weak, he is
anxious, always afraid to reveal himself, and easy to govern.
Thus he has replaced might with the majority, violence with
law, responsibility with elections.*

*It is clear that this weak and anxious creature could never
hold its own, no matter how great its numbers might be; in
view of its defining characteristics, it could never play any role
in the world but that of a herd of lambs between loose wolves.
Nevertheless, we see that even though bourgeois men find their
backs against the wall the moment truly powerful figures take
charge, still they are never destroyed, at times they even seem
to dominate the world. How is that possible? Neither the large
size of their herd, nor their virtue, nor their "common sense"
(to use the English term), nor their organization would be
strong enough to save them from destruction. Someone whose
vital intensity is so thoroughly weakened from the start cannot
be kept alive by any medicine in the world. And yet the bourgeoisie lives, thrives, and prospers.—Why?*

*The answer is: Because of the Steppenwolves. In fact, the
vital force of the bourgeoisie does not by any means derive
from the characteristics of its ordinary members, but rather*

*from those of its extraordinarily numerous "outsiders," who
can still be subsumed into the bourgeoisie by virtue of its neb-
ulous and malleable ideals. There are always a large number
of strong and wild characters living amid the bourgeoisie. Our
Steppenwolf Harry is a typical example. He, who has cultivated his individuality to a far greater degree than is possible
for a bourgeois man; he, who knows the bliss of meditation as
well as the somber joys of hatred and self-hatred; he, who dis-
dains law, virtue, and common sense, nonetheless remains captive to the bourgeoisie, and cannot escape it. And so the great
mass of the true bourgeoisie is surrounded by wide swaths of
humanity, many thousands of lives and intellects, each of them
in principle called to lead an unconditional life after having
outgrown the bourgeoisie, yet each of them at the same time
firmly rooted in that same bourgeoisie, drawn to it by infantile
feelings, a bit infected by its weakening of their vital intensity,
thus somehow remaining dependent, obligated, in service of
the bourgeoisie. For the principle of the bourgeoisie is counter
to that of great men: Whoever is not against me is with me!*

*If we examine the soul of the Steppenwolf from this per-
spective, we see him as a man whose high degree of individuation already sets him apart from the bourgeoisie—for
individuation, when pushed to the extreme, turns against the
self, and tends instead toward its destruction. We see that he
has strong dispositions toward both the saint and the libertine, but some weakness or inertia has prevented him from
making the leap into wild, free outer space, and instead he
remains stranded on the heavy, motherly star of the bourgeoisie. This is his place in the universe, it holds him fast. The vast
majority of intellectuals and the greater portion of all artists are of the same type. Only the strongest among them can
pierce through the atmosphere of the bourgeois earth to enter*

the cosmos; the others become resigned or make compromises, they disdain the bourgeoisie but still belong to it and even strengthen and glorify it, since in the end they must affirm it if they are to live. These countless existences do not rise to the level of tragedy, but they can certainly complain of quite considerable misfortune and unlucky stars, and in this hell their talents are cooked through and brought to fruition. Those few who manage to break free find their way to an unconditional life that ends in the most marvelous destruction; these are the tragic ones, their number is small. But the others, those who remain bound to the bourgeois life, whose talents are often held in great esteem by the bourgeoisie, may have recourse to a third realm, an imaginary but sovereign world: humor. Those Steppenwolves who find no peace, who endure constant, tremendous suffering, who lack the necessary power to break out into the cosmos, who feel called to the unconditional, yet unable to live there: when their spirit has grown strong and resilient from suffering, they can find relief and reconciliation in humor. Humor always remains somehow bourgeois, although the real bourgeois man is incapable of understanding it. In the imaginary sphere of humor, the vexed, manifold ideal of all Steppenwolves is realized: here it is possible not only to embrace the saint and the libertine simultaneously, to bend these two poles until they meet, but also to extend this embrace to encompass the bourgeois man. After all, it is quite possible for the religious zealot to embrace the criminal, and vice versa, but it is quite impossible for either of them, or for anyone else who lives an unconditional life, to also embrace the neutral, lukewarm middle ground, the bourgeoisie. Only humor, the magnificent invention of those who have been hindered in their calling to greatness—those nearly tragic figures, those most highly gifted misfortunates—only humor (perhaps the most peculiar and ingenious invention of man-kind) achieves the impossible, encompassing and uniting all domains of human existence in the beams of light from its prisms. To live in the world as if it were not the world; to obey the law and yet to stand above it; to own "as if one did not own"; to abstain as if it were no sacrifice—all of these well-loved and frequently formulated principles of great worldly wisdom can be realized by humor alone.

And if the Steppenwolf, who by no means lacks the neces-sary gifts and inclinations, should succeed in cooking up and sweating out this magic potion in the sultry bowels of his hell, then he would be saved. He still has a long way to go. But the possibility, the hope, is there. Whoever loves him, whoever cares for him, may wish him this salvation. True, he would thus remain forever rooted in the bourgeois world; but his suf-fering would be bearable, it would be fruitful. His relationship to the bourgeois world, in love and hate, would shed its senti-mentality, and his bondage to this world would cease to cause him constant torment and disgrace.

In order to achieve this, or perhaps to muster the courage to make the leap into outer space after all, such a Steppenwolf would have to be brought face-to-face with himself, he would have to gaze deeply into the chaos of his own soul and come to full self-consciousness. His questionable existence would then reveal itself to him in all its finality, and it would become impossible for him to take refuge from the hell of his instincts time after time in the consolations of sentimental philoso-phy, and to take refuge from these consolations in turn in the blind intoxication of his wolfish nature. Man and wolf would be compelled to acknowledge each other without the deceptive masks of feelings, to look each other nakedly in the eye. Then either they would explode and part ways for all time, so that there would be no more Steppenwolf, or they would enter into a marriage of convenience beneath the dawning light of humor.

One day Harry may be presented with this final possibility. One day he may learn to acknowledge himself, perhaps because one of our little mirrors has found its way into his hands, perhaps because he has encountered the immortals, or perhaps because he has found the key to the liberation of his depraved soul in one of our magic theaters. A thousand such possibilities await him, his fate irresistibly attracts them, all such outsiders of bourgeois society live in the atmosphere of these magical possibilities. Nothing is all it takes for lightning to strike.

And the Steppenwolf knows all of this very well, even if he never actually sees this sketch of his inner biography. He senses his place in the edifice of the world, he senses and knows the immortals, he senses and fears the possibility that he will encounter himself, and he knows about that mirror that he so bitterly needs to gaze into, and lives in mortal fear of what he will find there.

In concluding our study, it will be necessary to dispel one last fiction, one fundamental misconception. Of course all "explanations," all psychology, all attempts at understanding require explanatory aids, theories, mythologies, lies; and a respectable author should not neglect to dispel these lies as thoroughly as possible at the conclusion of his presentation. For instance, when I say "above" or "below," even that is a claim that requires explanation, since above and below exist only in thought, only in the abstract. The world itself knows no above or below.

And by the same token, briefly stated, the "Steppenwolf" is

*a fiction. If Harry feels that he is a wolf-man and believes that
he is composed of two hostile and contradictory natures, this is
merely a simplifying myth. Harry is not a wolf-man, and if we
seem to have adopted this lie that he himself has concocted and
believed, if we have attempted to actually regard and interpret
him as a being of two natures, it was only in hopes of making
ourselves more easily understood that we have employed this
misconception, which we shall now attempt to rectify.*

*The dichotomy of wolf and man, of instinct and intellect,
that Harry employed to make his fate more intelligible is a
very crude oversimplification, one that defiles the real in favor
of a plausible but erroneous explanation of the contradictions that this man finds in himself and that he takes for the
source of his not insignificant suffering. Harry finds within
himself a "man," that is, a world of thoughts, of feelings, of
culture, of tamed and sublimated nature, and alongside this
he finds a "wolf," that is, a dark world of instincts, of wildness,
barbarism, of unsublimated, raw nature. But in spite of this
apparently clear division of his being into two mutually hostile spheres, he has observed again and again how wolf and
man could get along with each other for a while, for one happy
moment. If Harry wanted to determine—for each individual moment of his life, for each of his deeds, for each of his
sensations—which portion belonged to the man, and which to
the wolf, he would immediately find himself in a predicament,
and his lovely wolf theory would fall apart entirely. For there
is no man, not even the most primitive Negro, not even the
idiot, who is so congenially simple that his entire nature can
be expressed as the sum of only two or three primary elements;
and it is a hopelessly childish undertaking to explain such a
sophisticated man as Harry with the naïve dichotomy of wolf
and man. Harry consists not of two natures, but of a hundred,*

of thousands. His life (like all human lives) does not swing between just two poles, such as instinct and intellect or saint and libertine, it swings between thousands, between countless pairs of poles.

The fact that such an intelligent and learned man as Harry can take himself for a "Steppenwolf," that he considers it possible to accommodate the rich and complex structure of his life in such plain, brutal, and primitive terms, ought not to come to us as a great surprise. Men are not capable of great feats of mind, and even the most intellectual and educated man always views the world and himself through filtered lenses, employing very naïve simplifications and distortions—but he does this to himself most of all! For all men have a truly compulsive and seemingly innate urge to conceive of the self, the "I," as a unity. No matter how frequently and how severely this delusional confidence might be shaken, it always makes itself whole again. The judge who sits across from the murderer and looks him in the eyes, who for a moment hears the murderer speaking with his own (the judge's) voice, who discovers all of the murderer's feelings, capabilities, possibilities within himself as well, returns to himself the next moment, becomes one again, becomes the judge, slips quickly back into the shell of his own imagined self, does his duty and sentences the murderer to death. And whenever some sense of this multiplicity begins to dawn in particularly gifted and finely configured human souls, when these people, like every genius, break through the delusion of the unified personality and see themselves as multiple, as a bundle of many "I"s, no sooner have they expressed this than the majority locks them up, calls on science for support, issues a diagnosis of schizophrenia, and protects mankind from having to hear a cry of truth from the mouths of these unfortunate people. Now, why waste words here, why say things that any thinking person already knows, but that good manners forbid us to express?—So, whenever a man takes this step forward, whenever he expands the imaginary unity of this "I" into a duality, even this step suffices to make him almost a genius, in any case a rare and interesting exception. But in reality, no "I" is a unity, not even the most naïve, every "I" is a richly varied world, a small, starry firmament, a chaos of forms, of degrees and conditions, of inheritances and possibilities. The fact that every individual endeavors to see this chaos as a unity, and speaks of his own "I" as if it were a simple, firmly formed, clearly defined phenomenon: this misconception, which afflicts every man (even the highest), seems to be a necessity, a basic condition of life, like breathing and eating.

This misconception results from a simple transference. Every man is one in body, but never in soul. Literature, too, even the most refined literature, traditionally presents people who appear to be whole, who appear to be unified. Of all the literature to date, experts and connoisseurs give pride of place to drama, and rightly so, since it offers (or could offer) the greatest possibilities for representing the "I" in its multiplicity— if only this were not contradicted by the crude illusion that each individual person in a drama represents a unified whole, simply because each character is inevitably stuck in a single, unified, self-contained body. And naïve aesthetics reserves the highest place of all for so-called character dramas, in which each character appears as a fully recognizable and discrete entity. Only slowly do some individuals begin to perceive, as if from afar, that all of this may be a cheap, superficial aesthetic, that we are mistaken when we praise our own great dramatists by invoking magnificent standards of beauty that are not our own, but rather imported from the classical age, which always took the physical body as its starting point, and thus truly invented the fiction of the "I," of the person. This concept is wholly unknown in the literature of ancient India; the heroes of the Indian epics are not people, but rather tangles of people, chains of incarnation. And in our modern world there are works of literature in which the attempt is made— surely without the author's full awareness—to represent the multiplicity of the soul behind the veil of the play of people and characters. Anyone who wishes to see this must resolve to consider the characters of such a work not as individual beings, but rather as parts, as sides, as various aspects of a higher unity (which we might call the author's soul). For instance, anyone who considers Faust in this manner will see Faust, Mephisto, Wagner, and all of the others as a single entity, a superperson, and only in this higher unity, not in the individual figures, is there some indication of the true nature of the soul. When Faust delivers the maxim that is famous among schoolteachers, and admired by trembling philistines—"Two souls, alas, are housed within my breast!"—he is forgetting Mephisto and quite a few other souls who also live in his breast. Of course, our Steppenwolf also believes that he carries two souls (wolf and man) within his breast, and he finds that even this makes his breast unpleasantly crowded. After all, the breast, the body, is always one; but in fact the souls that dwell there do not number only two or five, they are countless—man is an onion with a hundred skins, a tissue woven of many threads. This was well known and recognized in ancient Asia, and Buddhist yoga has a very precise technique for exposing the delusion of the personality. How comical and multifarious is the game of mankind: even as India devoted vast efforts over thousands of years to exposing this delusion, the Occident devoted equal efforts to supporting and strengthening it.

If we consider the Steppenwolf from this standpoint, it

becomes clear to us why his laughable dual nature causes him so much suffering. He believes, as Faust does, that even two souls are too much for a single breast, and that the breast must be torn asunder. On the contrary, two souls are far too few, and Harry brutally defiles his poor soul when he attempts to capture it in such a primitive image. Although he is a highly educated man, in this matter Harry behaves a bit like a savage who can't count higher than two. He calls one piece of himself man, another piece wolf, and believes that with that he has reached the end and offered an exhaustive account of himself. He crams everything spiritual, sublimated, or cultivated that he finds within himself into the "man," and anything instinctive, wild, and chaotic into the wolf. But real life is not as simple as it appears in our thoughts, nor as crude as it sounds in our poor, idiotic language, and Harry is deceiving himself twice over when he employs this wolfish method as a Negro might. Harry, we fear, counts as "man" entire regions of his soul that are far from attaining the status of man, and counts as wolf parts of his nature that have progressed far beyond the wolf.

Like all men, Harry thinks that he knows very well what a man is, and yet in truth he hasn't the slightest idea, although he often senses it in his dreams and other recalcitrant states of consciousness. He ought not to forget these insights, he ought to strive to make them his own! For man is not a fixed and enduring construction (as the classical ideal had it, despite the dissenting insights of the wise), rather he is an attempt and a transition, he is nothing other than the narrow, perilous bridge between nature and spirit. His innermost sense of purpose drives him to the spirit, to God—his inmost desire pulls him back to nature, to the mother: his life teeters, fearful and trembling, between these two powers. The meanings that men themselves associate with the term "man" are never more than a temporary, bourgeois consensus. Certain instincts, the rawest ones, are rejected and frowned upon by this convention; a certain amount of consciousness, civilization, and taming of the bestial instincts is required; a bit of spirit is not only permitted but actually demanded. The "man" of this convention, like every bourgeois ideal, is a compromise, a timorous, slyly naïve attempt to cheat both the evil primal mother, nature, and the burdensome primal father, spirit, of their harsh demands, and to dwell in the lukewarm middle ground between the two. That is why the bourgeois man allows and tolerates what he calls "personality," but at the same time surrenders that personality to the Moloch of the state, always playing off the one against the other. That is why the bourgeoisie burns a man today as a heretic, hangs him as a criminal, but builds monuments to him the day after tomorrow.

The insight that "man" is not a finished creation, but a demand of the spirit—a distant possibility, as much yearned for as it is feared—and that the path to that goal can only be traveled one short stretch at a time, in the face of the most frightful agonies and ecstasies, and only by those rare individuals for whom the scaffold is erected today, and a monument tomorrow—this insight lives within the Steppenwolf as well. But that thing within him that he calls "man," in contrast to his "wolf," is for the most part none other than the mediocre "man" of bourgeois convention. The path to the true man, the path to the immortals, is something that Harry can very well sense, and now and then he takes a tiny, tentative step along that path, for which he then atones with intense suffering, with painful loneliness. But to affirm and strive for that highest demand of all—to become truly human, the highest aspiration of the spirit—to travel the one narrow path that leads to immortality, is something that Harry fears in the depths of his soul. He feels quite clearly that that would lead to even greater suffering, to ostracism, to the ultimate renunciation, perhaps to the scaffold—and even if immortality beckons to him from the end of this path, still he is unwilling to endure all this suffering, to die all these deaths. Although he understands the aim of becoming human more clearly than the bourgeoisie, he closes his eyes and refuses to know that his desperate clinging to the "I," his desperate avoidance of death, is in fact the most certain path to eternal death, whereas the ability to die, to shed one's outer husk, to abandon oneself eternally to change, leads to immortality. When he worships his favorites among the immortals, such as Mozart, he ultimately still sees them through bourgeois eyes, and he is inclined to explain Mozart's perfection just as a schoolteacher would—as a product of his exceptional, specialized talents, rather than as a product of his great abandon and willingness to suffer, of his indifference to bourgeois ideals and his endurance of that most extreme loneliness that causes the bourgeois atmosphere around the man who suffers, the man becoming truly human, to grow as rarefied as the icy ether above the earth, that loneliness in the Garden of Gethsemane.

Still, at least our Steppenwolf has discovered this Faustian duality within himself, he has found that the unity of his body does not house a unified soul, that at best he is on the path, on the long pilgrimage that leads to this ideal of harmony. He would like to either vanquish the wolf within him and become fully human, or relinquish the man in order at least to live a unified, undivided life as a wolf. Presumably he has never closely observed a real wolf, for if he had, he might have seen that even animals do not have unified souls—that in them, too, behind their taut, elegant bodies, a multitude of aspirations and conditions can be found, that the wolf, too, has abysses within him, that the wolf, too, suffers. No, "Back to nature!" always leads man down the wrong path, a path of suffering and despair. Never again will it be possible for Harry to become fully wolf, and if he did, he would see that even the wolf is not a simple and primordial thing, but rather something manifold and very complex. Even the wolf has two, and more than two, souls in his wolfish breast, and whosoever wishes to be a wolf is guilty of the same forgetfulness as the man with his song: "Oh, how blissful still to be a child!" The sympathetic but sentimental man who sings the song of the blissful child also wishes to return to nature, to innocence, to the beginning, and he has completely forgotten that children are by no means blissful, that they are full of conflicts, that they are capable of many contradictions and every sort of suffering.

But there is no way back, neither to the wolf nor to the child. What lies at the origin of all things is not innocence and simplicity; everything that is created, even the most seemingly simple thing, is already guilty, is already rich in contradictions, it has been thrown into the dirty stream of becoming, and can never, never swim back upstream. The path to innocence, to the uncreated, to God, does not lead backward, but rather forward, not to the wolf or the child, but rather deeper into sin, deeper into the human. Even suicide will not be of much real use to you, poor Steppenwolf, you will have to follow the longer, more laborious, more difficult path of becoming human, to further and further multiply your duality, to further and further complicate your complexity. Rather than narrow your world, rather than simplify your soul, you will have to take more and more world—and finally the entire world—into your painfully expanded soul, in order perhaps to finally reach the end, to come to rest. This is the path that

Buddha followed, that every great man followed—sometimes consciously, sometimes unconsciously—as far as it would take him. Every birth means severing ties with the universe, means sundering, separation from God, becoming painfully new. To return to the universe, to undo this painful individuation, to become God means: to expand the soul to such an extent that it can again encompass the universe.

We are not speaking of man as he is studied in school, in political economy, in statistics, of the men who walk the streets by the millions, who should be regarded no differently than the sand at the beach or the splashes of the tide: a few million more or less would make no difference, they are material, nothing more. No, we are speaking here of man in the elevated sense, the end point of the long path of becoming human, the kingly man, the immortal. Genius is not so rare as it often appears to us, though surely it is also not nearly so common as literary histories and world histories, let alone the newspapers, would suggest. The Steppenwolf Harry, it seems to us, would be enough of a genius to follow this path, to take the risk of becoming human, rather than sniveling about his stupid Steppenwolf at the first sign of any difficulty.

The fact that people with so much potential would resort to Steppenwolves and "Two souls, alas!" is just as surprising and dismaying as the fact that they so often cultivate their cowardly love of the bourgeois life. A man who is capable of comprehending Buddha, a man who has a notion of the acmes and abysses of human existence, should not live in a world dominated by common sense, democracy, and bourgeois education. He only lives there out of cowardice, and when these dimensions close in on him, when his cramped bourgeois living-room becomes too cramped for him, then he blames the wolf, refusing to admit that at times the wolf is the very best part of him.

He calls all that is wild in him wolf, and he sees this as evil, as dangerous, as iconoclastic—but he, who takes himself for an artist of refined sensibilities, is unable to see that many other things live within him aside from the wolf, behind the wolf, and that not everything that bites is a wolf—that is, that the fox, the dragon, the tiger, the ape, and the bird of paradise live there as well. And that this whole world, this whole paradisal garden of lovely and terrible, large and small, strong and delicate creatures is crushed and held captive by the fairy tale of the wolf, just as the true man within him is crushed and held captive by the false, bourgeois man.

Imagine a garden with hundreds of varieties of trees, thousands of flowers, hundreds of fruits, hundreds of herbs. If the caretaker of this garden knew no botanical distinction but "edible" and "weed," then he would not know what to make of nine-tenths of his garden, he would pull up the most enchanting flowers and chop down the loftiest trees, or he would hate them and look askance at them. And this is what the Steppenwolf does with the thousand flowers of his soul. If something does not fit under the headings "man" or "wolf," he simply does not see it. And to think of all the things he counts as "man"! Everything cowardly, everything simian, everything stupid and petty, unless it is distinctly wolfish, he counts as "man," just as he counts everything strong and noble as wolfish, simply because he has not yet managed to make himself its master.

So we take our leave of Harry, we let him continue on his way alone. If he had already found his place among the immortals, if he were already at the point to which his toilsome path appears to lead, how he would stare in bemusement at this back-and-forth, this wild, indecisive zigzag path, how he would smile at this Steppenwolf—encouraging, chiding, pitying, amused!

WHEN I HAD FINISHED READING, IT OCCURRED to me that one night a few weeks earlier I had written a somewhat unusual poem that also concerned the Steppenwolf. I looked for it amid the drift of papers piled upon my desk, found it, and read:

I, the Steppenwolf, trot and trot,
white snow lies all around,
from the birch tree's bough a raven takes flight,
but no hare and no deer can be found!
I love the deer with all my heart,
if only I could find her!
My teeth, my hands would play their part,
for truly no feast could be finer.
I would be so kind to that lovely one
into her haunches my teeth would sink,
her bright red blood would be my drink,
and then I would howl through the night, alone.
Even a hare would do me good,
his warm flesh tastes so sweet in the night—
oh, where have all those pleasures fled
that can bring to my life just a bit of delight?
The hair of my tail has already gone gray,
my sight is no longer so clear,
it's been many years since my wife passed away.

Now I trot and I dream of the deer,
I trot and I dream of the hares,
hear the wind of the winter night howl,
drink the snow when my burning thirst sears,
oh, the devil may take my poor soul.

NOW I HAD TWO PORTRAITS of myself in my hands, one a self-portrait in doggerel, sad and anxious just like its creator, the other drawn coolly, with the appearance of great objectivity, by an external observer, from outside and from above, written by someone who knew more, yet also less, than I myself knew. And these two portraits together—my own melancholy, stammering poem and the insightful study written by an unknown hand—both grieved me, both of them were correct, both gave an unvarnished impression of my bleak existence, both showed clearly how unbearable and untenable my situation had become. This Steppenwolf had to die, he had to put an end to his abhorrent existence by his own hand—or he had to transform himself, melted down in the deadly crucible of renewed self-examination, he had to tear off his mask and become himself all over again. Oh, this process was hardly new or unfamiliar to me—I knew it, I had already experienced it several times, each time in a period of extreme desperation. Each time, in this phase of intense agitation, the "I" that I had been was shattered to pieces, each time it was shaken and destroyed by powers of the deep, and each time, in the process, a part of my life—a part that I had particularly loved and cherished—betrayed me and was lost to me. The first time, I lost my reputation in society, along with my fortune, and I had to learn to do without the respect of those who had previously doffed their hats to me. The second time, my family life fell apart overnight; my wife, who had descended into mental illness, had driven me from house and home, love and trust had suddenly been transformed into hate and deadly combat, my neighbors watched me leave with pity and scorn. That was the beginning of my isolation. And years later—hard, bitter years later, after I had built myself a new, ascetic and spiritual life and ideal in the midst of my austere loneliness and arduous self-discipline, when I had once again achieved a certain tranquility and eleva- tion in life, through devotion to abstract thought exercises and a strict discipline of meditation—this newly crafted life fell to pieces once more, it lost its noble, elevated meaning once and for all; I was dragged into the world again on wild and arduous journeys, new forms of suffering piled up, and new guilt. And each time, the removal of the mask, the collapse of an ideal was preceded by this dreadful emptiness and silence, this fatal constriction and iso- lation, this lack of all relationships to others, this empty, desolate hell of lovelessness and desperation, through which I now had to wander once again.

Every time that my life had undergone this sort of convulsion, I had gained something in the end—that could not be denied, it had given me greater freedom, greater spirit, greater depth, but also greater loneliness, greater coldness, a greater sense of being mis- understood. From a conventional perspective, my life had been a constant decline from one of these convulsions to the next, grow- ing ever more remote from what was normal, what was permissi- ble, what was healthy. Over the years, I had lost my job, my family, my home, I lived outside of all social groups, alone, loved by none, disliked by many, in constant, bitter conflict with public opinion and morality, and even though I still lived within the bourgeois system, all my feelings and thoughts made me a stranger in the midst of this world. Religion, fatherland, family, and state had lost their value, they no longer concerned me; the pretentions of scholarship, the guilds, and the arts disgusted me; my views, my taste, my whole way of thinking, which had once distinguished

me as a gifted and popular man, had grown depraved and gone to
seed, and they were now regarded as suspect. Perhaps I had gained
something invisible and immeasurable in the course of all these
painful transformations—but I had had to pay dearly for it, and
each time, my life had become harder, more difficult, more lonely,
more perilous. In truth, I had no reason to wish that this path
would continue, this path that led me into thinner and thinner
air, like the smoke in Nietzsche's autumn song.

Oh yes, I was familiar with these experiences, these transformations that fate has ordained for its problem children, its most
precarious children—I knew them all too well. I knew them as
an ambitious but unsuccessful hunter might know the stages of a
hunting expedition, as an old stock market player might know the
stages of speculation: of winning, of uncertainty, of instability, of
bankruptcy. Was I really supposed to endure all that again? All
that agony, all that mad misery, all those glimpses of the baseness
and worthlessness of my own self, all that terrible fear of defeat,
all that fear of death? Would it not be wiser and easier to prevent
the repetition of so much suffering, to cut and run? Certainly, it
would be easier and wiser. Whether or not the claims made in
the Steppenwolf booklet about "suicides" were true, no one could
deny me the pleasure of using coal gas, a straight razor, or a pistol
to spare myself the repetition of a process whose bitter anguish
I had had to taste often and deeply enough. No, for the devil's
sake, there was no power in the world that could have asked me
to go through another encounter with myself, with all the atten-
dant specters of death, another transformation, a new incarnation, when its goal and end would be not peace and tranquility,
but only yet another self-destruction, yet another self-formation!
However stupid, cowardly, and shabby, however inglorious and
disgraceful suicide might be as an emergency exit—every exit
from this mill of suffering, even the most ignominious, was dearly

to be wished for; there was no longer any theater of nobility and heroism, I was now confronted with the simple choice between a little fleeting pain and an unthinkably burning, endless suffering. Often enough in my difficult, crazy life I had played the noble Don Quixote, placing honor before pleasure and heroism before reason. Enough of that!

The morning was already yawning through the windows, the leaden, cursed morning of a rainy winter day, when I finally went to bed. I took my resolution to bed with me. But just as I was on the verge of falling asleep, at the very threshold of consciousness, that curious passage about the "immortals" from the Steppenwolf booklet flashed up before me, and with it came a sudden memory of how many times, even just recently, I had felt so close to the immortals that I could taste all of their cool, bright, grimly smiling wisdom in a measure of old music. That insight surfaced, glowed, went out, and then sleep settled on my brow, heavy as a mountain.

When I woke around noon, I found myself in the same situation I have just described: the little book lay on the nightstand along with my poem, and my resolution peered out at me from the turmoil of my recent life, friendly and cool, grown round and firm overnight while I slept. There was no need to hurry, my decision to die was not the whim of an hour, it was a ripe, long-lasting fruit, slowly grown and hanging heavy, gently tossed by the wind of fate, at whose next gust it was bound to fall.

I had an excellent painkiller in my first-aid kit, a particularly strong opiate that I indulged in only on the rarest of occasions, and often abstained from for months at a time; I only took this powerful narcotic when my physical pain became unbearable. Unfortunately, it was not suitable for suicide—I had put it to the test once several years ago. Back then, during a period when I was again overcome by despair, I had swallowed a fair amount of it, enough to kill six men, and yet it hadn't managed to kill me. I did fall asleep, and I lay there completely unconscious for some hours, but then, to my terrible disappointment, I was half awakened by violent convulsions of my stomach, I vomited up all the poison without quite regaining consciousness, then fell back asleep, only to wake up for good in the middle of the next day in a ghastly state of sobriety, my brain burned and empty, with almost no memory at all. Apart from a period of insomnia and an unpleasant stomachache, the poison had no lingering effects.

So that remedy was out of the question. But now I put my decision in these terms: as soon as I had reached the point where I needed to resort to that opiate again, I would permit myself to swallow not that brief redemption, but the great one, death—a certain, reliable death, by bullet or by razor. That settled the matter— waiting until my fiftieth birthday, as the Steppenwolf booklet had smartly suggested, seemed too long to me, it was still two years away. But whether it was a year from now or just a month, or even as soon as tomorrow—now the gate was standing open.

I CANNOT SAY THAT this "resolution" changed my life drastically. It made me a bit more indifferent to discomfort, a bit less cautious in my consumption of opium and wine, a bit more curious about the limits of what I could bear, that was all. My other experiences from that evening had a more lasting effect. I reread the Steppenwolf treatise from time to time, sometimes with devotion and gratitude, as if I knew that an invisible magus were wisely guiding my destiny, sometimes with scorn and contempt for the sobermindedness of the treatise, which did not seem to comprehend the specific mood and tension of my life at all. What was written there about Steppenwolves and suicides might be quite good and clever, but it applied to the genus, to the type, it was brilliant abstraction;

my person, on the other hand, my actual soul, my own individual fate, seemed to me too unique to be caught in such a coarse net.

But what preoccupied me more profoundly than anything else was that hallucination or vision on the wall of the church, the auspicious announcement in those dancing letters of light, which found its echo in the words of the treatise. Many things had been promised to me there, the voices of that strange world had piqued my curiosity immensely, I spent many long hours pondering it, completely absorbed in thought. And then the warning in those inscriptions spoke to me more and more clearly: "Not for everyone!" and "Only for the insane!" So I had to be insane and far removed from "everyone" if those voices were to reach me, if those worlds were to speak to me. My God, hadn't I long since left that life behind—the life of "everyone," the existence and the thinking of the normal ones—hadn't I been isolated and insane enough for some time now? And yet, in my innermost being, I understood this call quite well, the call to go insane, to cast aside reason, inhibition, and propriety, to surrender to the surging, lawless world of the soul, of the imagination.

One day, after I had once again combed the streets and squares of the city in vain for the man with the sign on the pole and prowled a number of times past the wall with the invisible door, I came upon a funeral procession in the neighborhood of St. Martin's, outside the old city walls. As I looked at the faces of the mourners plodding along behind the funeral carriage, my thought was: Where in this city, where in this world is anyone whose death would represent a loss to me? And where is anyone to whom my death might matter? To be sure, there was Erika, my girlfriend, true enough; but our relationship had been stretched thin for some time now, we rarely saw each other without quarreling, and at the moment I did not even know her whereabouts. Occasionally she came to see me, or I traveled to see her, and since we are both lonely and difficult people, somehow bound together by our souls and their afflictions, we maintained a sort of attachment in spite of everything. But wouldn't she perhaps breathe a sigh of relief if she were to learn of my death? I didn't know, nor was I fully confident in the reliability of my own feelings. One must live in the realm of the normal and the possible if one wishes to know about such things.

In the meantime, on a whim, I had joined the funeral procession and trotted along behind the mourners to the cemetery, a modern municipal cemetery built of concrete, with a crematorium and all the trappings. However, our dead man was not cremated, rather his coffin was unloaded beside a simple hole in the ground, and I watched the pastor and the rest of the vultures, the funeral parlor employees, as they carried out their duties, which they sought to imbue with an air of solemnity and mourning, but they took their theatricality and awkwardness and mendacity so far that the whole thing became comical: I saw how their black professional garb billowed about them, and how they strove to put the mourners in the right mood and move them to bow before the majesty of death. It was a wasted effort, no one cried, it seemed that they had all found the dead man expendable. Nor could anyone be cajoled into a pious mood, and when the pastor repeatedly addressed the company as "dear fellow Christians," all those merchants and master bakers and their wives lowered their silent working faces toward the ground in pained earnestness, awkward and mendacious, moved by no other wish than that this uncomfortable event might soon come to an end. Well, it did come to an end, the two most prominent fellow Christians shook the speaker's hand, they scraped their shoes on the nearest curbstone to remove the damp clay in which they had laid the dead man, their faces promptly became ordinary and human again, and one of them suddenly seemed familiar to me—it was, it seemed to me, the man who had been carrying the sign back then, and who had pressed that little book into my hand.

The moment I thought I recognized him, he turned around, bent down, started tugging at his black pants, which he awkwardly rolled up over the tops of his shoes, and then hurried away, an umbrella tucked under his arm. I ran after him, caught up with him, nodded to him, but he didn't seem to recognize me.

"Isn't there any evening entertainment tonight?" I asked, trying to wink at him as those who share secrets do. But it had been too long since I regularly practiced that sort of mimicry—after all, my way of life was such that I had practically forgotten how to speak—and even I could feel that my expression was nothing but a silly grimace.

"Evening entertainment?" the man grumbled, looking me in the face without recognition. "Go to the Black Eagle if you need something, pal."

Indeed, I was no longer sure whether he was the right person. Disappointed, I continued on my way, not knowing where to go, I had no goals, no aspirations, no duties. Life tasted dreadfully bitter, I felt how the disgust that had been welling up within me for so long was reaching its peak, how life was casting me out and throwing me away. I walked angrily through the gray city, everything seemed to me to smell of damp earth and burial. No, none of those birds of the dead would be allowed to stand by my grave, with their gowns and their sentimental cackling to their fellow Christians! Oh, no matter where I might look, no matter where my thoughts might travel, no joy was waiting for me anywhere, no voices were calling out to me, no enticement was awaiting me, everything reeked of lazy dissipation, of lazy half-and-half satisfaction, everything was old, withered, gray, limp, exhausted. Dear God, how was this possible? How could it have come to this for me, the youthful prodigy, the poet, the friend of the muses, the wanderer of the world, the ardent idealist? How had this so slowly crept over me—this paralysis, this hatred of myself and of all others, this constipation of all my emotions, this deep, wicked despondency, this filthy hell of empty-hearted despair?

As I was passing by the library, I ran into a young professor I had previously engaged in conversations with now and then, I had even called on him at home on several occasions the last time I was staying in this city, some years ago, to discuss Oriental mythologies, a field that occupied a great deal of my attention at the time. The scholar approached me in his stiff and somewhat nearsighted way, and he only recognized me when I was just about to pass him by. He set upon me with a hearty greeting, and I, in my pitiful condition, was half-and-half grateful to him for it. He was delighted and grew animated, he reminded me of details from our previous conversations, assured me that he owed a great deal to my suggestions and that he had often thought of me; he had seldom had such lively and productive discussions with colleagues since then. He asked how long I had been in town (I lied: just a few days) and why I hadn't come to see him. I looked into this pleasant man's good, learned face, really found the whole scene quite ridiculous, but like a starved dog I enjoyed this bit of warmth, this sip of love, this morsel of recognition. Touched, the Steppenwolf Harry grinned, his slobber ran down his dry gullet, his sentimentality bent his back against his will. Yes, I eagerly lied, I told him that I was here only temporarily for my studies, and that I also hadn't been feeling so well, otherwise I certainly would have paid him a visit. And when he then warmly invited me to at least spend that evening with him, I gratefully accepted, asked him to send my regards to his wife, and in the process my cheeks began to ache, because they were no longer accustomed to the effort of all that eager talking and smiling. And while I, Harry Haller, was standing there on the street, surprised and flattered, polite and solicitous, and smiling into the good, nearsighted face of that friendly man, the other Harry was standing beside me, also grinning, standing there grinning and thinking what a peculiar, perverse, and mendacious fellow I was after all, thinking how just two minutes ago I had been grimly baring my teeth at the whole damned world, and now, at the first summons, at the first harmless greeting from a respectable gentleman, I was saying please and thank you, feeling touched and overeager, and wallowing like a piglet in this little bit of goodwill, respect, and kindness. Thus the two Harrys, both of them extraordinarily unsympathetic figures, stood facing the pleasant professor, mocking each other, observing each other, spitting on the ground in front of each other and (as they always did in such situations) once again asking themselves the question: Was all of this simply human stupidity and weakness, the general human condition, or was all of it—this sentimental egoism, this lack of character, this emotional impurity and ambivalence—a merely personal, Steppenwolfian specialty? If this piggishness was the common condition of humanity, well, then my contempt for the world could be unleashed again with renewed force; but if it was only my personal weakness, then it would provide the occasion for an orgy of self-contempt.

In the midst of this quarrel between the two Harrys, the professor was nearly forgotten; suddenly he began to annoy me again, and I hastened to rid myself of him. I watched him for a long time as he walked away along the leafless avenue with the good-natured and somewhat comical gait of an idealist, a believer. The battle was raging fiercely within me, and while I mechanically curled and stretched my stiff fingers again, combating the gout that was secretly gnawing at me, I had to admit that I had allowed myself to be duped, that I had now saddled myself with an invitation to dinner at half past seven, where I would have an obligation to exchange pleasantries, to engage in scholarly chitchat, and to contemplate the happiness of other people's families. I went home in a huff, mixed cognac with water and used it to swallow my gout pills, lay down on the divan, and tried to read. When I had finally managed to read for a while in *Sophie's Journey from Memel to Saxony*, a delightful eighteenth-century bestseller, I suddenly remembered the invitation, and that I hadn't shaved, and that I had to get dressed. God knows why I had done this to myself! So, Harry, stand up, put down your book, lather up, scrape your chin raw, get dressed, and take pleasure in human company! And while I was lathering up, I thought of that filthy hole in the cemetery ground that they had lowered that unknown man into today, and of the grimaces on the faces of all those bored fellow Christians, and I couldn't even bring myself to laugh about it. That, it seemed to me, was where it ended—that filthy hole in the ground, with the preacher's stupid, awkward words, with the stupid, awkward faces of the assembled mourners, with the dreary sight of all those crosses and plaques of tin and marble, with all those artificial flowers of wire and glass—that was not only where the unknown man had ended up; that was not only where I, too, would end up, tomorrow or the day after tomorrow, buried, with a bit of dirt tossed on top of me while those in attendance watched, awkward and mendacious; no, that was how everything ended, all our striving, all our culture, all our faith, all our joy in life and lust for life, which was so very sick and would soon lie there beneath the dirt as well. Our cultural world was a cemetery, here Jesus Christ and Socrates, Mozart and Haydn, Dante and Goethe were only obscure names on rusting metal plaques, surrounded by awkward and mendacious mourners who would have given a great deal if they could believe again in the metal plaques that had once been sacred to them, who would have given a great deal if they could speak at least one honest, serious word of mourning and despair about this lost world, and who instead were left with nothing to do but grin awkwardly as they stood around a grave. In my rage, I nicked the same spot I always do on my chin, then tried to stop the bleeding with a styptic pencil, but I still had to change the fresh collar I had just put on—and I had no idea why I was doing any of this, since I didn't feel the slightest desire to accept the invitation. But one part of Harry was playing a role again, calling the professor a congenial fellow, longing for a bit of human smell, conversation, and companionship, remembering the professor's pretty wife, finding the thought of an evening with friendly hosts quite heartening after all, and helping me apply a sticking plaster to my chin, helping me get dressed and tie a proper tie, and gently dissuading me from indulging my real desire to stay home. At the same time I thought: The way that I am now getting dressed and going out, visiting the professor and exchanging more or less disingenuous pleasantries with him, all without actually wanting to, is the very same way that most people act and live and behave day after day, hour after hour, driven by compulsion rather than will, paying visits, having discussions, putting in hours at some official post or office, all compulsorily, mechanically, involuntarily, all of this could just as well be done by machines, or not done at all; and it is this eternal, perpetual mechanism that prevents them from subjecting their own lives to critique as I do, from recognizing and feeling life's stupidity and shallowness, its hideously grinning dubiousness, its hopeless sadness and desolation. Oh, and these people are right, infinitely right, to live that way, playing their games and running after whatever they think is important, instead of resisting that dismal mechanism and staring despondently into space as I do, now that I have run off the rails. If I sometimes disdain and mock people in these pages, let no one think that I am placing the blame on them, that I am accusing them, that I am holding others responsible for my own personal misery! But I—having already gone so far that I stand at the very edge of life, where it drops off into the fathomless

darkness—I would be committing an injustice and lying if I tried
to pretend, to myself and to others, that the mechanism was still
running for me, too—as if I, too, still belonged to that sweet,
childlike world of the eternal game!

The evening turned out as wonderfully as expected. I stopped
for a moment in front of my acquaintance's house and gazed up
at the windows. This, I thought, is where the man lives, and he
keeps on doing his work year after year, reading and annotating
texts, searching for connections between Near Eastern and Indian
mythologies, and he does it with pleasure, because he believes in
the value of what he is doing, he believes in the scholarly discipline to which he has devoted himself, he believes in the intrin-
sic value of knowledge, of its accumulation, because he believes in
progress, in development. He did not share in the experience of
the war, nor of Einstein's demolition of the previous foundations
of thought (which, in his view, concerns only the mathematicians),
he does not see how the preparations for the next war are under-
way all around him, he considers Jews and Communists detestable, he is a good, thoughtless, cheerful, self-important child, he
is very much to be envied. I pulled myself together and entered,
was received by a maid in a white apron (acting on some premonition, I made a precise note of where she put my hat and coat),
then I was led into a warm, well-lit room and asked to wait, and
instead of saying a prayer or taking a little nap, I yielded to a playful impulse and picked up the nearest object that presented itself
to me. It was a small, framed picture that stood on the round table,
with a stiff cardboard flap that forced it to lean at an angle. It was
an etching that depicted the poet Goethe as an old man full of
character, with a shock of hair befitting a genius and a beautifully
contoured face that lacked neither the famously fiery eyes nor the
touch of slightly courtly loneliness and tragedy—indeed, the artist
had taken particular care to represent them. He had succeeded in

giving this demonic old man (his depth notwithstanding) a somewhat professorial or even thespian air of composure and decency,
and in making him, all in all, a truly handsome old gentleman, a
suitable decoration for any bourgeois home. This picture was probably no dumber than all pictures of its kind—all the noble saviors,
apostles, heroes, intellectual giants, and statesmen turned out by
industrious artisans—and perhaps it was only thanks to a certain
virtuosic skill that it had such a provocative effect on me; in any
case, be that as it may, I was already in a sufficiently irritated and
charged state, and so this vain and self-satisfied portrayal of the
old Goethe immediately cried out to me, it sounded an awkward,
jarring note, telling me that I was not in the right place. This was
the home of handsomely stylized old masters and national heroes,
not Steppenwolves.

   If the master of the house had entered at that moment, I might
have succeeded in making my exit on some acceptable pretext.
However, it was his wife who came in, and I surrendered to my
fate, despite a premonition of disaster. We greeted each other,
and the first false note was followed by many more. The professor's wife commented that I was looking well, while I was only
too aware of how much I had aged in the years since we had last
seen each other; even as she was shaking my hand, the pain in
my gouty fingers offered an unpleasant reminder of that. Yes, and
then she asked how my dear wife was doing, and I had to tell her
that my wife had left me and we had gotten a divorce. We were
both glad when the professor came in. He likewise greeted me
warmly, and the awkwardness and comedy of the situation soon
found the finest expression imaginable. In his hands he was holding a copy of the newspaper he subscribed to, the organ of the
militaristic, warmongering party, and after shaking my hand he
pointed to the paper and told me that it said something about a
namesake of mine, a journalist named Haller, who must be an

awful wretch and an unpatriotic rascal, since he had made fun of
the Kaiser and voiced the opinion that his own fatherland bore
no less guilt for the outbreak of the war than the hostile powers.
What a wretch he must be! Well, now the chap had gotten what
he deserved, the editors had quite swiftly dispatched and pillo-
ried that pest. But when he saw that the topic did not interest me,
we moved on to other things, and the two of them did not even
remotely consider the possibility that the monster in question
could be sitting right in front of them, and yet this was indeed the
case, I myself was that monster. Well, what's the point of making a fuss and alarming people! I laughed to myself, but at the
same time I abandoned all hope of experiencing anything pleasant that evening. I remember the moment clearly. For at that very
moment, while the professor was speaking of the traitor Haller,
the terrible feeling of depression and despair that had been growing and gathering strength inside me ever since I witnessed that
scene at the cemetery became concentrated into a ferocious pressure, a physically perceptible distress (in my abdomen), a choking,
anxious sense of fate. Something was lying in wait for me, I felt,
some danger was creeping up on me from behind. Fortunately,
word came that dinner was ready. We went into the dining room,
and while I was making an effort to say and ask only the most
harmless things, I ate more than was my custom, and felt more
miserable with each passing moment. My God, I kept thinking,
why are we trying so hard? I had the distinct impression that my
hosts were not feeling well, either, and that their cheerfulness was
costing them some effort, whether because I was so exhausting
or because something else was amiss in the house. They asked me
all sorts of questions to which I could not give an honest answer,
and soon I found that I had lied myself into a corner, and I was
wrestling with my disgust at every word. Finally, to change the
subject, I began to talk about the funeral I had witnessed today.

But I didn't strike the right tone, my attempts at humor had a disconcerting effect, we drifted further and further apart, inside me the Steppenwolf was laughing and grinning, and all three of us were quite silent as we ate dessert.

We returned to the first room to drink coffee and brandy, which perhaps would help to warm us up a bit. But then the prince of poets caught my eye again, although he had been set to one side on a chest of drawers. I simply could not get away from him, and I took him in my hands again and began to grapple with him—though not without hearing some voices of caution within me. I was practically obsessed with the feeling that the situation was unbearable, that now I must succeed either in winning over my hosts, sweeping them along and bringing them into accord with me, or else in causing a full-blown explosion.

"Let us hope," I said, "that Goethe did not really look like that! That vanity and that noble pose, that dignity that coquets with the honored company, and all that precious sentimentality beneath the masculine surface! One can certainly have a lot against him, I often have a lot against that pompous old man myself, but to portray him like that, no, that's going too far."

The lady of the house poured the rest of the coffee with a deeply pained expression on her face, then she hurried out of the room, and her husband, half embarrassed, half reproachful, told me that the picture of Goethe belonged to his wife and that she was particularly fond of it. "And even if you were objectively correct, which, by the way, I dispute, you had no right to express yourself so bluntly."

"You're right about that," I admitted. "Unfortunately, it's a habit, a vice of mine to always opt for the bluntest possible expression, which, by the way, Goethe also did in his finer moments. Of course, this sweet, smug salon Goethe never would have used a blunt, authentic, direct expression. I sincerely apologize to you and your wife—please tell her that I am a schizophrenic. And with that, I would ask your permission to take my leave."

The disconcerted gentleman did raise a few objections, he also spoke again about how wonderful and stimulating our earlier conversations had been, indeed, how my conjectures about Mithras and Krishna had made a profound impression upon him back then, and how he had hoped that today we would also . . . and so on. I thanked him and said that these were very kind words, but that unfortunately my interest in Krishna as well as my desire for scholarly conversation had completely faded, that I had lied to him several times today, for example, I had been here in the city for more than a few days—for many months, in fact—but I was living alone, on my own terms, and was no longer fit to consort with better houses, because, first, I was always in a very bad mood and suffering from gout, and second, I was usually drunk. Furthermore, in order to clear the air and at least not depart as a liar, it was necessary for me to tell the honored gentleman that he had quite seriously insulted me today. With regard to Haller's opinions, the professor had adopted as his own the stupid, bullnecked view that he had read in a reactionary newspaper—a position worthy of an unemployed officer, but not of a scholar. But this "chap," this unpatriotic rascal Haller, was me, and it would be better for our country and for the world if at least the few people who were capable of thinking would commit themselves to reason and the love of peace instead of blindly and obsessively setting the course for a new war. Well then, Godspeed.

With that, I rose, bid farewell to Goethe and the professor, snatched my things from the coat hook outside, and hurried away. The wolf in my soul was howling loudly with schadenfreude, a tremendous drama was taking place between the two Harrys. For it was immediately clear to me that this disagreeable evening had much more significance for me than it did for the indignant professor: for him, it was a disappointment and a minor annoyance;

but for me, it was one final failure and flight, it was my farewell to the bourgeois, the moral, the learned world, it was an absolute victory for the Steppenwolf. And I was saying my farewells as a fugitive and a vanquished foe, declaring bankruptcy before myself, bidding farewell without consolation, without humor. I had bid farewell to my former world and home, to gentility, propriety, and scholarship, in just the same way as a man with a stomach ulcer bids farewell to roast pork. Seething, I walked beneath the lanterns, seething and deathly downcast. What a bleak, shameful, miserable day it had been, from morning to evening, from the cemetery to the scene at the professor's house! Why? What for? Was there any point in taking on more of these days, in eating up more of these soups? No! And so tonight I would put an end to this farce. Go home, Harry, and cut your throat! You have waited long enough.

I walked up and down the streets, driven by misery. Of course it had been stupid of me to spit on the good people's salon decorations, it was stupid and ill-mannered, but I just couldn't help it, I couldn't stand this tame, mendacious, well-mannered life any longer. And since it seemed that I could no longer bear loneliness, either, since even my own company had become so unspeakably odious and revolting to me, since I was suffocating as I flailed about in the airless space of my own private hell, what other escape was possible? There wasn't any. O father and mother, O distant, sacred fires of my youth, O you thousand joys, works, and goals of my life! None of that was mine anymore, not even remorse, there was only revulsion and pain. Never, it seemed to me, had the mere obligation to live caused so much pain as in this hour.

I rested for a moment in a dreary neighborhood tavern, drank water and cognac, then walked on again, with the devil at my heels, up and down the steep, crooked alleys of the old town, along the avenues, across the train station square. Get away from here!

I said to myself, went into the station, stared at the timetables on the walls, drank some wine, tried to collect my thoughts. I began more and more closely, more and more clearly to see the specter that I feared. It was the return home, the return to my room, the paralysis in the face of despair! Even if I walked around for many hours, I would not be able to escape it when I returned to my door, to the table piled with books, to the divan with the picture of my beloved hanging above it, I could not escape the moment when I would have to sharpen my razor and cut my throat. This image appeared before me more and more clearly—and more and more clearly, with my heart pounding wildly, I felt the fear of all fears: the fear of death! Yes, I had a dreadful fear of death. Although I could see no other way out—although revulsion, suffering, and despair towered up around me, although nothing held any appeal for me anymore, nothing could bring me joy and hope—still I felt an unspeakable dread at the thought of that execution, that final moment, that cold, gaping cut into my own flesh!

I could see no way to escape that dreaded conclusion. Even if today, in the battle between despair and cowardice, cowardice might take the upper hand, despair would stand before me anew tomorrow and every day thereafter, further exacerbated by self-contempt. I would take up the knife and cast it aside again, over and over, for as long as it might take until the job was finally done. Then better to do it today! I reasoned with myself as with a frightened child, but the child did not listen, he ran away, he wanted to live. As if in a fit, I was dragged further through the city, I gave my apartment a wide berth, always thinking of returning home, always putting it off. Now and then I stopped in at a bar for a drink, two drinks, then I was driven onward, making a wide circle around my destination, around the razor, around death. Dead tired, I sometimes sat down on a bench, on the edge of a fountain, on a guard stone, listened to my heart beating, wiped the sweat from my forehead, then walked on again, filled with mortal fear, filled with a flickering longing for life.

And so, late at night, in an outlying neighborhood that I hardly knew, I was drawn to a tavern where lively dance music could be heard through the window. As I entered, I read an old sign that hung above the door: The Black Eagle. Inside, the bar was still in full swing despite the late hour, with a noisy crowd, smoke, a haze of wine and voices, and dancing in the back room, where the music was raging. I stayed in the front room, which was full of ordinary people, some of them poorly dressed, while more elegant people could be seen in the ballroom at the rear. Pushed across the room by the crowd, I was shoved up against a table beside the bar, where a pretty pale girl was sitting on the bench along the wall, wearing a thin, low-cut ball gown, with a wilted flower in her hair. The girl gave me an attentive, friendly glance when she saw me coming, smiling as she moved aside a bit to make room for me.

"May I, ma'am?" I asked, sitting down beside her.

"Certainly, dear, you may," she said, "who are you, anyway?"

"Thank you," I said, "I can't possibly go home, I can't, I can't, I want to stay here, with you, if you'll let me. No, I can't go home."

She nodded as if she understood me, and as she nodded, I examined the curl that fell from her forehead past her ear, and I saw that the wilted flower was a camellia. Music was blaring from across the room, and the waitresses were hurriedly shouting out orders at the bar.

"Just stay here then," she said, and her voice did wonders for me. "Why can't you go home, anyway?"

"I can't. There's something waiting for me at home—no, I can't, it's too terrible."

"Then let it wait and stay here. But wipe off your glasses first, you can't see a damn thing. Here, let me see your handkerchief. So, what're we drinking? Burgundy?"

She wiped off my glasses; now I could finally see her clearly, the pale, firm face with the mouth painted blood-red, with the light gray eyes, with the smooth, cool forehead, with the short, tight curl in front of the ear. She took care of me with kindness and a slight hint of mockery, ordered wine and clinked glasses with me, looking down at my shoes as she did so.

"My God, where'd you come from? You look like you walked here all the way from Paris. That's no way to arrive at a ball."

I said yes and no, laughed a bit, let her talk. I liked her very much, which surprised me, since until then I had always avoided young girls like that and tended to regard them with suspicion. And the way she treated me was just what I needed at that moment—oh, and she has treated me the same way every hour since. She treated me just as gently and just as mockingly as I needed. She ordered a sandwich and commanded me to eat it. She poured me a drink and told me to take a sip, but not too quickly. Then she praised me for my obedience.

"You're a good boy," she said encouragingly, "you don't make it difficult. I bet it's been a long time since you've had to obey anyone."

"Yes, ma'am, you won the bet. How did you know?"

"Nothing to it. Obeying is just like eating and drinking—when you've gone without it for a long time, there's nothing better. You like to obey me, don't you?"

"Very much so, ma'am. You know everything."

"You make it easy. Hey, friend, maybe I could also tell you what it is that's waiting for you at home that's got you so afraid. But you already know that yourself, we don't need to talk about it, do we? Stupid stuff! Either people hang themselves, okay, then they hang themselves, they must have some good reason. Or else they keep on living, and then they just have their lives to worry about. Nothing could be simpler."

"Oh," I cried, "if only it were that simple! For God's sake, I've worried enough about life, but to no avail. It might be hard to hang yourself, I don't know. But living is much, much harder! God knows how hard it is!"

"Well, you're gonna see that it's child's play. We're already off to a good start, you've cleaned your glasses, you've had something to eat and drink. Now we're gonna brush off your pants and shoes a bit, they need it. And then you're gonna dance a shimmy with me."

"There, you see," I burst out, "I was right all along! There's nothing that I want to do less than disobey one of your commands. But that is one that I cannot obey. I can't dance a shimmy, or a waltz, or a polka, or whatever they're called; I've never learned to dance in my life. Now do you see that it's not all as simple as you think?"

The pretty girl smiled with her blood-red lips and shook her firm head with its boyish hairstyle. As I looked at her, it seemed to me that she resembled Rosa Kreisler, the first girl I'd fallen in love with as a boy, except that Rosa was tan and dark haired. No, I didn't know who this strange girl resembled, I only knew that it was someone from my very early youth, from my boyhood.

"Slow down," she cried, "slow down! So you can't dance? Not at all? Not even a one-step? Oh, but God knows how much effort you've put into life, isn't that what you were saying? You were lying, my boy, you shouldn't do that anymore at your age. How can you say you've made an effort to live when you don't even want to dance?"

"But what if I can't do it! I've never learned."

She laughed.

"But you've learned to read and write, haven't you, and to do arithmetic and probably Latin and French and all those kinds of things, too? I'll bet you sat in school for ten or twelve years, maybe went to the university after that, maybe got a doctorate, you speak Chinese or Spanish. Don't you? Okay. But you couldn't find the time and money for a few dance lessons? Huh!"

"It was my parents," I said in my defense, "they had me learn Latin and Greek and all that stuff. But they didn't have me learn to dance, that wasn't how we did things, my parents never danced themselves."

She looked at me coldly, scornfully, and once again something in her face reminded me of my early youth.

"There you go, it must be your parents' fault! Did you ask them if you could come to the Black Eagle tonight, too? Did you? What's that, they're long dead? Well then! If you didn't want to learn to dance when you were young because you were such a good boy, fair enough! Although, I don't believe you were such a good boy back then. But after that—what've you been up to all these years?"

"Oh," I confessed, "I don't even know anymore myself. I studied, made music, read books, wrote books, traveled—"

"You've got some funny views of life! You've always done the hard stuff, right, the tricky stuff, but you've never learned the simple things? Didn't have time? Didn't feel like it? Well, fair enough, thank God I'm not your mother. But then you make like you've put life through the paces and haven't found a single thing to like about it—no way, you can't do that!"

"Don't scold me, ma'am!" I begged. "I already know I'm insane."

"Oh come on, don't tell me any stories! You're not insane at all, Herr Professor, in fact, you're not nearly insane enough for me! You're smart in such a dumb way, it seems to me, just like a professor. Come on, eat another roll. You can tell me more later."

She got me another roll, salted it a bit, spread some mustard on it, cut off a piece for herself, and told me to eat. I ate. I would have done anything she told me to, anything but dance. It felt incredibly good to obey someone, to sit next to someone who asked questions, who gave orders, who laid me bare. If the professor or his wife had done that a few hours ago, I would have been spared a great deal. But no, it was good this way, I would have missed a great deal!

"What's your name, anyway?" she suddenly asked.

"Harry."

"Harry? A little boy's name! And you're a little boy, too, Harry, even if you've got a few gray patches in your hair. You're a little boy, and you should have someone to look after you a bit. I won't say any more about dancing. But look at your haircut! Don't you have a wife or a girlfriend?"

"I don't have a wife anymore, we're divorced. I do have a girlfriend, but she doesn't live here, I hardly ever see her, we don't get along very well."

She whistled softly through her teeth.

"Seems like you're a pretty difficult character, nobody wants to stay with you. But tell me: what was the special occasion this evening that had you wandering around the world in a daze? Did you get into a fight? Gamble away your money?"

That was hard to say.

"See," I began, "it was really a petty thing. I was invited to a professor's house—but I'm not a professor myself—and I really shouldn't have gone at all, I'm not used to sitting and chatting with people like that anymore, I've forgotten how to do it. Even as I was going into the house, I had a feeling that it would not go well—as I was hanging up my hat, it occurred to me that I might need it again soon. Yes, and at this professor's house there was a picture on the table, a stupid picture that irritated me . . ."

"What kind of picture? Why did it irritate you?" she interrupted me.

"Yes, it was a picture of Goethe—you know, the poet Goethe. But it didn't show him as he really looked—we don't know exactly what he looked like, he's been dead for a hundred years. Instead, some modern painter had painted a sanitized Goethe just the way he imagined him, and it was that picture that annoyed me and disgusted me so much—I don't know if you understand?"

"I understand very well, don't worry. Go on!"

"Even before that I had my issues with the professor; like almost all professors, he's a great patriot, and during the war he did his duty and helped lie to the people—in good faith, of course. But I'm opposed to war. Well, anyhow. On we go. I wouldn't have even needed to look at the picture . . ."

"You certainly wouldn't."

"But first of all, I was offended on Goethe's account, because he is very, very dear to me; and then, well, then I thought——then I thought or felt something like this: Here I am, sitting with people whom I consider my equals, and who I thought would love Goethe as I do, and whose image of Goethe I thought would be similar to mine, but now they have this tasteless, bastardized, saccharine picture sitting there, and they think it's wonderful, and they don't even realize that the essence of this picture is the very opposite of the essence of Goethe. They think the picture is wonderful, and they can, for all I care—but in that case, any trust that I might have in these people, any friendship I might feel for them, any sense of kinship and belonging, is over and done with. Besides, we never had much of a friendship anyway. So then I started to feel angry and sad, and I saw that I was all alone and no one appreciated me. Do you understand?"

"That's easy to understand, Harry. Then what? Did you smash the picture over their heads?"

"No, ma'am, I said my piece and ran away, I wanted to go home, but——"

"But there wouldn't have been a mama there to comfort or scold her silly boy. Oh, Harry, I almost feel sorry for you, I've never seen such a child."

Certainly, I understood that, it seemed to me. She gave me a glass of wine to drink. She really was like a mama to me. But now and then I saw for a moment how young and pretty she was.

"So," she began again, "so Goethe died a hundred years ago, and Harry's very fond of him, and he makes a lovely image in his mind of what Goethe might have looked like, and Harry has the right to do that, doesn't he? But the painter, who also adores Goethe and makes his own picture of him, has no right to do that, and neither does the professor, or anybody else, because that doesn't suit Harry, he can't bear it, he has to scold them and run away! If Harry had half a brain, he'd just laugh about the painter and the professor. If he were insane, he'd smash their Goethe in their faces. But since he's just a little boy, he goes running home and wants to hang himself——. I've understood your story well, Harry. It's a funny story. It makes me laugh. Stop, don't drink so fast! You have to drink Burgundy slowly, otherwise you'll get too hot. I have to tell you everything, don't I, little boy."

The look in her eyes was stern and admonishing, like that of a sixty-year-old governess.

"Oh yes," I begged her eagerly, "please, tell me everything."

"What do you want me to tell you?"

"Anything you like, ma'am."

"All right, I'll tell you something. For the past hour you've heard me talking to you like you're my friend, and you're still talking to me like I'm a stranger or some fine lady. Always Latin and Greek, always as complicated as possible! When a girl talks to you like a friend and you don't find her unpleasant, you answer her the same way. So, there, you've learned something. And second: for the past half hour I've known that your name is Harry. I know because I asked you. But you don't want to know my name."

"Oh yes I do, I want to know very much."

"Too late, little man! If we ever meet again, you can ask me then. I'm not going to tell you today. Okay, now I want to dance."

When I saw that she was preparing to stand up, suddenly my mood sank very low, I was afraid that she would go away and leave me alone, and then everything would go back to the way it had been before. Just as a toothache that has faded away for a while can suddenly return and burn like fire, in an instant that fear and horror were there again. Oh God, could I have forgotten what awaited me? Had anything really changed?

"Stop," I pleaded, "ma'am—friend, please don't go! Of course you can dance all you want, but don't stay away for long, come back, come back!"

Laughing, she stood up. She was not as tall as I had expected—she was slim, but not tall. Once again she reminded me of someone—who was it? I couldn't pin it down.

"Are you going to come back?"

"I'll come back, but it may be a while, half an hour or even an hour. I'll tell you what: close your eyes and get a bit of sleep; that's what you need."

I moved aside for her, and she slipped out; her short skirt brushed against my knees; as she went, she glanced into a tiny, round pocket mirror, raised her eyebrows, dabbed at her chin with a little powder puff, and disappeared into the dance hall. I glanced around: strange faces, smoking men, little pools of beer spilled on the marble tabletop, yelling and screaming from all sides, dance music from the next room. I should sleep, she had said. Ah, dear child, what do you know about my sleep, which is even more elusive than a weasel! To sleep amid this carnival, sitting at the table, between those clinking mugs of beer! I sipped at my wine, pulled a cigar out of my pocket, looked around for matches, but I really wasn't interested in smoking, so I set the cigar on the table in front of me. "Close your eyes," she'd told me. God knows where the girl got that voice, that sort of deep, kind voice, a motherly voice. It was good to obey that voice, I had found. Obediently, I closed my eyes, leaned my head against the wall, heard a hundred loud noises roaring around me, smiled at the idea that I could sleep in this place,

decided to go to the door to the next room and catch a glimpse
of the dance hall—I had to see my pretty girl dance, after all—
moved my feet under my chair, but realized for the first time how
infinitely tired I was from all those hours of wandering around,
and remained seated. And then I was already asleep, true to my
mother's command, sleeping greedily and gratefully, dreaming,
dreaming more clearly and sweetly than I had dreamt in a long
time. I dreamt:

I was sitting and waiting in an old-fashioned antechamber. At
first I knew only that I had an appointment with some Excellency
or other, then I remembered that it was Herr von Goethe who
was to receive me. Unfortunately, I was not here entirely on my
own account, but rather as a correspondent for a magazine, which
disturbed me greatly, and I could not understand what devil had
gotten me into this situation. I had also been unsettled by a scorpion that I had seen just moments ago, and that had been trying
to climb up my leg. I had defended myself against the little black
creature and shaken it off, but I didn't know where it was now, and
I didn't dare touch anything.

Besides, I wasn't entirely sure that someone had not acciden-
tally scheduled my appointment with Matthisson instead of
Goethe, though in my dream I confused Matthisson with Bürger,
and credited him with the poems to Molly. Incidentally, I would
have very much liked to meet Molly, I imagined her to be wonderful, gentle, musical, with a certain evening charm. If only I had
not been sitting there on behalf of that accursed editor! My displeasure about this grew and grew, and gradually it extended to
Goethe himself, so that suddenly my view of the man began to
be colored by all sorts of objections and accusations. That could
make for a fine audience! But the scorpion might not be so bad
after all, even if it was dangerous, and perhaps hiding in my imme-
diate vicinity; it seemed to me that it might also be a friendly sign,

it seemed very possible to me that the scorpion had something to do with Molly, that it was a kind of messenger that she had sent, or her heraldic animal, a beautiful, dangerous emblem of femininity and sin. Couldn't the animal's name perhaps be Vulpius? But then a servant opened the door, and I rose and entered.

There stood old Goethe, small and very stiff, with a hefty star of honor prominently displayed upon his classical chest. It seemed that he was still presiding, still receiving audiences, still watching over the world from his Weimar museum. For no sooner had he seen me than he nodded his head, bobbing it like an old raven, and spoke solemnly: "Well, I don't suppose you young people agree very much with us and our endeavors?"

"Quite right," I said, feeling the chill of his ministerial gaze. "Indeed, we young people are not in agreement with you, old sir. You are too solemn for us, Your Excellency, and too vain and pompous and not sincere enough. That might be the essential thing: not sincere enough."

The little old man leaned his stern head slightly forward, and as his hard, officiously pursed lips relaxed in a little smile and came delightfully to life, my heart suddenly skipped a beat, for all at once I remembered the poem "Dusk Has Fallen from on High," and remembered that this was the man and this was the mouth that had uttered those words. To tell the truth, at that moment I was already thoroughly disarmed and overwhelmed, and I would have preferred to kneel down before him. But I maintained my composure, and from his smiling mouth I heard the words: "Oh, so you're accusing me of insincerity? Those are some strong words! Wouldn't you like to explain yourself further?"

Yes, I wanted very much to do that.

"Herr von Goethe, like all great thinkers, you acutely perceived and sensed the dubiousness, the hopelessness of human life: the glory of the moment and the misery of its fading, the impossibility of attaining beautiful heights of feeling without atoning for them in the prison of everyday life, the burning desire for the realm of the spirit, which is locked in eternal, mortal combat with an equally burning and equally sacred love of the lost innocence of nature, all this terrible drifting in emptiness and uncertainty, where we are condemned to ephemerality, to an existence that is never fully valid, that remains forever provisional and dilettantish—in short, the utter futility, the absurdity, and the burning desperation of the human condition. You knew all this, you testified to it again and again, and yet with your whole life you preached the opposite, you expressed faith and optimism, you fooled yourself and others into believing that our intellectual endeavors are endowed with longevity and meaning. You rejected and suppressed those who bore witness to those depths, the voices of that desperate truth, in yourself as well as in Kleist and Beethoven. For decades, you pretended that your accumulation of knowledge and collections, your writing and collecting of letters, your whole autumnal existence in Weimar was actually a way to render the moment eternal, when in fact all you could do was mummify it—you pretended that it was a way to imbue nature with spirit, when in fact all you could do was stylize it into a mask. That is the insincerity for which we reproach you."

The old privy councilor looked me thoughtfully in the eyes, his mouth still smiling.

Then, to my astonishment, he asked: "Then you must find Mozart's *Magic Flute* quite unpleasant?"

And before I could protest, he continued: "*The Magic Flute* presents life as an exquisite song, it extols our feelings, which are of course transient, as if they were eternal and divine, it agrees with neither Herr von Kleist nor Herr Beethoven, rather it preaches optimism and faith."

"I know, I know!" I cried in a rage. "God knows what made you think of *The Magic Flute* of all things, which is the dearest thing in the world to me! But Mozart didn't live to be eighty-two, and he didn't demand the same things as you in his personal life: longevity, order, stiff dignity! He wasn't so self-important! He sang his divine melodies and he was poor and he died young, poor, unrecognized——"

I was running out of breath. There were a thousand things that needed to be said in ten words now, sweat was beginning to bead on my forehead.

Goethe, however, said very kindly: "The fact that I reached the age of eighty-two may indeed be unforgivable. However, I took less pleasure in it than you might imagine. You are right: I always had a great desire for longevity; I always feared death and fought against it. I think that the fight against death, the unconditional and stubborn will to live, is what has driven all exceptional people in their actions and their lives. But the fact that one must still die in the end, my young friend, is something that I demonstrated just as conclusively at the age of eighty-two as I would have by dying as a schoolboy. And if I may offer some justification, I would like to say this: there was much in my nature that was childlike, great curiosity and drive to play, a great desire to waste time. So it just took me a while to see that at some point it was time to stop playing."

As he said this, he smiled slyly, almost roguishly. His figure had grown taller, his stiff posture and the tense dignity in his face had vanished. And the air around us was now filled with many melodies, many Goethe songs, I could clearly hear Mozart's "Violet" and Schubert's "Bush and vale thou fill'st again." And Goethe's face was now rosy and young and laughing, and it resembled Mozart's one moment, Schubert's the next, as if he were their brother, and the star on his chest was made entirely of meadow flowers, a yellow primrose blossomed joyfully and jauntily from its center.

It did not quite suit me that the old man wished to evade my questions and accusations in such a joking fashion, and I cast him a reproachful glance. Then he bent forward and brought his mouth, the mouth that had already grown quite childlike, up close to my ear and whispered softly into it: "My boy, you take old Goethe much too seriously. You ought not to take old people seriously when they have already died, it does them an injustice. We immortals don't love to be taken seriously, we love to have fun. Seriousness, my boy, is a question of time; it arises, this much I will tell you, from an overestimation of time. I, too, once overestimated the value of time; that's why I wanted to live to be a hundred years old. But in eternity, you see, there is no time; eternity is a moment, just long enough to have fun."

Indeed, it was impossible to exchange another serious word with the man, he was merrily and nimbly prancing back and forth, with the primrose shooting out of his star like a rocket one moment, shrinking and disappearing the next. While he was performing his dazzling dance steps and figures, I had to admit that at least he had not neglected to learn to dance. He could do it beautifully. Then I remembered the scorpion, or rather Molly, and I called out to Goethe: "Tell me, isn't Molly here?"

Goethe laughed out loud. He went to his desk, opened a drawer, took out a precious leather or velvet case, opened it, and held it out for me to see. There, on the dark velvet, lay a tiny woman's leg, pristine and gleaming, a delightful leg, a bit bent at the knee, the foot pointed downward, tapering into the daintiest of toes.

I reached out, wanting to pick up the little leg, which I was quite enamored of, but as soon as I tried to grab it with two fingers, the toy appeared to give a little twitch, and suddenly it occurred to me that this might be the scorpion. Goethe seemed to understand, he even seemed to have wanted and intended precisely that—that profound perplexity, that quivering tension between desire and fear. He held the charming little scorpion very close to my face, saw me yearn for it, saw me recoil from it, and this seemed to give him great pleasure. While he was teasing me with that lovely, dangerous thing, he had grown quite old again, ancient, a thousand years old, with snow-white hair, and the old man's withered face was laughing silently, laughing uproariously to itself, with an old man's inscrutable humor.

WHEN I AWOKE, I had forgotten the dream, only later did it come back to me. I must have been asleep for nearly an hour at that barroom table, surrounded by the music and the hustle and bustle, I would never have thought it possible. The dear girl was standing in front of me, one hand resting on my shoulder.

"Give me two or three marks," she said, "I had something to eat over there."

I gave her my wallet, she walked away with it and soon returned.

"Well, now I can sit with you a little longer, then I have to go, I have a date."

I was taken aback. "With whom?" I asked quickly.

"With a gentleman, little Harry. He's invited me to the Odeon Bar."

"Oh, I thought you weren't going to leave me alone."

"Then you should have asked me out. Somebody beat you to it. Well, you're saving a good bit of money. You know the Odeon? Only champagne after midnight. Club chairs, Negro band, very nice."

I hadn't thought of all that.

"Oh," I said, pleading, "let me take you out! I thought that would go without saying, since we're friends now. Let me take you out, wherever you want, I beg you."

"That's nice of you. But look, my word is my word, and I said I'd go, so I'll go. Don't give it another thought! Come on, take another sip, we still have wine in the bottle. Drink it up and then go home and go to sleep. Promise me."

"No, you know I can't go home."

"Oh, you and your stories! You still haven't gotten over Goethe?" (At that moment, the Goethe dream came back to me.) "But if you really can't go home, then just stay here, they've got some guest rooms upstairs. Shall I get you one?"

I was content with that, and I asked where I could see her again. Where did she live? She wouldn't tell me. All I had to do was look around a bit, I'd find her soon enough.

"Can't I take you out?"

"Out where?"

"Wherever you like, whenever you like."

"Okay. We'll have dinner on Tuesday at the Old Franciscan, second floor. See you then!"

She gave me her hand, and only then did I notice that hand, a hand that entirely matched her voice, beautiful and full, wise and kind. She laughed mockingly when I kissed her hand.

And at the last moment, she turned back to me and said: "There's one other thing I want to tell you, it's about Goethe. See, the same thing that happened to you with Goethe, when you couldn't stand that picture of him, that happens to me sometimes with the saints."

"With the saints? Are you that pious?"

"No, sadly I'm not pious, but I used to be, and I will be again someday. After all, there's just not enough time to be pious."

"Not enough time? Do you need time for that?"

"Oh yes. Being pious takes time—in fact, it takes more than that: independence from time! You can't be seriously pious and still live in reality and take it seriously: time, money, the Odeon Bar, and all that stuff."

"I understand. But what about the saints?"

"Well, there are some saints I especially like: Stephen, St. Francis, and some others. Now sometimes I see pictures of them, and also of the Savior and Our Lady—all those phony, fake, foolish pictures—and I find them just as unbearable as you find that picture of Goethe. When I see such a sweet, stupid Savior or St. Francis, and see how other people think these pictures are so beautiful and edifying, it feels to me like an insult to the real Savior, and I think: Oh, why did he have to live and endure all that terrible suffering, if such a stupid picture of him is good enough for these people! But at the same time I know that even my image of the Savior or of Francis is only a human image, and it can't come close to the original image, and that my personal image of the Savior would seem just as stupid and inadequate to the Savior himself as all those cloying copies seem to me. I'm not telling you all that to prove you right for the way you felt about the picture of Goethe, for all your resentment and rage; no, you're wrong about that. I'm just saying it to prove that I can understand you. You scholars and artists have all kinds of outlandish things in your heads, but you're human just like everybody else, and the rest of us have our own dreams and games in our heads, too. Because I noticed, O learned sir, that you were a little uncertain about how to tell me your Goethe story—you had to try pretty hard to explain your abstract ideas to such a simple girl. Well, so then I wanted to show you that you don't have to try so hard. I understand you quite well. So, that's it! Now it's your bedtime."

She left, and an aged porter led me up two flights of stairs, or rather, first he asked after my luggage, and when he heard that I didn't have any, I had to pay what he called "bedroom rent" in advance. Then he took me up an old, dark staircase to a small room and left me alone. There was a rickety wooden bed, very short and hard, and hanging on the wall were a saber and a full-color portrait of Garibaldi, as well as a withered wreath from some organization's party. I would have given a great deal for a nightshirt. At least water and a small towel were provided, so I could wash myself, then I lay down on the bed fully clothed, leaving the light on, and had time to think. So now I was reconciled with Goethe. How lovely that he had come to me in a dream! And this wonderful girl—if only I had known her name! Suddenly there was a human being, a real live human being, who had shattered the cloudy glass dome of my deadly numbness and held out her hand to me, a good, beautiful, warm hand! Suddenly there were things that mattered to me again, things I could think about with joy, with worry, with excitement! Suddenly a door was open, and life could stream in to me! Perhaps I could live again, perhaps I could become human again. My soul, which had fallen asleep in the cold and had nearly frozen to death, was breathing again, drowsily beating its small, weak wings. Goethe had been here with me. A girl had ordered me to eat, drink, sleep, had shown me kindness, had laughed at me, had called me a stupid little boy. And that wonderful friend had also told me about the saints, she had shown me that I was not alone and misunderstood, even in my most incredible eccentricities, that I was not a pathological exception, that I had brothers and sisters, that I was understood. Would I ever see her again? Yes, certainly, she was someone I could count on. "My word is my word."

And already I was sleeping again, I slept four, five hours. It was after ten o'clock when I awoke in rumpled clothes, exhausted, tired, with a vague memory that something terrible had happened yesterday, but I was alive, hopeful, full of good thoughts. When I returned home to my apartment, I no longer felt any of the horrors that this homecoming had held for me the day before.

In the stairwell, above the Norfolk Island pine, I bumped into the "aunt," my landlady, whom I rarely saw face-to-face, but whose friendly demeanor I liked very much. It was an awkward encounter for me, since after all I was a bit bedraggled and bleary-eyed, unkempt and unshaven. I said hello and made as if to keep going. Ordinarily, she always respected my desire to be left alone and unnoticed, but today it seemed that a veil between me and the world around me had truly been torn in two, that a barrier had fallen—she laughed and paused on the stairs.

"You've been out and about, Mr. Haller, you didn't go to bed at all last night. You must be pretty tired!"

"Yes," I said, and had to laugh, too," things got a bit lively last night, and since I didn't want to disturb the character of your house, I slept in a hotel. I hold the peace and respectability of your house in high regard, sometimes I feel very much like an outsider here."

"Don't make fun, Mr. Haller!"

"Oh, I'm just making fun of myself."

"That's exactly what you shouldn't do. I don't want you to feel like an 'outsider' in my house. You should live as you please, and do what you like. I have had many very, very respectable lodgers, jewels of respectability, but none of them have been quieter, or disturbed us less, than you do. And now—will you have some tea?"

I didn't resist. In her salon, with its fine grandfather pictures and grandfather furniture, she served me tea, we chatted a bit, and without actually asking, the friendly woman learned various things about my life and my thoughts, and she listened with that attitude—that combination of respect and a mother's knack for taking things not quite seriously—that smart women reserve for men's eccentricities. We also talked about her nephew, and she led me into an adjoining room to see his latest after-work project, a radio set. That diligent young man had spent his evenings sitting there piecing that device together, captivated by the idea of wirelessness, bowing down on his pious knees before the god of technology who, after millennia, had managed to discover and most imperfectly represent things that every thinker has always known and put to wiser use. We talked about that, because the aunt is slightly inclined to piety, and not averse to religious conversations. I told her that the omnipresence of all forces and deeds had been very well known to the people of ancient India, and that technology had only brought one small facet of that phenomenon to more widespread attention, by constructing a transmitter and receiver for it—that is, for the sound waves—a transmitter and receiver that remained dreadfully imperfect at present. The most important facet of that ancient knowledge, the unreality of time, had not yet been considered from a technological perspective, but eventually, of course, it too would be "discovered" and fall into the hands of the hardworking engineers. It would be discovered, perhaps very soon, that not only are we constantly surrounded by a flood of current, contemporary images and events—such that music from Paris and Berlin can now be heard in Frankfurt or Zurich—but everything that has ever happened is registered and preserved in exactly the same way, so that one day, with or without a wire, with or without distracting background noise, we will be able to hear King Solomon and Walther von der Vogelweide speak. And all this, just like the advent of radio today, would only enable people to flee from themselves and their purpose and to surround themselves with an ever denser web of distractions and useless pursuits. But I said all these things, which were commonplace to me, not with my customary tone of bitterness and scorn for time and technology, but jokingly and playfully, and the aunt smiled, and we sat together for probably an hour, drinking tea and feeling content.

I had invited the pretty, mysterious girl from the Black Eagle to go out with me on Tuesday evening, and it cost me quite a bit of effort to kill the time until then. And by the time Tuesday finally rolled around, it had become shockingly clear to me how important my relationship with the unknown girl was. I thought only of her, I expected everything of her, I was prepared to sacrifice

everything to her and lay it at her feet, and yet I wasn't the slightest
bit in love with her. All I had to do was imagine that she might
break or forget our date, and then I saw clearly how things stood
with me; the world would be empty again, one day would be as
gray and worthless as the next, I would be surrounded again by
all that dreadful silence and numbness, and the only way out of
this silent hell would be the razor. And the razor had grown no
more appealing to me over these past few days, it had lost nothing
of its horror. That was just what made it all so ugly; I had a deep,
heartrending fear of slitting my throat, my fear of death was just as
ferocious, tenacious, pugnacious, and rebellious in its strength as
if I had been the healthiest man alive and my life had been a paradise. I recognized my condition with full, unsparing clarity, and
realized that it was the unbearable tension between not being able
to live and not being able to die that made her—that stranger, that
pretty little dancer from the Black Eagle—so important to me. She
was the little window, the tiny crack that let light into my dark
cave of fear. She was my salvation, my escape. She had to teach me
to live or teach me to die, she had to touch my frozen heart with
her firm, pretty hand, so that it would either blossom or crumble
to ashes beneath her living touch. As for what gave her these powers, what was the source of her magic, why she had mysteriously
taken on this profound significance for me, that was something I
couldn't think about, and it didn't matter, either; I didn't care to
know. I no longer had the slightest interest in any knowledge, in
any insight, those were just the things I had in excess; and that was
precisely what caused me the keenest, most humiliating torment
and disgrace: the fact that I saw my own condition so clearly, that I
was so acutely aware of it. I saw this fellow, this Steppenwolf beast,
before me like a fly in a web, and I watched his fate approach a
decisive turning point as he hung ensnared and defenseless in that
web, I saw the spider poised to bite, and I saw a hand extended

in rescue that seemed equally near. I could have said the cleverest and most insightful things about the contexts and causes of my suffering, the sickness of my soul, my affliction and neurosis; the mechanics were transparent to me. But it was not knowledge and understanding that I needed, that I so desperately longed for, but experience, decision, a push and a leap.

Although I never doubted, during those few days of waiting, that my friend would keep her word, on the last day I was very agitated and uncertain; never in my life have I waited more impatiently for evening to come. And while the excitement and impatience grew almost unbearable for me, at the same time they felt wonderful: It was something inconceivably beautiful and new for me—a disenchanted man who had gone so long with nothing to wait for, nothing to look forward to—it was wonderful to run back and forth all day long, filled with restlessness, anxiety, and eager anticipation, to imagine in advance how we would meet, what we would talk about, where the evening would lead, to shave and dress for it (with special care, a new shirt, a new tie, new shoelaces). Whoever this clever, mysterious girl might be, however she might have gotten into this relationship with me, it was all the same to me; she was there, the miracle had occurred, I had found someone again, and found a new interest in life! The only important thing was for this to continue, for me to abandon myself to this attraction, to follow this star.

That unforgettable moment when I saw her again! I was sitting in the cozy old restaurant, at a small table that I had needlessly called ahead to reserve, studying the menu, with two beautiful orchids that I had bought for my friend sitting in a glass of water. I had to wait quite a while for her, but I felt sure that she would come, and I was no longer agitated. And now she came, stopped in front of the cloakroom, and greeted me only with an alert, somewhat searching look from her light gray eyes. I suspiciously observed the waiter's behavior toward her. No, thank God, there was no familiarity, no lack of distance, he was unfailingly polite. And yet they knew each other, she called him Emil.

When I gave her the orchids, she was delighted, and laughed. "That's sweet of you, Harry. You wanted to give me a present, didn't you, and you didn't quite know what to choose, you didn't quite know to what extent you were actually entitled to give me a present, whether I might not be offended, and so you bought orchids, which are only flowers, but quite expensive ones. Well, thank you very much. By the way, I want to tell you this up front: I don't want any gifts from you. I live off of men, but I don't want to live off of you. But look how you've changed! I hardly even recognize you. The other day you looked as if you'd just been cut down from the noose, and now you're practically human again. Oh, by the way, did you obey my order?"

"What order?"

"Are you really that forgetful? I mean, can you dance the fox-trot now? You told me there was nothing you wanted more than to take orders from me, you liked nothing better than to obey me. Remember?"

"Oh yes, and that's still true! I meant it!"

"And yet you haven't learned to dance yet?"

"Is that something you can do so quickly, in just a few days?"

"Of course. You can learn the fox in an hour, the Boston in two. The tango takes longer, but you don't even need that one."

"But now I finally need to know your name!"

She looked at me for a while in silence.

"You might be able to guess it. I'd like it very much if you would guess it. Pay attention and take a good look at me! Haven't you noticed yet that I sometimes have a boy's face? Right now, for example?"

Yes, now that I looked closely at her face, I had to admit that she was right, it was a boy's face. And when I gave myself a minute, her face began to speak to me, it reminded me of my own boyhood, and of a friend I had back then whose name was Hermann. For a moment, it seemed as if she had been completely transformed into this Hermann.

"If you were a boy," I said in amazement, "your name would have to be Hermann."

"Who knows," she said playfully, "maybe I really am a boy, just in disguise."

"Is your name Hermine?"

She nodded, beaming, pleased that I had guessed it. Just then the soup came, we began to eat, and it gave her a childlike pleasure. Of all the things about her that charmed and enchanted me, the most endearing and unusual thing was the way that she could suddenly go from the most profound seriousness to the most whimsical gaiety and vice versa, without changing or straining herself at all, as if she were a gifted child. Now she was cheerful for a while, teasing me about the fox-trot, even tapping me with her feet, enthusiastically praising the food, noting that I had put some effort into my attire, but still finding plenty to criticize about my appearance.

I interjected to ask her: "How did you do that, the way you suddenly looked like a boy and I could guess your name?"

"Oh, you did that all by yourself. Don't you understand, you learned gentleman, that the reason you like me, and the reason I'm important to you, is that I'm a kind of mirror for you, that there's something inside of me that responds to you and understands you? Really, people should always be mirrors like that for each other, they should always respond and correspond to each other like that, but oddballs like you are so eccentric, you get carried away and enchanted so easily that you can't see anything or read anything in other people's eyes anymore, it doesn't make any difference to you anymore. And when an oddball like you suddenly finds a face that really looks at him again, in which he detects some kind of response and kinship, then of course he's delighted."

"You know everything, Hermine," I exclaimed in amazement. "It's just as you say. And yet you're so completely different from me! You're just the opposite of me; you have everything I lack."

"That's what you think," she said laconically, "and that's just how it should be."

And now her face, which really did seem like a magic mirror to me, was darkened by a heavy cloud of earnestness; suddenly her entire face spoke only of earnestness, of tragedy, it was unfathomable, like the empty eyes of a mask. Slowly, as if she were only reluctantly uttering each word, she said:

"Don't forget what you told me! You told me that I should give you orders, and that it would be your pleasure to obey them all. Don't forget! You must know, little Harry: just as you feel that my face responds to you, that something in me suits you and makes you trust me—you make me feel the same way. When I saw you come into the Black Eagle the other day, so tired and distant and practically lost to the world, I could feel it right away: there's a man who will obey me, he's yearning for me to give him orders! And I'll do it, too, that's why I started talking to you, and that's why we became friends."

Her speech was filled with such grave earnestness, with such tremendous pressure from the soul, that I couldn't quite keep up, and I tried to calm her down and distract her. She only shook off my efforts with a twitch of her eyebrows, fixed me with a compelling stare, and continued in a very cold voice: "I'm telling you, little one, you'd better keep your word, or you'll regret it. You will receive many orders from me, and you will follow them, nice orders, pleasant orders, it will be your pleasure to obey them. And in the end, you will also obey my final command, Harry."

"I will," I said, half submissively. "What will your final command for me be?" I had already guessed it, though, God knows why.

She shivered, as if she had a slight chill, and it seemed that she was slowly waking from her reverie. Her eyes would not let me go. Suddenly her mood grew even darker.

"It wouldn't be smart for me to tell you that. But I don't want to be smart, Harry, not this time. I want something else entirely. Listen up! You'll hear it, you'll forget it, you'll laugh about it, you'll cry about it. Listen up, little boy! I want to play a game of life and death with you, little brother, and I want to show you my cards before we even start to play."

How beautiful her face was, how otherworldly, when she said that! A knowing sorrow swam in those eyes, cool and bright; those eyes seemed to have already suffered every conceivable sorrow, and to have said yes to it. Her mouth spoke heavily, as if with an impediment, the way a person speaks whose face is frozen by a heavy frost; but there was something that contrasted with her gaze and her voice; between her lips, in the corners of her mouth, in the play of the tip of her tongue, which was only rarely visible, there flowed a sweet, playful sensuality, an intense desire for pleasure. A short curl hung down over her calm, smooth forehead, and from there, from that corner of her forehead with its curl, that wave of boyishness, of hermaphroditic magic flowed out from time to time like living breath. I listened to her fearfully, and yet as if in a daze, as if I were only half there.

"You like me," she continued, "for the reason I already told you: I broke through your loneliness, I caught you just outside the gates of hell and brought you back to life. But I want more from you, much more. I want to make you fall in love with me. No, don't contradict me, let me speak! You like me very much, I can feel it, and you're grateful to me, but you're not in love with me. I want to make you fall in love with me, that's part of my job; I make my living by making men fall in love with me. But listen up, I'm not doing this because I think that you of all people are so delightful. I'm not in love with you, Harry, any more than you are with me. But I need you, just as you need me. Right now, you need me because you're desperate, and you need a push to throw you into the water and bring you back to life. You need me so that you can learn to dance, learn to laugh, learn to live. But I need you, too— not today, later—for something very important and fine. When you're in love with me, I'll give you my final command, and you'll obey, and that will be good for you and for me."

She lifted one of the violet-brown orchids with its green veins a bit in the glass, tilted her face over it for a moment, and stared at the flower.

"You will not have an easy time of it, but you will do it. You will do my bidding and *you will kill me*. That is it. Ask me no more!"

Still looking at the orchid, she fell silent, her face relaxed, released from pressure and tension, it unfurled like an opening bud, and suddenly a delightful smile played on her lips, while her eyes remained fixed and spellbound for a moment. And now she shook her head with its little boy curl, drank a sip of water, suddenly noticed again that we were eating, and fell upon the food with a joyful appetite.

I had heard her uncanny speech very clearly, word for word, I had even guessed her "final command" before she spoke it, so it did not come as a shock to me when she reached the words "You will kill me." Everything she said sounded persuasive and portentous to me, I accepted it and did not resist it, and yet, in spite of the dreadful earnestness with which she had spoken, none of it seemed fully real and earnest to me. One part of my soul absorbed her words and believed them, another part of my soul nodded appeasingly and noted that even Hermine, as clever, healthy, and confident as she was, had her fantasies and twilight states. Hardly had her last word been spoken than a layer of irreality and inconsequentiality blanketed the whole scene.

All the same, I could not leap as lightly back into the world of the probable and the real as that tightrope walker Hermine did.

"So I'm going to kill you someday?" I asked, still quietly lost in my dream, while she was already laughing again and eagerly cutting up her poultry.

"Of course," she nodded in passing, "enough of that, it's dinnertime. Harry, be a dear and order me something else, a bit of green salad! Don't you have any appetite? I think you have to learn everything that comes naturally to other people, even the joy of eating. So look, little one, this here is a duck leg, and when you pull the nice, shiny meat off the bone, it's a feast, and it should make your heart feel just as hungry and excited and grateful as a lover's does when he helps his girl out of her jacket for the first time. Do you understand? No? You're a sheep. Look, I'll give you a piece of this lovely duck leg, you'll see. Now, open your mouth!—Oh, what a rascal you are! God knows, now he's been peering over at the other people, wondering if they won't see when he takes a bite off of my fork! Don't worry, you prodigal son, I'm not going to embarrass you. But if you need other people's permission before you can enjoy yourself, then you really are a poor rascal."

The scene that had just taken place was growing more and more unreal, it was more and more unbelievable that only minutes earlier those eyes had been staring so gravely and dreadfully. Oh, in that respect Hermine was like life itself: always one moment at a time, impossible to predict in advance. Now she was eating, and the duck leg and the salad, the tart and the liqueur were being taken seriously, they had become the object of pleasure and judgment, of conversation and fancy. As soon as the plate was taken away, a new chapter began. This woman, who had seen through me so completely, who seemed to know more about life than all the wise men put together, had made a practice of childishness, the little game of life lived in the moment, and practiced it with such artistry that I became her disciple without further ado. Whether this be supreme wisdom or the simplest naïveté: anyone who knew how to live in the moment like that, who lived so fully in the present, who so kindly and carefully cherished each little flower along the path, who knew the value of each playful little moment, had nothing to fear from life. But this joyful child, with her good appetite, with her playful gourmandism, was also, at the very same time, supposed to be a dreamer and hysteric who longed for death, or a vigilant and calculating woman who consciously, coldheartedly desired to make me her slave in love? That could not be. No, she was simply so utterly devoted to the moment that, just as she was open to every amusing inspiration, she was also open to every fleeting, dark chill from the remote depths of the soul, and she would let it play itself out.

This Hermine, whom I was seeing today for only the second time, knew everything about me, it seemed impossible to me that I could ever keep a secret from her. It may be that she would not have fully understood my intellectual life; she might not have been able to follow me in my relationships to music, to Goethe, to Novalis or Baudelaire—but even that was very doubtful, even that probably would not have cost her any effort. And even if it had—what was left of my "intellectual life," anyway? Wasn't it all lying in pieces, hadn't it lost all meaning? But I had no doubt that she would understand all of my other, personal problems and concerns. Soon I would talk to her about the Steppenwolf, about the treatise, about anything and everything that had existed for me alone until now, which I had never spoken a word about to anyone. I could not refrain from starting right away.

"Hermine," I said, "a curious thing happened to me the other day. A stranger gave me a little printed booklet, the kind you get at a carnival, and it had my entire story inside, everything about me, described in detail. Say, isn't that strange?"

"What's the little book called?" she asked casually.

"It's called *Treatise on the Steppenwolf.*"

"Oh, Steppenwolf is fantastic! And that's you, the Steppenwolf? That's supposed to be you?"

"Yes, that's me. I'm someone who's half man and half wolf, or who at least believes himself to be."

She didn't answer. She looked into my eyes with searching attentiveness, looked at my hands, and for a moment the deep seriousness and somber passion from earlier returned to her eyes and her face. I thought I could read her mind, she was wondering if I was wolf enough to carry out her "final command."

"Of course it's your imagination," she said, adopting a cheerful tone again, "or poetry, if you will. But there's something to it. You're not a wolf today, but the other day, when you came into that dance hall looking like you'd just fallen from the moon, you really were a bit of a beast, and that's exactly what I liked about you."

She interrupted herself with a sudden realization and said, with a sense of shock: "It sounds so stupid to use words like 'beast' or 'predator'! We shouldn't talk about animals that way. It's true that they're often horrible, but they're still much more real than people."

"What's 'real'? What do you mean?"

"Well, look at an animal, a cat, a dog, a bird, or even one of those beautiful bigger animals in the zoo, like a puma or a giraffe! You have to see that all of them are real, not a single animal is awkward or unsure of what to do or how to behave. They're not trying to flatter you, they're not trying to impress you. There's no performance. They are what they are, like stones and flowers or like stars in the sky. Do you understand?"

I understood.

"Animals are usually sad," she went on. "And when a person is very sad, not because he has a toothache or he's lost money, but because for just an hour he really feels how everything is for a change, the whole of life, and then he's really, truly sad, he always looks a bit like an animal—then he looks sad, but also more real and more beautiful than usual. That's how it is, and that's how you looked, Steppenwolf, the first time I saw you."

"Well, Hermine, so what do you think about that book that describes me?"

"Oh, you know, I don't like to think all the time. We'll talk about that some other time. You can give it to me to read one of these days. Or no, if I ever get around to reading again, give me one of those books you've written yourself."

She ordered coffee and seemed inattentive and distracted for a while, then suddenly she lit up, and she seemed to have come to some conclusion in her musings.

"Hello," she exclaimed joyfully, "I've got it!"

"Got what?"

"The fox-trot thing, I couldn't stop thinking about it the whole time. So tell me: do you have a room where the two of us could dance for an hour every now and then? It's all right if it's small, that doesn't matter, but there can't be anyone living right below you who would come up and make a fuss if his ceiling started shaking a little. All right, very good! Then you can learn to dance at home."

"Yes," I said shyly, "so much the better. But I thought you needed music for that."

"Of course you do. So listen, you'll buy the music, that won't cost any more than dance lessons with a teacher. And you won't need a teacher, I'll do that myself. Then we'll have music as often as we want, and we'll get to keep the gramophone, too."

"The gramophone?"

"Of course. You'll just buy one of those little gadgets and a couple of dance records to go with it . . ."

"Wonderful," I cried, "and if you really succeed in teaching me to dance, you'll get the gramophone as your fee. Agreed?"

I said it very decisively, but it didn't come from the heart. I couldn't imagine a device like that in my study next to all the books, a device I couldn't stand, and I had plenty of objections to the dancing, too. I had thought that we could perhaps try it once in a while, although I was convinced that I was much too old and stiff and would never be able to learn it at this age. But now, all at once, it was just too fast and furious for me, and I felt everything in me putting up a fight—everything that I, as an old, spoiled music connoisseur, had against gramophones, jazz, and the latest dance music. The idea that now, in my study, next to Novalis and Jean Paul, in my intellectual sanctuary and refuge, American dance hits should be heard, and that I should dance to them, was really more than anyone could ask of me. But it was not "anyone" who demanded this; it was Hermine, and she had the right to give orders. I obeyed. Of course I obeyed.

We met up the next afternoon in a café. Hermine was already sitting there drinking tea when I arrived, and she smiled and showed me a newspaper where she had found my name. It was one of the reactionary smear-sheets from my native country, one of the papers where fierce diatribes against me were always making the rounds from time to time. During the war I had been a pacifist, after the war I had occasionally called for calm, patience, humanity, and self-criticism, and I had defended myself against the nationalist agitation that was growing harsher, more ridiculous, and wilder by the day. This was another one of those attacks, poorly written, half of it drafted by the editor himself, the other half lifted from the many similar essays that had appeared in publications of that ilk. It is well known that no one writes as poorly as the defenders of outdated ideologies, no one practices his craft with less diligence and care. Hermine had read the essay and had learned from it that Harry Haller was a pest and an unpatriotic rascal, and that of course things could only get worse for the fatherland as long as such people and such thoughts were tolerated, and as long as the youth continued to be indoctrinated with sentimental ideals of humanity instead of violent revenge against our hereditary enemy.

"Is that you?" asked Hermine, pointing to my name. "Well, you've done a nice job of making enemies there, Harry. Does that bother you?"

I read a few lines, it was the usual, I'd been hearing every single one of those clichéd insults ad nauseam for years.

"No," I said, "it doesn't bother me, I got used to it a long time ago. On a few occasions, I expressed the opinion that it was incumbent upon every people, and even upon every single individual, that they stop lulling themselves to sleep with dishonest political 'questions of guilt,' and that they instead look within themselves to see to what extent they shared the blame for the war and for all the other misfortunes in the world, on account of their mistakes, their failures, and their bad habits; that is the only way that we might perhaps avoid the next war. They can't forgive me for that, because of course they themselves are completely innocent: the Kaiser, the generals, the big industrialists, the politicians, the newspapers—nobody has the slightest thing to blame himself for, nobody bears any guilt! You'd think that everything in the world was wonderful, except that there are twelve million murdered people lying beneath the ground. And look, Hermine, even if diatribes like that don't make me angry anymore, they do sometimes make me sad. Two-thirds of my countrymen read those kinds of newspapers, every morning and every evening they hear those tones, every day they're being worked on, admonished, incited, riled up, and the goal and purpose of it all is another war, the next war, the coming war, and it will probably be even more hideous than the last. It's all very clear and simple, anyone could understand it, anyone could reach the same conclusion if he would just spend a single hour of his time thinking about it. But nobody wants to do that, nobody wants to avoid the next war, nobody wants to spare himself and his children the next slaughter of millions, unless he can do it at an even lower cost to himself. An hour of reflection, a period of introspection about our own involvement in the disorder and wickedness of the world, our own complicity— look, nobody wants that! And so it will go on, and many thousands of people will keep eagerly working each day to prepare the next war. For as long as I've understood that, it has paralyzed me and plunged me into despair, I have no 'fatherland' and no ideals anymore, that's all just window dressing for the bosses who are preparing the next slaughter. There's no point in thinking, saying, writing anything humane, there's no point in thinking positive thoughts—for every two or three people who do that, there are a thousand newspapers, magazines, speeches, meetings held in public or in secret, that are all striving for the opposite and achieving it, day after day."

Hermine had been listening attentively.

"Yes," she said then, "you're quite right. Of course there will be another war, you don't have to read the newspapers to know that. You can be sad about it, of course, but that doesn't do any good. It's just like being sad about the fact that you'll inevitably have to die one day, no matter what you might do to prevent it. The fight against death, dear Harry, is always a beautiful, noble, wonderful, and honorable cause, and that means that the fight against war is as well. But it's always hopelessly quixotic, too."

"That may be true," I burst out, "but if you go around telling truths like that—that we're all going to die soon anyway so it's all a wash and nothing matters—you just make the whole of life shallow and stupid. Oh, so maybe we should just throw it all away, renounce all intellect, all aspiration, all humanity, let ambition and money continue to rule, and sit there with our glass of beer while we wait for the next mobilization?"

The look that Hermine gave me now was a strange one, a look full of amusement, full of mockery and mischief and sympathetic camaraderie, but at the same time so full of gravitas, knowledge, and unfathomable earnestness!

"You shouldn't do that," she said in a motherly tone. "It won't make your life shallow and stupid to know that your struggle is going to be unsuccessful. It's much shallower, Harry, if you fight for something good and ideal in the belief that you have to succeed. Are ideals there to be realized? Do we humans live in order to abolish death? No, we live to fear it and then again to love it, and it is precisely because of death that our little bit of life sometimes shines so beautifully for an hour. You are a child, Harry. Now, be a good boy and come with me, we have a lot to do today. I'm not going to worry about the war and the newspapers anymore today. Are you?"

Oh no, I was ready, too.

We went together—it was our first joint outing in town—to a music shop and looked at gramophones, opened them and shut them, asked to hear them played, and when we'd found one that was very suitable and nice and well priced, I wanted to buy it, but Hermine wasn't so easy to please. She held me back, and first I had to go to a second store with her and see and hear all the systems and sizes there, too, from the most expensive to the cheapest, and only then did she agree to go back to the first store and buy the contraption we'd found there.

"You see," I said, "we could have made this easier on ourselves."

"You think so? And then maybe tomorrow we would've seen the same contraption for sale in another window for twenty francs less. And besides, shopping is fun, and when something is fun, you should savor it. You still have a lot to learn."

With the help of a porter, we brought our purchase back to my apartment.

Hermine carefully examined my living room, complimented the heating stove and the divan, tested the chairs, picked up books, paused for a long time in front of the photograph of my girlfriend. We'd placed the gramophone on a chest of drawers between piles of books. And now my lesson began. She played a fox-trot, showed me the first steps, took my hand, and began to lead me. I trotted along obediently, bumping into chairs, listening to her commands, not understanding them, stepping on her toes, and being as clumsy as I was dutiful. After the second dance, she threw herself down on the divan, laughing like a child.

"My God, you're so stiff! Just keep moving, the way you do when you go for a walk! You don't have to make any effort at all. Are you getting hot already? Well, let's just rest for five minutes! Look, if you know how to do it, dancing is just as simple as thinking, and it's a whole lot easier to learn. Now you won't be so impatient with all those people who don't want to learn to think, who'd rather just call Mr. Haller a traitor to his country and quietly wait for the next war to come."

She left after an hour, assuring me that it would go better next time. I begged to differ, and I was very disappointed in my own stupidity and clumsiness; it seemed to me that I'd learned nothing at all from that lesson, and I didn't think I'd do any better on the next attempt. No, dancing required skills that I completely lacked: cheerfulness, innocence, lightheartedness, swing. Well, that's what I'd thought all along.

But behold, it really did go better the next time, and I was even starting to enjoy it, and at the end of the lesson Hermine claimed that I could do the fox-trot now. But when she added that that meant I'd have to go dancing with her at a restaurant the next day, I was horrified, and I put up a vigorous fight. She coolly reminded me of my vow of obedience, and ordered me to meet her for tea the following day at the Hotel des Balances.

That evening I sat at home, I wanted to read but I couldn't. I was dreading the day to come; I was horrified at the thought that I, an old, timid, sensitive misfit, should not only visit one of those dreary modern tea and dance halls with jazz music, but even present myself there, among strangers, as a dancer, despite the fact that I was still so utterly incompetent. And I confess that I laughed at myself and felt ashamed of myself when, alone in my quiet study, I cranked up the machine and let it run, as I softly repeated the steps of my fox-trot in my stocking feet.

The next day, at the Hotel des Balances, there was a little band playing, and people were drinking tea and whiskey. I tried to bribe Hermine, offered her cakes, tried to invite her to share a bottle of wine with me, but she was adamant.

"You're not here for your own amusement today. This is dance class."

I had to dance with her two or three times, and in between dances she introduced me to the saxophone player, a dark, handsome young man of Spanish or South American extraction who she said could play all the instruments and speak all the languages in the world. This señor seemed to be a close acquaintance and friend of Hermine's, he had two saxophones of different sizes sitting in front of him, and he blew into first one, then the other, while his black, glistening eyes studied the dancers with interest and delight. To my own amazement, I felt something like jealousy toward this harmless, handsome musician—not romantic jealousy, since there was no question of romance between Hermine and me, but more of an intellectual jealousy between friends, because it seemed to me that he was undeserving of the interest and the distinct admiration, even reverence, with which she treated him. I have to make some odd acquaintances here, I thought sullenly.

Hermine was asked to dance again and again, and I was left sitting alone with my tea, listening to the music, a kind of music that I had always found unbearable. Dear God, I thought, now I'm supposed to be brought into this world and make myself at home here, in this world that I find so strange and repulsive, this world of idlers and pleasure seekers, which I've always so carefully avoided and so deeply despised, this slick, clichéd world of marble tables, jazz music, cocottes, traveling salesmen! I dejectedly sipped my tea and scanned the halfway elegant crowd. Two beautiful girls caught my eye, both of them good dancers, and I watched them with admiration and envy as they danced, lithely, beautifully, cheerfully, and confidently.

Then Hermine appeared again, she was unhappy with me. She scolded me, said I hadn't come here to make faces like that and sit there motionless at the tea table, now if I would please just pull myself together and go out and dance. What, I didn't know anyone? Well, I didn't need to. Didn't I see any girls I liked?

I pointed one out to her, the prettier one, who was standing close to us and looked stunning in her little velvet skirt, with her short, thick blond hair and her full, womanly arms. Hermine insisted that I go over to her right away and ask her to dance. I resisted, feeling desperate.

"But I can't!" I said unhappily. "Sure, if I were a handsome young guy! But a stiff old fool like me who can't even dance—she'd laugh at me!"

Hermine gave me a scornful look.

"But of course you don't care if I laugh at you. You're such a coward! Anyone who approaches a girl runs the risk of being laughed at; those are the stakes. So take a chance, Harry, and if worse comes to worst, she'll laugh at you—if you don't do it, I'll lose my faith in your obedience."

She was unrelenting. Trembling, I stood up and walked toward the beautiful girl just as the music started up again.

"I'm already spoken for," she said, looking at me curiously with those big bright eyes, "but the man I'm dancing with seems to be stuck in the bar over there. All right, come on!"

I embraced her and danced the first steps, still amazed that she hadn't turned me away, but then she caught on to my situation and took the lead. She danced wonderfully, and I was swept away, for a few moments I forgot all about the rules and regulations I had learned for dancing, I just swam along, felt my dance partner's firm hips, her quick, limber knees, looked into her young, radiant face, and confessed to her that today was the first time in my entire life that I'd ever danced. She smiled and encouraged me, and responded to my rapt gazes and flattering words with wonderful grace, not with words, but with quiet, rapturous movements that drew us tantalizingly closer together. I placed my right hand firmly above her waist, joyfully and eagerly following the movements of her legs, her arms, her shoulders, to my astonishment I never once stepped on her feet, and when the music stopped we both stood and clapped until the dance began again and I once more eagerly, lovingly, and devoutly performed that rite.

When the dance was over, all too soon, the beautiful velvet girl withdrew, and suddenly Hermine, who had been watching us, was standing next to me.

"Do you notice anything?" she laughed approvingly. "Have you discovered that women's legs aren't table legs? Well, bravo! Now you can do the fox-trot, thank God, tomorrow we'll start on the Boston, and in three weeks there's a masquerade ball at the Globe Ballrooms."

The dance band was taking a break, we'd sat down, and now the handsome young Mr. Pablo, the saxophone player, came over as well, nodded to us, and sat down next to Hermine. He seemed to be a very good friend of hers. But I confess that I did not take a liking to the gentleman at all on that first encounter. He was handsome, that much could not be denied, handsome in build and handsome in countenance, but I could not identify any other virtues in him. Even with his multilingualism he took the easy way out—that is, he said nothing at all, just words like please, thank you, yes, certainly, hello, and so forth, which he did in fact know in several languages. No, he didn't say a thing, Señor Pablo, and he didn't seem to think much, either, that handsome caballero. His occupation was to play the saxophone in the jazz band, and he seemed to pursue this profession with love and passion, sometimes suddenly clapping his hands while playing or allowing himself other outbursts of enthusiasm, such as loudly singing words like: "oh oh oh oh, ha ha, hello!" But apart from that, he was clearly on this earth for no other purpose than to be beautiful, to please women, and to wear the latest fashion in collars and ties, along with many rings on his fingers. His conversation consisted of sitting with us, smiling at us, looking at his wristwatch, and rolling cigarettes, which he did with considerable dexterity. His dark, handsome Creole eyes and his black curls concealed no romantic disposition, no problems, no thoughts—seen from up close, this beautiful, exotic demigod was an affable and somewhat spoiled boy with pleasant manners, nothing more. I talked to him about his instrument and about the tonal qualities of jazz music, I wanted him to see that he was dealing with an old hand and a connoisseur where music was concerned. But he didn't pursue the question at all, and when I launched into something like a music-theoretical defense of jazz out of courtesy to him, or actually to Hermine, he smiled benignly at me and my efforts, presumably he was completely unaware that there had ever been any other kinds of music before or besides jazz. He was nice, nice and pleasant, his big, empty eyes smiled sweetly; but he and I seemed to have nothing in common—nothing that was important and sacred to him could be that way to me, we came from opposite sides of the world, our languages had not a word in common. (But later Hermine told me something strange. She told me that after that conversation, Pablo had said that she should be very careful with me, since I was so very unhappy. And when she asked him where he'd gotten that idea, he said: "Poor, poor man. Look at his eyes! Can't laugh!")

Once the black-eyed man had excused himself and the music had started again, Hermine stood up. "Now you could dance with me again, Harry. Or don't you want to anymore?"

I danced more lightly, more freely, and more happily with her now, too, though I was not as unburdened and carefree as I had been with the other girl. Hermine allowed me to lead, and she followed, her body clinging to mine as tenderly and delicately as a flower petal, and now I could find and feel all those same beautiful qualities in her, drawing near to me one moment, pulling away the next—she, too, gave off a scent of woman and love, her dance, too, tenderly and intimately sang the sweetly alluring song of sex—and yet I could not respond with complete freedom and joy to all of this, could not fully forget myself and surrender myself to it. Hermine was all too close to me, she was my partner, my sister, my equal, she resembled me and my childhood friend Hermann, the dreamer, the poet, my ardent partner in intellectual exercises and excesses.

"I know," she said when I spoke of it later, "I know very well. I'm still going to make you fall in love with me eventually, but there's no hurry. For the time being we're partners, we're people who hope to become friends, because we've recognized each other. For now we both want to learn from each other and play with each other. I show you my little theater and teach you to dance and to be a little cheerful and dumb, and you show me your thoughts and some of your knowledge."

"Oh, Hermine, there isn't much to show, you know so much more than I do. What an extraordinary person you are, girl! You understand everything about me, and you're always a step ahead of me. Do I mean anything to you? Don't you find me boring?"

She looked down glumly at the ground.

"I don't like it when you talk like that. Think of that evening when you were so broken and filled with despair, and in your anguish and loneliness you crossed my path and became my partner! Why do you think I was able to recognize you and understand you then?"

"Why, Hermine? Tell me!"

"Because I'm like you. Because I'm just as alone as you are, and it's just as hard for me as it is for you to love life and people and myself and take them seriously. After all, there are always some people like that who demand the utmost from life and find it hard to put up with its stupidity and crudity."

"Yes, my friend!" I cried out, deeply astonished. "I understand you, partner, no one understands you the way I do. But you're still a mystery to me. You live your life so playfully, you have such wonderful respect for the little things and pleasures, you're such an artist in life. How can you suffer from life? How can you despair?"

"I don't despair, Harry. But suffering from life—oh yes, I know a thing or two about that. You're surprised that I'm not happy, because I can dance and I know my way around the surface of life so well. And I'm surprised, friend, that you're so disappointed in life, since you make yourself at home in the most beautiful and deepest things of all, in the intellect, in art, in thought! That's why we were drawn to each other, that's why we're brother and sister. I'll teach you to dance and play and smile and remain unsatisfied all the while. And you'll teach me to think and know and remain unsatisfied all the while. Do you know that we're both children of the devil?"

"Yes, that we are. The devil is the intellect, and we're his unfortunate children. We've fallen out of nature and we're dangling in the void. But that reminds me of something: in the Steppenwolf treatise that I told you about, it says something to the effect that if Harry thinks that he has one or two souls, if he thinks that he consists of one or two personalities, it's only his imagination. Every man, it says, is made up of ten, a hundred, a thousand souls."

"I like that very much," exclaimed Hermine. "In your case, for instance, the intellect is very highly developed, and yet you're very backward in so many of the little arts of life. Harry the thinker is a hundred years old, but Harry the dancer is hardly half a day old. We want to take him further now, along with all his little brothers, who are just as small and stupid and immature as he is."

Smiling, she looked at me. And asked softly, in a different voice:

"And how did you like Maria?"

"Maria? Who's that?"

"That's the girl you danced with. A pretty girl, a very pretty girl. It looked to me like you were a little bit in love with her."

"Do you know her then?"

"Oh yes, we know each other quite well. Did you really take a liking to her?"

"I liked her, and I was glad that she was so forgiving of my dancing."

"Well, if that's all it is! You ought to court her a little, Harry. She's very pretty, and she dances so well, and besides, you're already in love with her. I think you'll be successful."

"Ah, that's not what I'm aiming for."

"Now you're lying a little. I know you've got a girlfriend some-where out there in the world, and you see her every six months just to quarrel with her. It's very nice of you if you want to stay faithful to your strange girlfriend, but forgive me if I don't take it too seriously! In fact, I have my suspicions about you in general, I think you take love terribly seriously. You can do that, you can love as much as you want in your own ideal way, that's up to you, it's no concern of mine. What does concern me, though, is that you need to get a little better at the small, simple arts and games of life—that's what I'm going to teach you, and I'll teach you better than your ideal girlfriend did, you can count on that! You really need to sleep with a pretty girl again, Steppenwolf."

"Hermine," I cried in torment, "just look at me, I'm an old man."

"A little boy, that's what you are. And just like you were too comfortable to learn to dance until it was almost too late, you were also too comfortable to learn to love. Dear friend, you sure know how to love ideally and tragically, and you can do it very well, I have no doubt about that—good for you! But now you're going to learn to love in an ordinary, human way, too. You've already taken the first steps, soon you'll be ready to go to a ball. Well, you still have to learn the Boston, we'll start on that tomorrow. I'll be here at three o'clock. By the way, how did you like the music here?"

"It was outstanding."

"See, that's progress, too, you've learned something. Until now you couldn't stand all that dance and jazz music, it wasn't serious or deep enough for you, but now you've seen that you don't have to take it seriously at all, it can still be quite nice and delightful. By the way, the whole band would be nothing without Pablo. He leads it, he fires it up."

JUST AS THE GRAMOPHONE had befouled the air of intellectual asceticism in my study, just as the American dances had penetrated my cultivated world of music in a strange and disturbing, even crushing fashion, so new things—fearful things, devastating things—were beginning to penetrate my life from all sides, that life which had been so sharply delineated and strictly circumscribed until now. The Steppenwolf treatise and Hermine were right with their doctrine of the thousand souls, every day a few new souls showed up in me in addition to all the old ones, they made demands, made noise, and now I could see the madness of my old personality, I could see it clearly like a picture before my eyes. I had given exclusive priority to the few abilities and activities in which I happened to excel, and I had painted the picture of a Harry and lived the life of a Harry who was actually no more than a very finely trained specialist in poetry, music, and philosophy— as for the entire rest of my person, the whole remaining chaos of abilities, drives, and aspirations, I had found them burdensome, and had given them the name of Steppenwolf.

Nevertheless, this release from my delusion, this dissolution of my personality was by no means merely a pleasant and diverting adventure; on the contrary, it was often bitterly painful, almost unbearable. The gramophone often sounded truly diabolical in these surroundings, where everything else was tempered to such different tones. And sometimes, when I was dancing my one-steps in some fashionable restaurant among all the elegant playboys and charlatans, I felt like a traitor to everything that had ever been dear and sacred to me in life. If Hermine had left me alone for just eight days, I would have escaped in no time from all those tedious and ridiculous attempts at living a playboy lifestyle. But Hermine was always there; even though I didn't see her every day, I was always being seen by her, guided, observed, examined—she could even read all the angry fantasies of rebellion and escape that were written on my face, and she did so with a smile.

With the progressive destruction of what I had once termed my personality, I also began to understand why, despite all my despair, I had always had such a terrible fear of death, and I began to realize that this dreadful and shameful fear of death was just another aspect of my old, mendacious, bourgeois existence. The Mr. Haller who had hitherto existed—the gifted writer, the connoisseur of Mozart and Goethe, the author of noteworthy reflections on the metaphysics of art, on genius and tragedy, on humanity, the melancholy hermit in his cell piled high with books—was subjected to self-criticism one piece at a time, and he came up short in every respect. This gifted and interesting gentleman, Mr. Haller, had preached reason and humanity and protested against the savagery of war, and yet during the war he had not allowed himself to be lined up against the wall and shot, as his own thinking would have dictated; instead, he had found some way to adapt, an extremely decent and noble way, of course, but a compromise nonetheless. He was also opposed to power and exploitation, and yet he held shares in several industrial corporations that were just sitting in the bank, and he devoured the interest that they earned without a twinge of remorse. And so it was with everything. Harry Haller may have disguised himself wonderfully as an idealist and a misanthrope, as a melancholy hermit and a grumbling prophet, but fundamentally he was a bourgeois man, he found a life like Hermine's reprehensible, he chafed at the nights wasted in restaurants, and at the money squandered there as well, he had a guilty conscience, and in no way did he long for liberation and fulfillment; on the contrary, he had a fierce longing to return to the comfortable times when his intellectual exploits had still brought him pleasure and fame. It was exactly the same longing that was felt by those newspaper readers he despised and ridiculed—they longed for those ideal days back before the war, because they found such longing more comfortable than learning from what they had experienced. Devil take him, he was nauseating, that Mr. Haller! And yet I clung to him, or to his mask that was already dissolving, clung to his intellectual flirtations, to his bourgeois fear of disorder and randomness (which included death), and I scornfully and enviously compared the nascent, new Harry, this somewhat shy, eccentric dilettante of the dance halls, with that former, falsely ideal image of Harry, in whom the new Harry had now succeeded in identifying all the fatal flaws that had so disturbed him when he saw them in the professor's Goethe etching. He himself, the old Harry, had been just that sort of bourgeois ideal of Goethe, just that sort of intellectual hero with an all-too-noble gaze, glistening with grandeur, intellect, and humanity as if with brilliantine, and nearly overwhelmed by the nobility of his own soul! But the devil take it, that fair image had developed some serious holes, the ideal Mr. Haller had been pitifully dismantled. He looked like a dignitary who had fallen into the hands of bandits and now stood there in tattered pants—who would have been wise to learn to play the derelict, but instead wore his rags as if they still sported medals, and continued to tearfully affect his lost dignity.

I kept running into Pablo the musician, and I was forced to revise my judgment of him, if only because Hermine was so fond of him and sought his company so eagerly. I had pegged Pablo in my memory as a handsome zero, a small, somewhat vain beau, a cheerful and carefree child who puffed joyfully into his carnival trumpet and could be manipulated easily with praise and chocolate. But Pablo never asked for my opinions, they meant no more to him than my musical theories. He was polite and friendly, always smiling as he listened to me, but he never gave me any real answers. Yet I still seemed to have attracted his interest, and he made an obvious effort to please me and show me goodwill. Once, when I became irritable and almost rude during one of those fruitless conversations, he looked me in the face with shock and dismay, took my left hand and stroked it, and offered me something to sniff from a small, gold-plated box, saying that it would do me good. I cast Hermine a questioning glance, she nodded, and I took the box and snorted. And soon I really did feel refreshed, more lively, there had probably been some cocaine in the powder. Hermine told me that Pablo had many remedies like that, which he obtained through secret channels and sometimes gave to friends, and that he was a master in mixing and measuring them: remedies for numbing pain, for sleeping, for inspiring beautiful dreams, for making people happy, for making people fall in love.

On one occasion I ran into him on the street, on the quay, and he joined me without further ado. This time, I finally managed to get him to talk.

"Mr. Pablo," I said to him, as he played with a thin, black and silver cane, "you're a friend of Hermine's, that's why I've taken an interest in you. But I must say that you don't make the conversation easy for me. I've tried to talk to you about music several times—I would have been interested in hearing your opinions, your objections, your judgments; but you've acted as if it's beneath you to give me even the slightest answer."

He gave a hearty laugh, and this time he didn't make me wait for the answer, but said nonchalantly: "You see, in my opinion, there's just no point in talking about music. I never talk about music. What should I have said in response to your wise, truthful words? You were so right about everything you said. But you see, I'm a musician, not a scholar, and I don't think that being right matters at all when it comes to music. In music, it doesn't make any difference whether you're right, or whether you have taste and education and all that."

"Well, all right. But what does make a difference then?"

"What makes a difference is making music, Mr. Haller, making music as well and as often and as intensely as possible! That's it, monsieur. If I have all the works of Bach and Haydn in my head and can say the smartest things about them, that doesn't do anyone any good. But if I take my horn and play a lively shimmy, the shimmy may be good or bad, but it will make people happy, it will get into their legs and their blood. That's all that matters. Just look at the faces in a ballroom sometime, at the moment when the music starts again after a long intermission—look how the eyes flash, the legs twitch, the faces start to laugh! That's what making music is all about."

"Very good, Mr. Pablo. But music isn't only for the senses, it's also for the mind and spirit. There isn't only the music of the moment, there's also immortal music that lives on, even when it isn't being played. A person can lie in his bed all alone and conjure up a melody from *The Magic Flute* or from the *St. Matthew Passion* in his mind, and then there's music playing, even if not a single person is blowing into a flute or bowing a violin."

"Certainly, Mr. Haller. And there are also many lonely dreamers who silently repeat 'Yearning' and 'Valencia' to themselves every night; even the poorest typewriter girl in her office has the latest one-step in her head, and she drums her keys to the beat. You're right, all the lonely people, I don't begrudge them all their silent music, be it 'Yearning' or *The Magic Flute* or 'Valencia'! But where do those people get their lonely, silent music? They get it from us, the musicians; first someone has to play it, and they have to hear it, and it has to enter their bloodstream, before they can sit at home in their rooms and think of it, and dream of it."

"Agreed," I said coolly. "Still, it's hardly acceptable to put Mozart and the latest fox-trot on the same level. And it makes a difference whether the music you play for the people is divine, eternal music or just the cheap music of the day."

When Pablo noticed the agitation in my voice, he immediately made his sweetest face, stroked my arm tenderly, and spoke in an incredibly gentle tone.

"Oh, my dear sir, you may be quite right about the levels. I certainly don't mind if you put Mozart and Haydn and 'Valencia' on any level you like! It makes no difference to me, I'm not the one who decides about the levels, nobody asks me. Maybe Mozart will still be played a hundred years from now and 'Valencia' won't survive even two years—I think we can leave that to the good Lord, for he is just and holds all of our life spans in his hands, even the life span of every waltz and fox-trot, surely he will do what is right. But we musicians have to do our part, our duty and our task: we have to play what people want to hear right now, and we have to play it as well and as beautifully and as powerfully as possible."

I gave up with a sigh. There was no arguing with this man.

THERE WERE MOMENTS WHEN old and new, pain and pleasure, fear and delight were strangely intermingled. One instant I was in heaven, the next in hell, usually both at once. At times the old Harry and the new lived in bitter conflict with each other, at times they lived in peace. Sometimes the old Harry seemed to be altogether dead, dead and buried, then suddenly he was standing there again, giving orders and acting the part of the tyrant who always knew better, and the new, small, young Harry was ashamed, he kept quiet and allowed himself to be pushed up against the wall. At other times, the young Harry seized the old one by the throat and gave it a valiant squeeze, unleashing waves of moaning and agony, and many thoughts of the razor.

But often sorrow and happiness crashed over me in a single wave. One such moment occurred a few days after my first attempt at dancing in public, when I entered my bedroom in the evening and—to my utter amazement, surprise, shock, and delight—found the beautiful Maria lying in my bed.

Of all the surprises to which Hermine had subjected me so far, this was the most intense. For I did not doubt for a moment that it was she who had sent me this bird of paradise. That evening I had not been with Hermine for a change, instead I had taken in a fine performance of old church music in the minster—it had been a beautiful and wistful journey into my former life, into the realms of my youth, into the domain of the ideal Harry. In the Gothic loftiness of the church, with its beautiful reticulated vaulting that swayed with a sort of spectral life in the play of the few candles, I had listened to pieces by Buxtehude, Pachelbel, Bach, Haydn, I had walked along those beloved old paths again, had heard the glorious voice of a Bach singer again, a woman with whom I had once been friends and experienced many extraordinary performances. The voices of the old music, their infinite grandeur and majesty had awakened in me all the exaltations, raptures, and enthusiasms of youth; sad and absorbed, I sat in the high chancel of the church, a guest for an hour in this noble, sacred world that I had once called home. During a Haydn duet, tears had suddenly come to my eyes, I had not waited until the end of the concert, I had forgone the opportunity for a reunion with the singer (oh, how many glorious evenings I had once spent with the artists after such concerts!), I had crept out of the minster and walked myself weary through those late-night alleys, where here and there, behind the windows of the restaurants, jazz bands played the melodies of my current life. Oh, what a dreary madness my life had become!

As I walked through the night, I had also spent a long time reflecting on my peculiar relationship to music, and I had once again recognized this relationship, as touching as it is tragic, as the fate of the entire German intelligentsia. The German intellect is subject to matriarchal law, bound to nature by a hegemony of music the likes of which no other people has ever known. We intellectuals—instead of resisting it like men and pledging our allegiance and attention to the intellect, the Logos, the word—all dream of a language without words that says the unspeakable, that depicts the unrepresentable. Instead of playing his own instrument as faithfully and honestly as possible, the German intellectual has always rebelled against the word and against reason, and flirted with music. And in music—in wonderful, blissful tonal compositions, in wonderful, noble feelings and moods that have never been forced into reality—the German intellect has wallowed, while neglecting the majority of its actual tasks. We intellectuals were not at home in reality, we were all alien and hostile to it, which is why the role of the intellect in our German reality, in our history, in our politics, in our public opinion was so pitiful. Well, I had often turned this thought over in my mind, not without occasionally feeling a strong yearning to help shape reality for a change, to take serious, responsible action for a change, instead of just squandering all my time on aesthetics and intellectual arts and crafts. But it always ended in resignation, in a fatalistic capitulation. The generals and captains of heavy industry were quite right: we "intellectuals" never amounted to anything, we were a superfluous, impractical, irresponsible society of witty windbags. The devil take us! Razor!

Thus filled with thoughts and echoes of music, my heart heavy with grief and a desperate longing for life, for reality, for meaning, for something irretrievably lost, I had finally returned home, climbed my stairs, lit the lamp in the living room, and tried in vain to read a little, thought of the promise I'd made to go to the Cécil Bar tomorrow evening for whiskey and dancing, and felt resentment and bitterness not only toward myself, but also toward Hermine. She might have had the best and kindest of intentions, she might be a wonderful creature—but she should have just let me go to seed from the start instead of dragging me in, deep down into this weird, twisted, shimmering fantasy world, where I would always remain a stranger, and where the very best part of me was wasting away and suffering!

And so I had sadly turned out the light, sadly made my way to my bedroom, sadly begun to undress, when I was startled by an unfamiliar scent, it smelled faintly of perfume, and looking around, I saw the beautiful Maria lying in my bed, smiling, a bit anxious, with big blue eyes.

"Maria!" I said. And my first thought was that my landlady would give me notice if she knew.

"I came," she said quietly. "Are you angry with me?"

"No, no. I know Hermine gave you the key. Very well."

"Oh, you're angry about it. I'll just be going."

"No, my beautiful Maria, stay! It's just that I'm very sad this particular evening; I can't be any fun today, but maybe I can again tomorrow."

I had bent down slightly toward her, when suddenly she grabbed my head with her two large, strong hands, pulled it down to hers, and kissed me for a long time. Then I sat down on the bed beside her, held her hand, asked her to speak quietly so that no one would hear us, and looked down into her full, beautiful face, which was lying there on my pillow, strange and wonderful like a giant flower. She slowly pulled my hand to her mouth, pulled it under the covers, and laid it on her warm chest, which was silently rising and falling.

"You don't have to be fun," she said. "Hermine already told me you were troubled. Anyone can understand that. Do you still like me, then? The other night, when we were dancing, you were very much in love."

I kissed her on the eyes, mouth, neck, and breasts. Just a moment ago I had been thinking of Hermine with bitterness and reproach. Now I was holding her gift in my hands, and I was grateful. Maria's caresses in no way detracted from the wonderful music I had heard today, they were worthy of it, they fulfilled it. I slowly pulled the covers off the beautiful woman, until I had kissed her all the way down to her feet. When I lay down with her, her flower of a face smiled at me knowingly and kindly.

I didn't sleep very much that night by Maria's side, but I slept deeply and soundly, like a child. And between my periods of sleep, I drank in her beautiful, carefree youth, and from our hushed pillow talk I learned many things worth knowing about her and

Hermine's lives. I had known very little about that sort of life and existence before; only in the theater had I occasionally encountered similar creatures, women as well as men, half artist, half demimonde. Now I could gain some insight into these strange, peculiarly innocent, peculiarly depraved lives. These girls, most of whom came from poor families, were too clever and too pretty to devote their entire lives to some poorly paid and joyless line of work, instead they all lived off odd jobs at some times, and off their own grace and charm at others. Such girls might sometimes sit behind a typewriter for a few months, or spend a while as the mistress of a wealthy man, they received pocket money and gifts, at times they lived in furs, cars, and grand hotels, at other times in garrets, and, although they might be persuaded to marry if the offer was generous enough, on the whole that was not their ambition at all. Some of them were devoid of desire when it came to love, bestowing their favors only reluctantly and always bargaining for the highest price. Others, including Maria, were unusually gifted in love and hungry for love, and most of these girls were also experienced in love with both sexes; they lived solely for the sake of love and always had other relationships that blossomed on the side, in addition to their official, paying companions. Hardworking and industrious, anxious and careless, clever yet lacking in sense, these butterflies lived their lives, as childlike as they were refined—they were independent, not just anyone could buy them, they expected to get the good fortune and good weather they had coming to them, they were in love with life and yet much less attached to it than the average member of the bourgeoisie—always ready to follow a fairy-tale prince to his castle, always half consciously anticipating a sad and difficult end.

Maria taught me many things on that first, incredible night, and in the days that followed—not only delightful new games and pleasures of the senses, but also new understanding, new insights, new

love. For me, as a hermit and an aesthete, the world of dance halls
and nightclubs, of cinemas, bars, and hotel tea halls still had something inferior, forbidden, and degrading about it; but for Maria, for
Hermine and her acquaintances, it was quite simply the world as
such, it was neither good nor evil, neither desirable nor despicable;
it was the world in which their short, passionate lives blossomed; it
was the world in which they were at home and experienced. They
loved a glass of champagne or a special plate in the Grill Room just
the way that one of us might love a composer or a poet, and they
lavished the same enthusiasm, passion, and emotion on a new dance
hit or on a jazz singer's sentimental, schmaltzy song that one of us
might lavish on Nietzsche or Hamsun. Maria told me about that
handsome saxophone player Pablo and an American song that he
had sometimes sung to them, and she sang its praises with a rapture,
admiration, and love that touched and gripped me far more than
some highly educated person's ecstasies about the carefully curated
pleasures of fine art. I was prepared to share her enthusiasm, whatever the song might be; Maria's adoring words and the desire that
bloomed in her eyes had opened up wide cracks in my aesthetics.
To be sure, there were some things of beauty, a few select things of
exquisite beauty, that seemed to me beyond all dispute and doubt—
Mozart, above all—but where to draw the line? Hadn't we connoisseurs and critics all ardently loved works of art and artists in our
youth that we found dubious and foolish today? Hadn't we been
through this with Liszt, with Wagner, in many cases even with Beethoven? Wasn't Maria's blossoming, childlike infatuation with this
American song an experience of art every bit as pure, beautiful, and
devoid of doubt as some schoolmaster's passion for *Tristan* or some
conductor's ecstasy about the Ninth Symphony? And didn't that
accord strangely well with Mr. Pablo's views, and prove him right?

That handsome Pablo—it seemed Maria also loved him very
much!

"He's a handsome man," I said, "I quite like him, too. But tell me, Maria, how can you love him and also love me, a boring old fellow who isn't handsome, who's even starting to get gray hair, and who can't blow a saxophone or sing love songs in English?"

"Don't say such ugly things!" she scolded. "It's only natural. I like you, too, there's something handsome and sweet and special about you, too, and you can't be any different than you are. It's better not to talk about stuff like that or ask for reasons. Look, when you kiss my neck or my ear, I can feel how much you like me, how much pleasure I give you; there's a certain way you have of kissing, there's something a little bit shy about it, and what that tells me is: he likes you, he's grateful that you're so pretty. And I like that very, very much. But then when I'm with some other man, what I like is just the opposite, I like it if he doesn't seem to care about me, and when he kisses me it's like he's doing me a favor."

We fell asleep again. I woke up again with my arms still wrapped around her, my beautiful, beautiful flower.

And yet—incredibly!—the beautiful flower was still the gift that Hermine had given me! She was still standing behind it, concealed by it as if by a mask. And suddenly I thought of Erika, my distant, bitter lover, my poor girlfriend. She was hardly less pretty than Maria, though she was not in such full bloom, not so liberated, and she was less gifted in the little, ingenious arts of love; for a time Erika's image rose up before me, clear and painful, beloved and deeply entwined with my fate, and then it sank down again into sleep, into oblivion, into a distance that half filled me with mourning.

And many more images of my life appeared before me in the course of that beautiful, tender night, after all the years that I had spent living a life that was empty, poor, and devoid of images. Now that eros had magically unleashed it, the flood of images poured out, deep and rich, and for moments at a time my heart stood still with delight and sorrow, as I saw how rich my life's picture gallery had been, how full of high, eternal stars and constellations the poor Steppenwolf's soul had been. My childhood and my mother gazed across at me, tender and transfigured, like part of a mountain range off in the infinite blue distance, the chorus of my friendships sounded out brazen and clear, beginning with the legendary Hermann, Hermine's soul brother; fragrant and unearthly, like sea flowers raising their damp blossoms from the water, the images of many women I had loved swam to the surface, women I had desired and extolled, only a few of whom I had won and sought to claim for my own. My wife appeared, too, the woman I had lived with for many years, who had taught me about companionship, conflict, resignation, the woman I had trusted deeply, in spite of all the hardships of life, with a trust that remained alive in me until the day when, having grown mad and ill, she suddenly abandoned me, taking flight in a wild outburst of revolt—and I realized how much I loved her, and how deeply I must have trusted her, if her betrayal of my trust could deal me such a heavy, life-altering blow.

These images—there were hundreds of them, named and nameless—were all there again, fresh and new, rising from the spring of this night of love, and I knew again what I had long forgotten in my misery, that the true richness and value of my life was contained in these things, which had endured indestructibly, these experiences that had been transformed into stars, which I could perhaps forget, but could never destroy, these things which, in their succession, recounted the saga of my life, which in their starry glow contained the indestructible value of my existence. My life had been arduous, erratic, and unhappy, it had led to renunciation and denial, it had tasted of the bitter salt that is the fate of all humanity, but it had been rich, proud and rich, even in its misery it had been a royal life. And even if the final, short stretch along the road to ruin should be miserably squandered, at its core it had been a noble life, it had a fine countenance and lineage, it had been devoted not to pennies, but to the stars.

Some time has passed, and many things have happened and changed since then, I can remember only a few details from that night, particular words that passed between us, particular gestures and acts of deep, loving tenderness, starry moments of awakening from the heavy sleep of lovers' lassitude. But that was the night when, for the first time since my decline, my own life gazed at me with its radiant, unblinking eyes, when I once again recognized contingency as fate, once again recognized in the wreckage of my existence a fragment of the divine. My soul could breathe again, my eyes could see again, and there were moments when I fervently felt that if I could only gather together this scattered world of images, if I could only raise my own life, the life of the Steppenwolf Harry Haller, to the status of an image, then I myself would be able to enter the world of images and be immortal. And wasn't that the goal that every human life set out to attain?

The next morning, after she had shared my breakfast, I had to smuggle Maria out of the house, which I managed to accomplish. That same day, I rented a small room for the two of us in a nearby part of town, for the exclusive purpose of our rendezvous.

Then my dance teacher Hermine diligently arrived, and I had to learn the Boston. She was strict and unrelenting, and she did not spare me a single lesson, because it had been resolved that I would attend the next masquerade ball with her. She had asked me for money for her costume, but refused to tell me anything about it. I was still forbidden to visit her, or even to know where she lived.

That period before the masquerade ball, roughly three weeks, was extraordinarily lovely. It seemed to me that Maria was the first real lover I'd ever had. I had always demanded that the women I loved be intellectual and educated, without ever quite realizing that even the most intellectual and relatively educated woman

never truly responded to the Logos within me, but always stood
in opposition to it; when I came to these women, I brought my
thoughts and problems along with me, and I would have found it
completely impossible to love a girl for more than an hour if she
had barely ever read a book, if she barely knew what reading was,
if she couldn't tell the difference between Tchaikovsky and Beethoven. Maria wasn't educated, she didn't need those circuitous
routes and alternative worlds, all of her problems sprang directly
from her senses. She made an art and purpose of using the senses
and the gifts she had been given—her particular figure, her col-
oring, her hair, her voice, her skin, her temperament—in order to
achieve as much sensual and amorous pleasure as possible; to seek
and summon forth from her lover an answer, an appreciation, and
a vigorous, exhilarating response to each and every one of her gifts,
to every tender curve and contour of her body. I had already sensed
that when I made my first shy attempt to dance with her, I had
smelled the scent of that brilliant, delightfully cultivated sensuality, and she had enchanted me. Certainly it was also no coincidence that Hermine, the all-knowing, had brought me this Maria.
Her scent, her whole nature, was summery, rosy.

I did not have the good fortune of being Maria's only lover, or
her favorite; I was one of several. She often had no time at all for
me, sometimes an hour in the afternoon, rarely a whole night.
She would not take any money from me, that was probably Hermine's doing. But she was happy to accept gifts, and if I gave her
a new little red patent-leather wallet, there might also be two or
three gold coins inside it. By the way, she had a good laugh at my
expense when I gave her that little red coin purse! It was lovely,
but it was a slow seller, long out of fashion. Those were things I'd
never known about or understood before, they were as foreign to
me as any Eskimo language, but I learned a great deal about them
from Maria. Above all, I learned that these little toys, these fashion

and luxury items are not mere trinkets and kitsch, or the invention of money-hungry manufacturers and merchants; rather, they
are fully justified, beautiful, and richly varied, they are a small, or
rather a large world of things that all exist for the sole purpose of
serving love, refining the senses, enlivening a dead world and magically endowing it with new organs of love, from powder and perfume to dancing shoes, from finger rings to cigarette boxes, from
belt buckles to handbags. This purse was not a purse, this wallet
was not a wallet, flowers were not flowers, this fan was not a fan,
everything was love, magic, excitation in tangible form, it was a
messenger, a smuggler, a weapon, a battle cry.

I often wondered who the real object of Maria's love might be.
Most of all, I think, she loved young Pablo with his saxophone,
with his lost, black eyes and his long, pale, delicate, melancholy
hands. I would have imagined this Pablo to be a somewhat sleepy,
spoiled, and passive lover, but Maria assured me that although he
was slow to catch fire, once he did he was firmer, harder, more masculine, and more demanding than any boxer or horseman. And so
I came to hear and know secrets about this and that person, about
the jazz musician, about the actor, about certain women, about the
girls and men of our milieu, I knew all kinds of secrets, saw connections and enmities beneath the surface, and over time I (who
had been a completely impartial outsider) became intimate with
this world, it pulled me in. I also learned a lot about Hermine. But
I saw Mr. Pablo especially frequently now, the man Maria loved
so much. She, too, needed some of his secret remedies now and
then, she even procured these pleasures for me from time to time,
and Pablo was always especially happy to serve me. Once he said
to me in no uncertain terms: "You are so much unhappy, this is
not good, one should not be like that. I'm sorry. Take little opium
pipe." My opinion of this cheerful, clever, childlike, yet inscrutable
man changed constantly, we became friends, and not infrequently

I accepted some of his remedies. He observed my infatuation with Maria with a certain bemusement. Once he threw a "party" in his room, the garret of a hotel in an outlying neighborhood. There was only one chair in the room, Maria and I had to sit on the bed. He gave us something to drink, a wonderful, mysterious liqueur that he had concocted from three bottles. And then, when I had gotten into a very good mood, he proposed to us, eyes sparkling, a ménage à trois. I brusquely refused, such a thing was not possible for me, but nevertheless I did glance over at Maria for a moment to see what she thought of it, and although she immediately concurred in my refusal, I saw the glimmer in her eyes and sensed that she regretted the missed opportunity. Pablo was disappointed that I declined, but he wasn't hurt. "Too bad," he said, "Harry thinks too much morally. Nothing to do. Would have been so nice, so very nice! But I know alternative." He let each of us smoke a few puffs of opium, and as we sat there motionless, our eyes open, all three of us experienced the scene he had suggested, and Maria trembled with delight. When I felt a bit unwell afterward, Pablo laid me on the bed, gave me a few drops of medicine, and when I closed my eyes for a few minutes, I felt a very fleeting whisper of a kiss on each eyelid. I accepted it as if I thought it was from Maria. But I knew very well that it was from him.

And one evening he surprised me even more. He showed up at my apartment, told me that he needed twenty francs, and asked me for the money. In exchange, he offered, Maria would be mine tonight, not his.

"Pablo," I said in shock, "you don't know what you're saying. Handing over your mistress to another man in exchange for money is the most shameful thing a man can do here. I didn't hear your proposal, Pablo."

He looked at me with pity. "You don't want to, Mr. Harry. Fine. You're always making things difficult for yourself. So you don't sleep with Maria tonight, if that's what you prefer, and you give me the money anyway, you will get it back. I need it desperately."

"What for?"

"For Agostino—you know, the kid who plays second violin. He's been sick for eight days now, and nobody's taking care of him. He doesn't have a penny, and right now I don't, either."

Out of curiosity, and partly also to punish myself, I went with him to see Agostino; Pablo brought him milk and medicine in his garret—a quite miserable garret—then shook out the bedding to freshen it up, aired out the room, and put a nice, proper compress around Agostino's feverish head, all of which he did quickly and delicately and expertly, like a good nurse. That same evening, I saw him playing music in the City Bar until the wee hours of the morning.

I often had long, detailed conversations with Hermine about Maria, about her hands, her shoulders, her hips, the way she laughed, kissed, danced.

"Has she shown you this one yet?" Hermine asked me once, and went on to describe a particular game that Maria played with her tongue when she kissed. I asked Hermine to show me herself, but she sternly rebuffed me. "That will come later," she said, "I'm not your lover yet."

I asked her how she knew about Maria's kissing skills and certain secret details of Maria's body that only a man who loved her would know.

"Oh," she cried, "we're friends, you know. Do you think we keep secrets from each other? I've slept with her and played with her often enough. Well, you've got yourself a fine girl there, she can do more than most."

"Hermine, I think that there are still some secrets, even between you and her. Or have you told her everything you know about me, too?"

"No, those are different kinds of things, she wouldn't understand. Maria's wonderful, you're lucky, but there are some things
between you and me that she doesn't have a clue about. I told her a
lot about you, of course, much more than you would have wanted
at the time—I had to seduce her for you, after all! But Maria will
never understand you as I understand you, friend, and neither will
anyone else. I've learned a few more things from her, too—I know
as much as Maria knows about you. I know you almost as well as if
we'd slept together many times."

The next time I was with Maria, it felt strange and mysterious
to know that she had had Hermine as close to her heart as she had
me, that she had felt, kissed, tasted, and tested Hermine's limbs,
hair, and skin just as she had mine. New relationships and connections appeared before me now, indirect and complicated ones, new
possibilities for love and life, and I thought of the thousand souls
of the Steppenwolf treatise.

IN THAT SHORT TIME between my first acquaintance with
Maria and the great masquerade ball, I was positively happy, and
yet I never had the feeling that I had been redeemed, that I had
finally attained a state of bliss; instead, I felt very clearly that all
of this was only a prelude, a preparation, that everything was
surging vigorously forward, that the important thing was yet
to come.

I had learned so many dances by now that I could actually imagine taking part in the ball, which was the subject of more and more
conversation each day. Hermine had a secret, she was determined
not to tell me what sort of costume she would be wearing. She said
that I would recognize her, and if I failed to, she would help me,
but I was not to know anything beforehand. She also showed no
curiosity about my masquerade plans, and I decided not to dress

up at all. When I tried to invite Maria to the ball, she explained to me that she already had a squire for this party, and she even had a ticket already, so I was somewhat disappointed to see that I would have to attend the party alone. It was the city's most distinguished costume ball, which took place annually in the Globe Ballrooms, sponsored by the Society of Artists.

I rarely saw Hermine during that time, but the day before the ball she spent a while at my apartment—she'd come to pick up her ticket, which I had bought—and she was just casually sitting in my room when the conversation took a turn that struck me as strange and made a profound impression on me.

"You're actually doing quite well now," she said, "the dancing agrees with you. If someone hadn't seen you in four weeks, they'd hardly recognize you."

"Yes," I admitted, "I haven't been this well in years. It's all thanks to you, Hermine."

"Oh, it isn't that beautiful Maria of yours?"

"No. And anyway, she was a gift from you, too. She's wonderful."

"She's just the lover you needed, Steppenwolf. Pretty, young, good-humored, very gifted in love, and not available every day. If you didn't have to share her with the others, if she didn't always keep her visits so brief, things wouldn't be so good for you."

Yes, I had to admit that, too.

"So, you actually have everything you need now, right?"

"No, Hermine, it isn't like that. I have something very beautiful and delightful, a great joy, a precious comfort. I'm positively happy . . ."

"That's it! What more could you want?"

"I want more. I'm not satisfied with happiness, I'm not made for it, that's not my destiny. My destiny is just the opposite."

"You mean to be unhappy? Well, you had plenty of that back when you couldn't go home on account of the straight razor."

"No, Hermine, it's different though. I was very unhappy back then, I admit. But that unhappiness was stupid, it was fruitless."

"Why's that?"

"Because it came with something that I didn't need—it made me fear death, even though I wished for it at the same time! The unhappiness that I need and long for is different; it makes me suffer with delight and die with passion. That's the unhappiness or happiness that I'm waiting for."

"I understand you. We're brother and sister in that way. But what do you have against the happiness you've found now with Maria? Why aren't you satisfied?"

"I don't have anything against this happiness, oh no, I love it, I'm grateful for it. It's beautiful, like a sunny day in the middle of a rainy summer. But I feel that there's no way it can last. This happiness is fruitless, too. It brings contentment, but contentment is not the food for me. It puts the Steppenwolf to sleep, it satiates him. But it's not a happiness worth dying for."

"So death must come then, Steppenwolf?"

"I think so, yes! I'm very content with my happiness, I can bear it for quite a while. But every now and then, when this happiness gives me an hour to wake up and start longing again, the goal of all my longing is not to hold on to this happiness forever, but to suffer again, only more beautifully and less wretchedly than before. I long for a kind of suffering that makes me ready and willing to die."

Hermine looked me tenderly in the eyes, with that dark gaze that could come over her so suddenly. Those wonderful, terrible eyes! Slowly, searching for the words one by one and stringing them together, she said—so softly that I had to strain to hear it:

"I want to tell you something today, something I have known for a long time, and you know it too, but perhaps you haven't told yourself yet. Now I'm going to tell you what I know about me and you and about our destiny. Harry, you were an artist and thinker, a person filled with joy and conviction, always following the path of the great and the eternal, never satisfied with things that were only nice and small. But the more this life has awakened you and brought you around to yourself, the greater your distress has become, and the more deeply you have plunged into suffering, anguish, and despair, up to your neck—and everything that you once knew and loved and revered as beautiful and holy, all the faith you once had in people and in our lofty purpose, couldn't help you, it all turned out to be worthless and just fell to pieces. Your faith couldn't find any more air to breathe. And suffocation is a cruel death. Isn't that right, Harry? Is that your destiny?"

I nodded, nodded, nodded.

"You had an image of life within you, a faith, a demand, you were prepared to perform great deeds, to endure great suffering and sacrifice—but then you gradually realized that the world didn't demand any deeds or sacrifices or anything else of you, that life wasn't an epic poem, with roles for heroes and all that, it was a nice bourgeois parlor where people were perfectly content with food and drink, with coffee and knitting, tarot games and radio music. And anyone who wants it otherwise, who has that in him— the heroic and the beautiful, the veneration of the great poets or the veneration of the saints—is a fool and a Don Quixote. Fine. And it was the same for me, my friend! I was a girl with many gifts, destined to live up to high ideals, to place great demands on myself, to perform virtuous tasks. I could take on a great calling, be the wife of a king, the mistress of a revolutionary, the sister of a genius, the mother of a martyr. Yet life has only allowed me to become a courtesan with reasonably good taste—and even that was hard enough for me! That's how it went for me. For a while I was inconsolable, and for a long time I tried to blame myself. After all, I thought, life must always be right, and if life had mocked my beautiful dreams, I thought, then my dreams must have simply

been stupid and wrong. But that didn't help at all. And because
I had good eyes and ears and I was also a little bit curious, I took
a close look at so-called life, at my acquaintances and neighbors,
at fifty or more people and their destinies, and Harry, what I saw
there was: my dreams had been right, a thousand times right, just
like yours. But life, reality, was wrong. The fact that a woman like
me had no choice but to grow old, pennilessly and pointlessly,
while sitting at a typewriter in the service of some moneymaker,
or to marry one of those moneymakers just on account of his
money, or to become a kind of prostitute, that was just as wrong
as it would be for a shy, lonely, desperate person like you to reach
for the razor. Maybe my misery was more material and moral, and
yours was more intellectual—but the path was the same. Do you
think I can't understand your fear of the fox-trot, your aversion
to the bars and dance halls, your distaste for jazz music and all
that stuff? I understand it all too well, just like I understand your
loathing of politics, your despair about all the useless talk and irresponsible behavior of the parties, the press, your anguish about the
war, about the past war and the coming wars, about the way people
think, read, build, make music, throw parties, and educate themselves today! You're right, Steppenwolf, a thousand times right,
and yet you must perish. You're much too demanding and hungry
for the simple, comfortable world of today, which is satisfied with
so little; it spits you out, you have one more dimension than it can
handle. Anyone who wants to live and enjoy his life today can't be
a person like you and me. Someone who demands music instead of
tootling, joy instead of pleasure, soul instead of money, real work
instead of busyness, authentic passion instead of playfulness, can
never be at home in this pretty little world here . . ."

She looked pensively down at the floor.

"Hermine," I cried tenderly, "sister, what good eyes you have!
And yet you taught me the fox-trot! But what do you mean when

you say that people like us, people with one dimension too many, can't live here? Why is that? Is it only true in our time? Or has it always been that way?"

"I don't know. Out of respect for the world, I'd like to suppose that it's just our time, it's just a sickness, a temporary misfortune. The leaders are working hard, and successfully, to prepare the next war, meanwhile the rest of us are dancing the fox-trot, earning money, and eating pralinés—in times like these, the world looks pretty lousy. Let's hope that other times were better and will be better again, richer, broader, deeper. But that doesn't help us. And maybe it's always been like this . . ."

"It's always been like today? Always just a world for politicians, racketeers, waiters, and playboys, without a single breath of air for real people?"

"Well, I don't know, nobody knows. It doesn't matter, either. But now, my friend, I'm thinking about your favorite, the person you've sometimes told me about, whose letters you've read to me— Mozart. What was it like for him? Who ruled the world in his day, who skimmed off the cream, who set the tone, who counted for something: Mozart or the profiteers, Mozart or the shallow, dime-a-dozen people? And how did he die, how was he buried? And I think that maybe it's always been that way and always will be, and what they call 'world history' in school, what you have to learn by heart for your education, with all the heroes, geniuses, great deeds and feelings—that's just a sham thought up by the schoolteachers for educational purposes and to keep the children busy with some-thing during the years they have to be there. It's always been that way and always will be: Time and the world, money and power belong to the small and shallow people, while the others, the real people, have nothing. Nothing but death."

"Nothing else at all?"

"Oh yes, eternity."

"You mean an immortal name, fame in the eyes of posterity?"

"No, Wolfie, not fame—is that worth anything? And do you think that every truly authentic, complete person has become famous and well known to posterity?"

"No, of course not."

"So, it isn't fame. Fame really only exists for the sake of education, it's something that schoolteachers care about. It isn't fame, oh no! But what I call eternity. Pious people call it the Kingdom of God. I always tell myself: We people—the more demanding ones, with our longings, with our one dimension too many—none of us would be able to live at all if there weren't some other air to breathe beyond the air of this world, if there weren't something beyond time—eternity, and that is the realm of the authentic. It includes the music of Mozart and the poems of your great poets, it includes the saints who performed miracles, who died martyrs' deaths and set a great example for mankind. But eternity also includes the image of every authentic deed, the power of every authentic feeling, even if no one knows about it and sees it and writes it down and preserves it for posterity. In eternity there is no posterity, we are all contemporaries."

"You're right," I said.

"Pious people," she continued reflectively, "have understood it best. That's why they came up with the saints and what they call 'the communion of saints.' The saints are the authentic people, the younger brothers of the Savior. We follow in their footsteps throughout our lives, with every good deed, with every brave thought, with every love. The communion of saints was depicted by the painters of ages past in a golden heaven, radiant, beautiful, and peaceful—and that's just what I called 'eternity' before. It's the realm beyond all time and appearances. That's where we belong, that's our home, the place our heart strives for, Steppenwolf, and that's why we long for death. That's where you'll find your Goethe again, and your Novalis and Mozart, and I'll find my saints, Christopher, Philip Neri, and all the rest. There are many saints who were terrible sinners at first, sin can also be a path to holiness—sin and vice. You'll laugh, but I often think to myself that my friend Pablo might also be a saint in disguise. Oh, Harry, we have to grope through so much filth and nonsense to get home! And we have no one to guide us, our only guide is homesickness."

Her voice had grown very soft again as she spoke these final words, and now the room was peaceful and quiet, the gold lettering on the spines of the many books in my library shimmered in the light of the setting sun. I took Hermine's head in my hands, kissed her on the forehead, and tilted her head so that her cheek was resting against mine, like brother and sister, and for a moment we remained in that position. I would have preferred to stay like that and not to leave the house again that day. But Maria had promised herself to me for the night, the last night before the big ball.

As I was on my way to see her, though, I was thinking not of Maria, but only of what Hermine had said. It seemed to me that perhaps these were not her own thoughts, but rather mine, which the clairvoyant had read and inhaled and was now returning to me, so that they took shape and stood there fresh before me. I was particularly grateful to her in that hour for expressing the thought of eternity. I needed that, I could not live or even die without it. The holy hereafter, the world without time, the world of eternal value, of divine substance, had been restored to me today by my friend and dance instructor. I had to think of my dream of Goethe, of the image of the old sage who had laughed in such an inhuman way and had his immortal fun with me. Only now did I understand Goethe's laughter, the laughter of the immortals. It had no object, this laughter, it was pure light, pure brightness, it was what remains when an authentic man has made his way through the sufferings, vices, errors, passions, and misunderstandings of men and has broken out into the eternal, into outer space. And this "eternity" was none other than the redemption of time—it was, so to speak, time's return to innocence, its transformation back into space.

I looked for Maria at the spot where we usually dined on our evenings together, but she hadn't arrived yet. I sat at the set table in the quiet little neighborhood tavern and waited, still thinking about our conversation. All those thoughts that had surfaced between Hermine and me seemed so deeply familiar, so intimate, so rooted in my own mythology and my own world of images! The immortals, the way that they inhabit their timeless space, transported, transformed into an image, encased in crystalline eternity as if in ether, and the cool, star-sparkling serenity of that extraterrestrial world—where had I encountered it all before? I brooded on it, and pieces from Mozart's *Cassations* and Bach's *Well-Tempered Clavier* came to mind, everywhere in that music the same cool, starry brilliance seemed to shine, the same ethereal clarity seemed to resonate. Yes, that was it, this music was something like time that had been frozen into space, and a superhuman serenity, an eternal, divine laughter, reverberated infinitely above it. Oh, and the old Goethe from my dream fit in so well! And suddenly I heard that unfathomable laughter around me, heard the immortals laughing. Enchanted, I sat there, enchanted, I fumbled for my pencil in my waistcoat pocket, searched for paper, found the wine list lying in front of me, turned it over, and wrote on the back, wrote lines of verse that I would find in my pocket the following day. They read:

The Immortals

From the deepest valleys of the earth
The steam of life drifts up to us again,

Wildest desperation, drunken mirth,
Bloody meals for scaffold-fated men,
Lustful spasms, cravings without end,
Murderers, usurers, worshippers lift their hands,
Whipped on by lust and fear, this human swarm,
Reeking dank and putrid, raw and warm,
Breathes in its bliss, breathes out a beastly shout,
Consumes itself and spits itself back out,
Gives birth to noble arts, gives birth to wars,
Adorns the burning whorehouse with its blights,
Along its way it gorges, feasts, and whores
Through this child's world of carnival delights,
Rises above the waves for each anew,
And one day falls to shit for each one, too.

We, though, have found a place we call our own
Amidst the starry ice of ether's cold,
The days, the hours remain to us unknown,
We are not man nor woman, young nor old.
Whatever sins you have, whatever fears,
Whatever murders and whatever joys
Appear to us like circling suns, like toys,
Each day to us is like a million years.
Softly nodding at your twitching lives,
Softly gazing at the star-swirled skies,
We take deep breaths, breathe in this cosmic winter,
The great celestial dragon is our friend,
Our being, cool and changeless, is forever,
Our laughter, cool and star-bright, knows no end.

Then Maria came, and after a fine meal we went together to
our little room. That evening she was more beautiful, warmer,

and more intimate than ever, and she treated me to affections and games that felt to me like the utmost in devotion.

"Maria," I said, "you're as indulgent as a goddess today. Make sure you don't kill us both—after all, tomorrow's the masquerade ball. Who's going to be your squire tomorrow? I fear, my dear little flower, that he'll be a fairy-tale prince, and he'll carry you off and you'll never find your way back to me. You're making love to me tonight almost the way good lovers do when they say goodbye, for the last time!"

She pressed her lips very close to my ear and whispered:

"Don't speak, Harry! Any time may be the last time. If Hermine takes you, you won't come back to me again. She may take you tomorrow."

Never did I experience the distinctive feeling of those days, that incredible, bittersweet, mixed emotion, more intensely than on the night before the ball. It was happiness that I felt: Maria's beauty and devotion, the opportunity to savor, touch, inhale a hundred fine, delicate sensual pleasures that I had only come to know so late in life, as I was already growing old, to splash in a gentle, rolling wave of pleasure. And yet that was only the shell: inside, everything was full of meaning, tension, fate, and while I was lovingly, tenderly occupied with the sweet, touching trifles of love, as I seemed to be swimming in such balmy happiness, I felt in my heart how my fate was rushing headlong forward, racing and bucking like a skittish horse, toward the abyss, toward the plunge, full of fear, full of longing, full of surrender to death. Just as until recently I had skittishly, fearfully resisted the pleasant frivolity of merely sensual love, just as I had trembled at Maria's laughing beauty, at her readiness to give herself to others, so now I felt a fear of death—but that fear itself already knew that it would soon give way to surrender and redemption.

While we were silently absorbed in our frantic games of love, more intimate with each other than ever before, my soul bid farewell to Maria, farewell to all that she had meant to me. Thanks to her, I had learned to be a child one last time before the end, to abandon myself to the play of surfaces, to seek out the most fleeting pleasures, to be a child and an animal in the innocence of sex—a state that had been only a rare exception in my earlier life, since sensual life and sex had almost always had a bitter aftertaste of guilt for me, the sweet but uneasy taste of the forbidden fruit, against which an intellectual man must be on his guard. Now Hermine and Maria had shown me this garden in its innocence, I had been a grateful guest there—but soon it would be time for me to move on, it was too pretty and warm in this garden. I was destined to continue vying for the crown of life, to continue atoning for the endless guilt of life. An easy life, an easy love, an easy death—that was not for me.

Based on some hints that the girls had dropped, I surmised that very special pleasures and debauchery were planned for the ball tomorrow, or afterward. Perhaps this was the end, perhaps Maria's hunch was right, and today would be the last time that we lay together, perhaps tomorrow the new chapter of our destiny would begin? I was full of burning desire, full of suffocating fear, and I clung desperately to Maria, ran down all the paths and thickets of her garden once more, quivering and ravening, and once more I sank my teeth deeply into the sweet fruit of the tree of paradise.

THE FOLLOWING DAY, I caught up on the sleep I had missed that night. I went to the public baths in the morning, went home, dead tired, closed my bedroom curtains, found my poem in my pocket while undressing, forgot it again, lay down at once, forgot about Maria, Hermine, and the masquerade ball, and slept through the whole day. When I got up that evening, it was only while I was shaving that I remembered that the masquerade ball was about to begin in just an hour and I still had to pick out a dress shirt. In a good mood, I got ready and went out to eat first.

It would be the first masquerade ball that I had actually taken part in. I had attended such parties from time to time in the past, and had sometimes found them quite nice, but I had never danced, I had only been a spectator, and the enthusiasm with which I had heard others talk about them and look forward to them had always seemed odd to me. But today's ball was an event that I, too, looked forward to with excitement, and not without trepidation. Since I had no lady to take to the ball, I decided to go late, which Hermine had also recommended to me.

The Steel Helmet Tavern, my former haunt, where disappointed men wasted their evenings, drank their wine, and played at being bachelors, was a place I had seldom visited of late; it no longer fit with the style of my current life. But tonight I was drawn to it again, entirely of my own accord; in that anxious-joyous mood that had taken hold of me at the moment, a mood suffused with fatefulness and farewell, all the stations and landmarks of my life once again acquired that painfully beautiful glow of things past— even the small, smoke-filled drinking house where until recently I had been one of the regulars, where until recently the primitive anesthetic of a bottle of table wine had been all I needed in order to go back to my lonely bed for another night, to endure life for another day. Since then, I had sampled other remedies, more pow- erful stimulants, sipped sweeter poisons. Smiling, I entered the old dive, where the tavernkeeper greeted me and the silent regulars welcomed me with a nod. A roasted chicken was recommended and then served to me, a bright young Alsatian wine flowed into my thick, rustic glass, the clean, white wooden tables and the old, yellow, wood-paneled walls regarded me kindly. And while I was eating and drinking, a feeling was growing within me, the feeling that I was wilting away, preparing to bid farewell, the sweet and painfully intimate feeling that I had formed a bond with all the places and things of my former life, a bond that had never been completely dissolved, but was now growing ripe for dissolution. The "modern" man calls this sentimentality; he no longer loves things, not even his most sacred possession, his automobile, which he hopes to be able to exchange for a better make as soon as possible. This modern man is dashing, capable, healthy, cool, and firm, an excellent fellow; he will acquit himself fabulously in the next war. That didn't matter to me, I wasn't a modern man, nor even an old-fashioned one, I had fallen out of time and was drifting along, close to death, with a will to die. I had nothing against sentimentalities, I was glad and grateful just to sense something like feelings in my burned-out heart. So I surrendered to the memories of the old tavern, to my attachment to the clunky old chairs, surrendered to the smell of smoke and wine, to the glow of familiarity, of warmth, of homeliness that all of it held for me. It is pleasant to bid farewell, it puts one in a tender mood. My hard seat was dear to me, my rustic glass, the cool, fruity taste of the Alsatian wine was dear to me, everything and everyone in this room I knew so well was dear to me, the faces of the drowsing drinkers, the disappointed men whose brother I had been for so long. These were bourgeois sentimentalities that I was feeling, lightly seasoned with a hint of the old-fashioned romantic tavern fantasies I had entertained in my boyhood, when taverns, wine, and cigars were still forbidden, unfamiliar, glorious things. But no Steppenwolf rose to bare his teeth and tear my sentiments to shreds. I sat there peacefully, in the glow of the past, the weak glow of a star that had already set.

A street vendor came in with roasted chestnuts, and I bought a handful from him. An old woman came in with flowers, I bought a few carnations from her and gave them to the tavernkeeper. Only when I wanted to pay, and reached in vain for the usual coat pocket, did I realize again that I was wearing a tailcoat. The masquerade ball! Hermine!

But it was still plenty early, I couldn't make up my mind to go to the Globe Ballrooms just yet. I also felt some of the same resistance and inhibition that I had with respect to all those pleasures recently: a reluctance to enter large, crowded, noisy spaces, a schoolboy's shyness toward that alien atmosphere, toward that playboy world, toward dancing.

As I was strolling along, I passed a movie theater, saw beams of light and giant colored posters gleaming, took a few more steps, then turned around and went inside. I could sit there quietly in the dark until about eleven o'clock. Led by a boy with a shuttered lantern, I stumbled through the curtains into the darkened theater, made my way to a seat, and suddenly found myself in the middle of the Old Testament. It was one of those films that are produced with great effort and skill, supposedly not to earn money but in the service of noble and holy goals—the kind that religion teachers might even take their students to see in the afternoon. It told the story of Moses and the Israelites in Egypt, and featured an enormous array of people, horses, camels, palaces, pharaonic splendor and Jewish travails in the hot desert sands. I saw Moses, his hair styled a bit like Walt Whitman's, a splendid, theatrical Moses, fiery and gloomy, striding through the desert like Wotan with his long staff, leading the Jews. I saw him pray to God at the Red Sea, and saw the Red Sea part to reveal a path, a narrow pass between the towering mountains of water (the confirmation candidates whose pastor had brought them to see this religious film could spend hours arguing about how the moviemakers had pulled off that feat), I saw the prophet and his fearful people walk through, and I saw Pharaoh's chariots appear behind them, saw the Egyptians on the shore of the sea pause and hesitate, then courageously venture down the same path, and saw the mountains of water crash down upon the magnificent Pharaoh in his golden armor and all his chariots and men, not without recalling a wonderful duet for two basses by Handel in which this event is gloriously recounted in song. Then I saw Moses climb Mount Sinai, a gloomy hero in a gloomy, rocky wilderness, and I watched as Jehovah delivered the Ten Commandments to him by means of storms, gales, and flashes of light, even as his worthless people erected the Golden Calf at the foot of the mountain and indulged in some rather raucous amusements. I found it so incredible and unbelievable to be present for this spectacle, and to see these sacred stories—with their heroes and miracles, which had once imbued our childhood with the first, dawning inkling of another world, a superhuman world—to see these stories played out here in front of a grateful audience who had paid the cost of admission and now sat quietly eating the sandwiches they had brought along, it was just one nice little snapshot of the tremendous junk heap and cultural clearance sale that is the present era. My God, in order to prevent a scandal like that, it would have been better if not only the Egyptians, but also the Jews and all the other people had perished back then, died a violent and respectable death, instead of suffering this gruesome, illusory, half-and-half death that we died today. Indeed!

My secret inhibitions, my repressed wariness of the masquerade ball, had by no means been diminished by the cinema and its excitements, rather they had been unpleasantly augmented, and I had to force myself finally to go to the Globe Ballrooms and set foot inside, summoning up Hermine in my mind. It was late, and the ball had been in full swing for quite a while by the time I arrived, sober and shy, and before I had even taken off my coat, I found myself caught up in a frenzy of masks, jostled about like an old friend, girls were inviting me to visit the champagne lounges, clowns were slapping me on the shoulder and addressing me in familiar tones. I didn't take the bait, I just fought my way through the crowded rooms to the coat check, and when I received my coat check number I tucked it into my pocket with great care, thinking I might need it again very soon, when I'd had enough of all this turmoil.

The party was roaring in every room of the sprawling building, people were dancing in all of the ballrooms and even in the basement, all of the corridors and stairwells were flooded with masks, dancing, music, laughter, and hustle and bustle. I crept through the throngs, from the Negro band to the peasant music, from the large, radiant grand ballroom to the hallways, staircases, bars, buffets, and champagne rooms. Most of the walls were hung with wild, spirited paintings by the latest artists. Everyone was there: artists, journalists, scholars, businessmen, and of course the entire demimonde of the city. Mister Pablo was sitting with one of the orchestras, blowing enthusiastically into his sinuous horn; when he recognized me, he sang out a loud greeting. Pushed by the crowd, I made my way to this room and that, up the stairs, down the stairs; the artists had transformed a corridor in the basement into hell, where an ensemble of devils was furiously drumming away. Eventually I began to keep an eye out for Hermine, for Maria, I went in search of them, I tried several times to reach the grand ballroom, but each time I failed, or the flow of the crowd swept me in the opposite direction. By midnight I still hadn't found anyone; although I hadn't danced yet, I was already hot and dizzy, I flung myself into the nearest chair, amid all the strangers, asked for wine, and concluded that taking part in such noisy festivities was not the thing for an old man like me. Resigned, I drank my glass of wine, stared at the bare arms and backs of the ladies, watched the many grotesque, masked figures drift by, allowed myself to be jostled by the crowd, and silently sent the few girls who wanted to sit on my lap or dance with me on their way. "Grumpy old man," one shouted, and she was right. I decided to drink myself into a better and bolder mood, but I didn't like the wine, either, I barely managed to down a second glass. And gradually I began to feel the Steppenwolf standing behind me, sticking out his tongue. There was nothing wrong with me, I was just in the wrong place. I had come here with the best of intentions, but I could not be happy here, and the loud, boisterous joy, the laughter, and all the frolicking around seemed stupid and forced to me.

So it was that at one o'clock I stalked back to the coat check, disappointed and angry, to put on my coat and depart. It was a defeat, a relapse into the Steppenwolf, and Hermine would hardly forgive me. But I couldn't help it. I had looked around carefully as I fought my way back through the crowd to the coat check, to see if any of my lady friends might be seen there. All for naught. Now I was standing at the counter, the polite man on the other side was already holding out his hand for my number, I reached into my waistcoat pocket—the number was gone! The devil take it, that was the last thing I needed. Several times as I was sadly wandering through the halls, as I was sitting with my insipid wine, I had reached into my pocket, fighting off the urge to leave, and each time I had felt that round, flat token right where it belonged. And now it was gone. Everything was stacked against me.

"Lost your number?" a little red and yellow devil next to me asked in a shrill voice. "Here, pal, you can have mine," and already he was holding it out to me. Even as I was mechanically reaching out my hand to take it and twiddling it between my fingers, the spry little fellow had already disappeared again.

But when I lifted the small, round cardboard token to my eye to look at the number, there was no number on it at all, just some tiny, scrawled handwriting. I asked the coat check man to wait, went to stand beneath the nearest chandelier, and tried to read. There was something scrawled there, in small, tumbling letters that were difficult to make out:

> *Tonight from four o'clock on—magic theater*
> *—only for the insane—*
> *Admission costs your sanity.*
> *Not for everyone. Hermine is in hell.*

Just as a marionette whose string has momentarily slipped from the puppeteer's hands collapses in a brief, limp death and stupor but then springs back to life—rejoins the game, dances and acts—so too I, pulled along by a magic string, ran back into the turmoil from which I had just escaped—no longer tired, listless, and old, but lithe, young, and eager. Never has a sinner been in a greater hurry to get to hell. Just a moment earlier my patent leather shoes had been pinching my feet, the thick, perfumed air had made me nauseated, the heat had made me limp; now I was walking briskly through all the halls, my feet bouncing in a one-step beat toward hell, I felt that the air was full of magic, I was cradled and carried along by its warmth, by all the roaring music, by the tumult of colors, by the scent of the women's shoulders, by the intoxication of hundreds of people, by the laughter, by the beat of the dance, by the gleam of all the fiery eyes. A Spanish dancer flew into my arms: "Dance with me!"—"I can't," I said, "I have to go to hell. But I'll gladly take your kiss along with me." The red mouth beneath the mask came toward me, and it was only from the kiss that I recognized Maria. I clasped her tightly in my arms, her full mouth blossomed like a ripe summer rose. And now we were already dancing, our lips still pressed together, and we danced past Pablo, who was lovingly draped over his tenderly wailing pipe, radiantly and half dreamily embracing us with his beautiful animal gaze. But before we had done even twenty dance steps, the music stopped, and I reluctantly let Maria out of my hands.

"I would have loved to dance with you again," I said, intoxicated by her warmth, "come along with me for a few steps, Maria, I'm in love with your beautiful arm, let me enjoy it a moment longer! But look, Hermine has called me. She's in hell."

"That's what I thought. Farewell, Harry, you'll always be dear to me." She took her leave. So that was the scent that had risen so ripe and full from the summer rose: the scent of departure, of autumn, of destiny.

On I ran, through the long corridors of caressing crowds, down the stairs, into hell. Wickedly lurid lamps were burning there on the pitch-black walls, and the band of devils was playing at a fever pitch. On a high barstool sat a handsome young man without a mask, dressed in a tailcoat, he eyed me briefly with a disdainful glance. I was pressed against the wall by the whirl of dancers, roughly twenty couples were dancing in the very crowded room. I greedily and anxiously observed all the women, most of them were still masked, some were laughing at me, but not one of them was Hermine. The handsome youth glanced over mockingly from the high barstool. During the next break in the dance, I thought, she would come and call me. The dance ended, but no one came.

I went over to the bar, which was tucked away in a corner of the small, low-ceilinged room. Leaning on the bar next to the young man's stool, I ordered a whiskey. As I drank, I regarded his youthful profile, it looked so familiar and lovely, like an image from a very distant time, a precious image seen through the silent, dusty veil of the past. Oh, then it came to me in a flash: it was Hermann, my childhood friend!

"Hermann!" I said hesitantly.

He smiled. "Harry? You found me?"

It was Hermine, only her hairstyle was slightly different and she was wearing light makeup, her knowing face looked distinguished and pale, framed as it was by the fashionable mandarin collar, her hands emerged so daintily from the wide black sleeves of the tailcoat and the white cuffs of the shirt, her feet emerged so delicately from the long black pants, sheathed in black-and-white men's silk stockings.

"Is this the costume you've chosen to make me fall in love with you, Hermine?"

She nodded: "So far, I've only made a few ladies fall in love. But now it's your turn. Let's have a glass of champagne first."

This we did, perched on our high barstools, while nearby the dancing continued and the hot, heavy string music swelled. And although Hermine didn't seem to be making any effort, I very soon fell in love with her. Since she was wearing men's clothes, I couldn't dance with her, I couldn't allow myself any tenderness, couldn't make any advances, but even as she appeared distant and indifferent in her male guise, her eyes, her words, and her gestures all combined to envelop me in the charms of her femininity. Without even touching her, I fell under her spell, and the power of this spell still played its part, it was hermaphroditic. For she spoke to me about Hermann and about childhood, mine and hers, about those years before sexual maturity in which the youthful capacity for love embraces not only both sexes, but everything and anything, sensual and intellectual, and endows everything with the magic of love and the fairy-tale capacity for transformation, which occasionally returns later in life, but only to the chosen and to the poets. She played the young man to the hilt, smoked cigarettes and chatted with ease and wit, often with a bit of mockery, but it was all suffused with eros, everything was transformed into a sweet seduction as it made its way to my senses.

How well, how thoroughly I had known Hermine, or taken myself to know her, and how fully new was the Hermine who revealed herself to me that night! How softly and imperceptibly she drew her net around me, the net I longed for, how playfully, like a mermaid, she gave me that sweet poison to drink!

We sat and chatted and drank champagne. We strolled through the halls as observers, as adventurous explorers, picking out couples and eavesdropping on their amorous games. She would point out women and urge me to dance with them, advising me on which arts of seduction to employ with this or that woman. We would present ourselves as rivals, both pursuing the same woman for a while, dancing with her in turn, both trying to win her for ourselves. And yet all of this was just a masquerade, just a game between the two of us, binding us more tightly together, inflaming both of us for each other. Everything was a fairy tale, everything was one dimension richer, one meaning deeper, everything was a game and a symbol. We saw a very beautiful young woman who appeared somewhat discontented and dissatisfied, Hermann danced with her, made her blossom, disappeared with her into a champagne lounge and told me afterward that she had conquered this woman not as a man, but as a woman, with the magic of Lesbos. But for me, this whole thundering palace of boisterous dance halls, this intoxicated crowd of masks was slowly becoming a fantastic dream paradise, one blossom after another wooed me with its fragrance, I playfully probed one fruit after another with my searching fingers, snakes gazed out at me seductively from the green shadows of the leaves, lotus blossoms floated ghostly above a black swamp, magic birds beckoned in the branches, and yet all of this was leading me to a single, longed-for destination, all of this was filling me anew with longing for the one and only. Once I danced with a girl I didn't know, I was glowing, wooing her, I swept her along in a frenzy of intoxication, and while we were suspended in that unreal state, she suddenly said with a laugh: "I hardly recognize you. Earlier this evening you were so dumb and bland." And I realized she was the girl who had called me "Grumpy old man" just a few hours ago. Now she thought she had me all to herself, but during the next dance I was already glowing for another girl. I danced for two hours or more, every dance, even dances I had never learned. Hermann, the smiling youth, would occasionally appear in my vicinity, nod to me, disappear into the crowd.

In that night at the ball I had an experience that had remained unknown to me for fifty years, although it's familiar to every teenage girl and university student: the experience of the party with its rush of collective intoxication, the secret of how the self dissolves into the crowd, the *unio mystica* of joy. I had often heard it spoken of, every housemaid knew about it, and I had often seen others' eyes light up as they spoke of it, and had always smiled, half in condescension, half in envy. A hundred times in my life I had seen that sparkle in the eyes of a man lost in drunken reveries, a man who had been liberated from himself, that smile and that half-crazed ecstasy on the face of a man absorbed in the intoxication of the collective, I had seen it in both refined and vulgar forms, in drunken recruits and sailors as well as in great artists, in the enthusiasm of their grand performances, and no less in young soldiers going off to war, and even more recently I had admired, loved, mocked, and envied that sparkle and smile of reverie in my friend Pablo as he bent blissfully over his saxophone in the intoxication of performing music with the orchestra, or watched the conductor, the drummer, the man with the banjo, enthralled, ecstatic. At times I had thought that such a smile, such a childlike sparkle, was possible only for very young people, or for those tribes and peoples who did not admit any strong individuation or differentiation of the one from the many. But today, in this blessed night, I myself, the Steppenwolf Harry, was flashing that sparkling smile, I myself was swimming in that deep, childlike, fairy-tale happiness, I myself was breathing that sweet dream and intoxication of connection, music, rhythm, wine, and passion, which I had so often heard recounted and praised in some student's recollection of a ball, and had always listened to with derision and a petty sense of superiority. I was no longer myself, my personality had dissolved in that festive intoxication like salt in water. I danced with this or that woman, but it was not only that one woman I held in my arms, whose hair brushed me, whose scent I inhaled, but rather all of them, all of the other women who were swimming in the same hall, in the same dance, in the same music as I was, whose radiant faces floated before me like large fantastic flowers, they all belonged to me, I belonged to all of them, we were all part of one another. And the men were a part of it, too, I was also in them, and they were not strangers to me, their smiles were mine, their flirtations were mine, and mine were theirs.

That winter a new dance tune, a fox-trot, had taken the world by storm, its title was "Yearning." This "Yearning" was played over and over again, and requested over and over again, we were all saturated and intoxicated by it, we all hummed along with its melody. I danced without stopping, with every woman who came my way, with quite young girls, with young women in full bloom, with women in the ripeness of summer, with women whose blossoms were wistfully fading away: I was enraptured by all of them, laughing, happy, radiant. And when Pablo, who had always regarded me as a pitiful, poor devil, saw me in that radiant state, his eyes flashed at me, he stood up enthusiastically from his seat in the orchestra, blew powerfully into his horn, climbed onto the chair, stood on top of it, and blew with his cheeks full of air, swaying back and forth wildly and blissfully with his instrument to the beat of that "Yearning," and my dancer and I blew him kisses and sang along in loud voices. Oh, I thought amid it all, whatever may happen to

me now, at least I too was happy once, I too was radiant, liberated
from myself, I was a brother of Pablo's, a child.

I had lost all track of time, I don't know how many hours or
moments that intoxicated happiness lasted. Nor did I notice that
the more animated the party became, the more tightly it drew
together. Most of the guests had already left, the corridors were
quiet now, and many of the lights had been extinguished, the stairwell was deserted, in the upper halls one band after another had
fallen silent and gone home; only in the grand ballroom and in
the hell below was the lively bacchanal still raging, its fervor constantly intensifying. Since I could not dance with Hermine, the
young man, we had only seen and greeted each other briefly during
breaks in the dancing, and in the end she had completely disappeared from my sight, not only from my eyes, but even from my
thoughts. There were no more thoughts. I was dissolved, swimming
in the drunken frenzy of the dance, encircled by scents, sounds,
sighs, words, seen and spurred on by unknown eyes, surrounded
by unknown faces, lips, cheeks, arms, breasts, knees, rhythmically
rocked back and forth by the music as if by a wave.

Now, halfway coming to my senses for a moment, I suddenly
saw—among the last remaining guests who were now packed into
one of the small halls, the last hall where music was still playing—
I suddenly saw a Pierrette dressed in black with a white-painted
face, a beautiful, fresh-faced girl, the only girl wearing a mask, a
lovely figure I had not seen even once in the course of the night.
While everyone else was showing the signs of the late hour in their
red, flushed faces, their wrinkled outfits, their wilted collars and
ruffs, the black-clad Pierrette stood there fresh and new, with her
white face behind the mask, in an unwrinkled costume with an
untouched ruff, bright crisp lace cuffs, and a fresh coiffure. I was
drawn to her, I embraced her, drew her into the dance, inhaled her
fragrance as her ruff tickled my chin, as her hair brushed my cheek,

her firm young body responded to my movements more tenderly and intimately than any other dancer had that night, she slipped away from me, playfully forcing and enticing me into ever new forms of contact. And suddenly, just as I was leaning over her in the midst of the dance, my mouth seeking hers, her mouth smiled a familiar, superior smile, and I recognized that strong chin, I happily recognized those shoulders, those elbows, those hands. It was Hermine, no longer Hermann, in new clothes, fresh, lightly perfumed and powdered. Our lips met passionately, for a moment her whole body, down to the knees, was pressed against me with desire and surrender, then she pulled her mouth away from me and danced, seeming tentative, withdrawn. When the music stopped, we remained locked in our embrace, all the enraptured couples around us clapped, stomped, shouted, urged the exhausted band to play "Yearning" again. And now we all suddenly felt the arrival of morning, we saw the pale light behind the curtains, we knew that the end of our pleasure was near, we sensed our impending fatigue, and once more we plunged blindly into the dance, into the music, into the flood of light, laughing and desperate, stepping furiously to the beat, couple pressed against couple, once again we blissfully felt that great wave crashing over us. In that dance, Hermine let her superiority, her mockery, her cool reserve fall away—she knew that there was nothing more she had to do to make me fall in love. I belonged to her. And she surrendered herself, in the dance, in her gaze, in her kiss, in her smile. All the women of that feverish night, all the women I had danced with, all the women I had set ablaze, who had set me ablaze, the women I had pursued, the women I had yearningly pressed myself against, all the women I had gazed after with amorous longing, had melted together and become one, blossoming in my arms.

This nuptial dance continued for some time. Twice, three times, the music subsided, the wind players lowered their instruments,

the piano player stood up from the grand piano, the first violin-
ist shook his head in surrender, and each time they were spurred
on again by the imploring frenzy of the last remaining dancers,
they played again, played faster, played wilder. Then—we were still
standing, entwined and panting from the last, ravenous dance—
the lid of the piano slammed shut with a bang, our arms fell wearily to our sides like those of the wind players and violinists, and
the flautist, blinking, packed his flute into its case, doors opened,
cold air rushed in, attendants appeared with coats, and the bar-
tender turned off the lights. Everyone drifted apart, a ghostly and
eerie dispersal, the dancers who had been glowing brightly just
moments ago now bundled themselves into their coats and turned
up their collars with a shiver. Hermine stood there, pale but smiling. She slowly raised her arms and brushed back her hair, her armpit gleamed in the light, a thin, infinitely delicate shadow ran from
there to her covered breast, and that little transitory line of shadow
seemed to me to sum up all her charms, all the games and possibilities of her beautiful body, like a smile.

We stood looking at each other, the last in the hall, the last in
the building. Somewhere downstairs I heard a door slam, a glass
shatter, giggling voices that got lost amid the nasty, hurried noise
of automobiles cranking up their engines. Somewhere, from
some uncertain distance and altitude, I heard a peal of laughter,
an uncommonly bright and joyful, yet eerie and alien laughter, a
laugh that seemed to be made of crystal and ice, bright and radiant, but cold and unrelenting. Where had I heard that strange
laughter before? I wasn't sure.

We both stood looking at each other. For a moment I was suddenly awake and sober, I felt the sweaty clothes hanging on my
body, repulsively damp and clammy, I saw my hands, red and
thickly veined, emerging from the wrinkled, sweaty cuffs of my
shirt. But all of this passed in an instant, one glance from Hermine

erased it. As she gazed at me, it seemed that it was my own soul looking at me, reality itself seemed to collapse, including the reality of my longing for her. Enchanted, we gazed at each other, my own poor little soul gazed back at me.

"You're ready?" asked Hermine, and her smile vanished, just as the shadow on her breast had vanished. High and distant, that strange laughter faded out in unknown spaces.

I nodded. Oh yes, I was ready.

Now Pablo, the musician, appeared in the doorway, and his joyful eyes shone at us, in truth they were animal eyes, but animal eyes are always serious, whereas his eyes always laughed, and their laughter made them human eyes. He beckoned to us with all his heartfelt friendliness. He had put on a colorful silk smoking jacket, and his sodden shirt collar and overtired, pale face appeared strangely withered and wan above its red lapels, but his shining black eyes canceled out that effect. They, too, canceled out reality, they, too, were enchanting.

Responding to his gesture, we went over to him, and in the doorway he said to me quietly: "Brother Harry, I'd like to invite you to join me for a bit of entertainment. Admission only for the insane, costs your sanity. Are you ready?" I nodded again.

Dear fellow! He tenderly and carefully took us both by the arm, Hermine on the right, me on the left, and led us up a staircase into a small, round room, which was lit from above with a bluish light and almost entirely empty, containing nothing but a small, round table and three armchairs, in which we took our seat.

Where were we? Was I sleeping? Was I at home? Was I sitting in a car and driving? No, I was sitting in the round, blue-lit room, in its rarefied air, in a layer of reality that had become very porous. Why was Hermine so pale? Why was Pablo talking so much? Could it be that I was making him speak, that I was speaking through him? Wasn't it just my own soul, that poor lost, frightened bird, that was gazing out at me from his black eyes, as it did from Hermine's gray eyes?

Our friend Pablo looked at us with all his good and somewhat ceremonious friendliness, and spoke at length, he had many things to say. He, whom I had never heard speak coherently, who took no interest in disputes or formulations, whom I had hardly thought capable of thinking—he spoke now, he spoke fluently and flawlessly in his kind, warm voice.

"Friends, I have invited you here for some entertainment that Harry has long desired, that he has long dreamed of. It is a bit late, and we are probably all a little tired. Therefore, let us first rest here a bit and gather our strength."

He took three glasses and a funny little bottle from a niche in the wall, as well as a small, exotic box made of several colors of wood, filled the three little glasses from the bottle, took three long, thin, yellow cigarettes out of the box, pulled a lighter from his silk jacket, and offered us a light. Now we all leaned back in our armchairs and slowly smoked our cigarettes, their smoke as thick as incense, and took small, slow sips of that bittersweet, incredibly unfamiliar and strange-tasting liquid, which proved to be immensely invigorating and exhilarating, as if we were being filled with gas, becoming weightless. So we sat, taking small drags of smoke, resting, sipping at our glasses, feeling ourselves grow light and happy. And Pablo spoke calmly in his warm voice:

"Dear Harry, it is my pleasure to be able to entertain you a bit today. You have often been very weary of your life. You have been yearning to get away from here, haven't you? You long to leave this time, this world, this reality, and to enter another reality that suits you better, a world without time. Do that, dear friend, I invite you to do that. After all, you know where this other world lies hidden, you know that it is the world of your own soul that you seek. The other reality that you long for lives only within you. I cannot give you anything that you do not already have within yourself, I cannot reveal to you any other gallery of images than that of your soul. I can give you nothing, only the opportunity, the impetus, the key. I can help you make your own world visible, that is all."

He reached into the pocket of his colorful jacket again and pulled out a round pocket mirror.

"You see: that's how you've always seen yourself!"

He held the little mirror before my eyes (a children's verse came to mind: "Mirror, mirror in the hand"), and I saw an image, somewhat bleary and cloudy, an uncanny image, an image in motion, violently seething and swirling: I saw myself, Harry Haller, and inside this Harry I saw the Steppenwolf, a wary and beautiful wolf, but with a lost and frightened look, its eyes glowing angrily one moment, sadly the next, and this wolf figure flowed through Harry in ceaseless motion, just as in a stream a tributary of a different color surges and churns, struggling, sorrowful, one gorging in the other, full of an unredeemed longing to take on form. Sadly, sadly, the flowing, half-formed wolf gazed out at me from its beautiful, wary eyes.

"That's how you've always seen yourself," Pablo repeated softly, sliding the mirror back into his pocket. I gratefully closed my eyes and sipped at the elixir.

"Now we've rested," said Pablo, "we've gathered our strength and we've chatted a bit. If you're not tired anymore, then I'd like to take you inside my peep box now and show you my little theater. Is it all right with you?"

We rose, and Pablo led the way, smiling; he opened a door, pulled aside a curtain, and we found ourselves standing in the curving, horseshoe-shaped corridor of a theater, right at the center; to either side, the hallway traced an arc past the narrow doors of a great many, unbelievably many box seats.

"This is our theater," Pablo explained, "a cheerful theater, hopefully the two of you will find all sorts of things to laugh about." At that, he laughed aloud, just a short burst, but it pierced right through me, it was that same bright, strange laughter that I had heard earlier, coming from above.

"My little theater has all the doors you could possibly want, ten or a hundred or a thousand, and behind each door, you will each find whatever you are looking for. Oh yes, my dear friend Harry, it's a lovely picture gallery, my good sir, but it would do you no good at all to visit it in your current state. You would be hindered and blinded by that thing you like to call your personality. No doubt you have long since divined that your wish—to overcome time, to be released from reality, or whatever else you might call it—amounts to nothing but a longing to shed your so-called personality. That is the prison in which you are confined. And if you were to enter the theater as you are, you would see everything through Harry's eyes, through the old glasses of the Steppenwolf. Therefore, my good sir, you are invited to take off your glasses and kindly leave your most distinguished personality here in the cloakroom, where you may retrieve it whenever you wish. The pleasant evening of dancing that you have just enjoyed, the treatise on the Steppenwolf, and finally, the little stimulant that we have just imbibed ought to have prepared you sufficiently. You, Harry, will have the left side of the theater at your disposal once you have cast off your precious personality, Hermine will have the right side, and you may meet again inside the theater whenever you like. Hermine, please go behind the curtain for the time being, I would like to take Harry in first."

Hermine disappeared to the right, past a huge mirror that completely covered the back wall all the way from the floor to the vaulted ceiling.

"So, Mr. Harry, come along now, and please be in good spirits. The purpose of this whole production is to put you in good spirits, to teach you to laugh—I hope you'll make it easy for me. You're feeling all right, aren't you? Yes? You're not afraid? All right, very well. Now, without fear, and with sincere pleasure, you will enter our world of illusion, you will make your entrance by committing a little mock suicide, as is the custom."

He pulled out the little pocket mirror again and held it in front of my face. Again, that confused, cloudy Harry stared back at me, with the writhing wolf still struggling inside him—it was an image that I knew well but truly did not care for, and the thought of its destruction caused me no grief.

"Dear friend, you will now destroy this mirror image, which is no longer needed; that is all you have to do. It will suffice, if your mood allows, for you to respond to this image with sincere laughter. You are in a school of humor here, you are here to learn to laugh. Well, all higher humor begins when you stop taking yourself seriously."

I looked squarely into the little mirror, mirror in the hand, where Harry the wolf was convulsing. For a moment I felt myself convulsing deep inside, quietly but painfully, a feeling like memory, like homesickness, like remorse. Then my slight trepidation gave way to a new feeling, as when a rotten tooth has been pulled from a jaw numbed with cocaine—a deep sigh of relief, and at the same time, a sense of amazement that it didn't hurt at all. And this feeling was accompanied by a fresh sense of exhilaration and an irresistible urge to laugh, so that I broke out in cathartic laughter.

The cloudy little image in the mirror flickered and disappeared, the small, round surface of the mirror suddenly looked as if it had been burned, it had turned gray and rough and opaque. Laughing, Pablo threw the piece of glass away, it rolled down the floor of the endless corridor and out of sight.

"Nice laugh, my dear Harry," cried Pablo, "you'll learn to laugh like the immortals yet. Now you've finally killed the Steppenwolf.

You can't do that with razors. Take care that he stays dead! Soon you'll be able to leave this stupid reality behind. We'll drink to our brotherhood the next chance we get, my dear, I've never liked you as much as I do today. And if you still want to, we can philosophize and debate with each other and talk all you want about music and Mozart and Gluck and Plato and Goethe. Now you understand why we couldn't do that earlier.—Hopefully you'll succeed in ridding yourself of the Steppenwolf for today. Because of course your suicide isn't final; we're in a magic theater, there are only images here, there's no reality. So choose the beautiful and joyful images, and show that you're truly not in love with your questionable personality anymore! However, if you should want it back after all, you need only look again into the mirror that I'm about to show you. But you know the wise old saying: One little mirror in the hand is better than two on the wall. Haha!" (Once again he let out that beautiful, terrible laugh.)—"And now there's just one funny little ceremony to perform. Now that you've cast off the glasses of your personality, come and look in a real mirror for once! It'll be fun for you."

Laughing and giving me a few playful caresses, he spun me around so that I was facing the huge mirror on the wall. I saw myself in it.

For a brief moment I saw the Harry I knew, only with an unusually good-humored, bright, laughing face. But no sooner had I recognized him than he fell apart, a second figure broke away from him, a third, a tenth, a twentieth, and the whole giant mirror was full of Harrys or pieces of Harry, countless Harrys, I was only able to look at each one and recognize him for one brief flash. Some of these many Harrys were as old as I was, some were older, some ancient, some quite young, youths, boys, schoolboys, little rascals, children. Fifty-year-old and twenty-year-old Harrys were running and jumping past one another, thirty-year-olds and five-year-olds,

serious and humorous, dignified and comical, well-dressed and
ragged and also completely naked, hairless and long-haired, and
all of them were me, and I saw and recognized each of them in
a flash and then they disappeared, scattering in all directions, to
the left, to the right, into the depths of the mirror, out of the mirror. One of them, an elegant young fellow, leaped at Pablo's chest
with a laugh, embraced him, and ran away with him. And one,
whom I particularly liked, a handsome, charming boy of sixteen or
seventeen, ran like lightning into the corridor, eagerly reading the
inscriptions on all the doors; I ran after him, he stopped in front of
one door, and I read the words:

> *All the Girls Are Yours!*
> *Deposit one mark*

The dear boy sprang up, plunged headfirst into the coin slot,
and disappeared behind the door.

Pablo, too, had disappeared, even the mirror seemed to have disappeared, and with it all the countless Harry figures. I felt that
I had now been abandoned to myself and to the theater, and I
stepped curiously from one door to the next, reading the inscription, the enticement, the promise on each one.

THE INSCRIPTION

> *Happy Hunting!*
> *Big-game hunting for automobiles*

attracted me, I opened the narrow door and stepped inside.

I was drawn at once into a noisy and turbulent world. On
the streets, automobiles, some of them armored, were chasing

pedestrians, running them down and grinding them to a pulp, crushing them against the walls of houses. I understood at once: it was the battle between men and machines—long prepared, long anticipated, long feared, now this battle had finally broken out. There were dead and dismembered people lying all around, there were smashed, twisted, half-burned automobiles everywhere, and airplanes were circling above this chaotic confusion, taking rifle and machine-gun fire from many rooftops and windows. There were wild, wonderfully provocative posters on all the walls, with giant letters that blazed like torches, calling on the nation to finally stand up for the people, against the machines, to finally put an end to the fat, well-dressed, fragrantly perfumed rich people who used their machines to squeeze the last ounce of fat out of everyone else—to kill those rich people along with their big, wheezing, ominously growling, diabolically purring automobiles, to finally set fire to the factories and clear out the desecrated earth and depopulate it a bit so that grass could grow again, so that the dusty cement world could once again give way to something like forest, meadow, heath, brook, and moor. Other posters, though—wonderfully painted, splendidly stylized, in more subtle, less childish colors, composed with extraordinary cleverness and wit—took the opposite view, movingly warning all propertied and prudent people against the impending chaos of anarchy, poignantly portraying the blessings of order, work, property, culture, and law, and praising machines as man's supreme and ultimate invention, with whose help they would become gods. I read the posters with reflection and admiration, both the red and the green ones, their fiery eloquence and compelling logic made a tremendous impression on me, they were right, and with deep conviction I stood before first one poster, then the next, quite disturbed nonetheless by the rather intense gunfire all around me. Well, the most important thing was clear: it was war, a fierce, furious, and highly congenial

war, not a war concerned with emperors, republics, national bor-
ders, flags, colors, and other such decorative and theatrical trappings—in other words, with dirty tricks—but rather one where
everyone who felt that the air was growing too snug for him and
life no longer held any appeal could give vent to his anger and try
to bring about the wholesale destruction of this tinny, civilized
world. I could see the lust for destruction and murder laughing
so brightly and forthrightly from everyone's eyes, and those same
wild, red flowers bloomed within me, tall and bold, and laughed
no less heartily. I joyfully joined the fight.

But best of all, who should suddenly appear beside me but my
school friend Gustav, who had been lost to me for decades, but he
had been my wildest and strongest friend, with the greatest thirst
for life, back when I was a young child. My heart laughed when I
saw his bright blue eyes twinkling at me again. He beckoned to
me, and I immediately, joyfully followed him.

"Dear God, Gustav," I cried out happily, "we meet again! What's
become of you?"

He laughed irritably, just as he had when he was a boy.

"You fool, do you have to start right in with questions and gossip again? I became a professor of theology—so, now you know,
but fortunately there's no theology anymore, my boy, just war.
Come on!"

Just then a small motorcar headed straight toward us, puffing as
it came; Gustav shot down the driver, jumped up into the driver's
seat as nimbly as a monkey, brought the car to a halt, and let me
climb aboard, then we drove quick as the devil between shotgun
pellets and overturned cars, making our way out through the city
and the outlying neighborhoods.

"Are you on the side of the industrialists?" I asked my friend.

"Oh, don't worry about that, that's a matter of taste, we'll talk
about that once we get out. But no, wait a minute, I'd rather we pick

the other side, although fundamentally, of course, it doesn't matter. I'm a theologian, and my forefather Luther supported the princes and the rich against the peasants in his day, so we can make up for that a little bit now. Bad car, I hope it can hold out a few more kilometers!"

Swift as the wind, that heavenly child, my friend Gustav grinned, we rattled for miles, passing into a quiet, green landscape, crossing a great plain, and then slowly ascending into a mighty mountain range. There we came to a stop on a smooth, glistening road that ran between a steep rock face and a low retaining wall, climbing in hairpin curves, high above a shining blue lake.

"Beautiful area," I said.

"Very pretty. We can call it Axle Street, it'll be piled high with broken axles soon enough, little Harry, watch out!"

There was a tall pine tree by the side of the road, and high up in the tree we saw something like a tree house built of boards, a lookout or a raised hunting stand. Gustav smiled at me, his bright blue eyes twinkling slyly, and we hastily got out of our car, climbed up the trunk of the tree, panting, and hid in the tree house, which we liked very much. There we found shotguns, pistols, boxes of shells. And no sooner had we cooled off a bit and settled into the hunting stand than the horn of a large luxury car could be heard blaring hoarsely and imperiously from around the next bend, the car was purring at high speed along the slick mountain road. We already had our shotguns in our hands. It was wonderfully exciting.

"Aim for the chauffeur!" Gustav quickly ordered, just as the heavy car was passing below us. I took aim and fired, hitting the driver in his blue cap. The man slumped over, the car sped on, hit the rock wall, bounced back, crashed against the low retaining wall as heavily and furiously as a big fat bumblebee, rolled over, and, with a brief, muffled thud, crashed over the wall and plunged down the side of the mountain.

"Done!" Gustav laughed. "I'll take the next one."

Already another car was speeding toward us, the three or four occupants sat small in their seats, a piece of veil was blowing straight back in the air behind a woman's head, a bright blue veil, I actually felt bad about it, who knows if the most beautiful woman's face wasn't laughing underneath it. My God, if we were going to play robbers, maybe it would have made a prettier and more proper scene if we had followed the example of great role models and spared the pretty ladies from our righteous blood lust. But Gustav had already fired. The chauffeur jerked, slumped down, the car sped up the rock face of the mountain, launched into the air, fell back, and slammed down onto the street, wheels in the air. We waited, nothing moved, the people lay silently under their car, as if caught in a trap. It was still purring and rattling and spinning its wheels whimsically in the air, but suddenly we heard a terrible bang and the car was consumed by dazzling flames.

"A Ford," said Gustav. "We have to go down and clear the road."

We climbed down and surveyed the burning wreck. It had burned out very quickly, in the meantime we had found some fresh-cut tree limbs to use as levers, and we hoisted the wreck to the side of the road and over the edge, down the side of the mountain, where it could still be heard crackling in the bushes for a long time. Two of the dead had fallen out as we were rolling the car, and they were lying on the road, their clothes partly burned. One wore a coat that was still in quite good shape, and I searched his pockets to see if we could find out who he had been. I found a leather wallet with calling cards inside. I took one out and read the words: "Tat tvam asi."

"Very funny," Gustav said. "But the names of the people we kill aren't really relevant. They're poor devils like us, their names don't matter. This world must go to pieces, and we'll go with it. Put the

whole thing under water for ten minutes, that'd be the most pain-
less solution. Now, let's get to work!"

We threw the dead bodies down after the car. Another car was
already approaching, honking its horn. We shot this one up from
right where we were standing on the street. It drunkenly careened
onward for a little while, then crashed and came to a halt, wheezing, with one of its occupants sitting motionless inside, but a pretty
young girl climbed out unharmed, though pale and trembling violently. We greeted her kindly and offered our services. She was far
too frightened to speak, and she stared at us for a while as if she
were mad.

"Well, let's check on the old gentleman first," Gustav said, turning to the passenger who was still slouched in his seat behind the
dead chauffeur. He was a gentleman with short gray hair, his bright,
light gray eyes were open, but he seemed to be badly injured, at
least there was blood flowing from his mouth, and he was holding
his neck in an unnaturally crooked, stiff position.

"By your leave, my dear old sir, my name is Gustav. We have
taken the liberty of shooting your chauffeur. May we ask with
whom we have the honor?"

The old man peered out coolly and sadly from his small gray eyes.

"I am Chief Prosecutor Loering," he said slowly. "You didn't
just kill my poor chauffeur, you killed me, too; I feel my end is
near. Why did you shoot at us, anyway?"

"For speeding."

"We were driving at normal speed."

"What was normal yesterday is no longer normal today, Mr.
Chief Prosecutor. Today we believe that a car is always moving too
fast, regardless of its speed. Now we're destroying all the cars, and
the other machines, too."

"Even your shotguns?"

"Their turn will come, too, if we have time for that. We'll

probably all be done in tomorrow or the next day. As you know, our part of the world was horribly overpopulated. Well, now there should be some air."

"Do you shoot everyone, then, indiscriminately?"

"Absolutely. Of course it might be a shame in some cases. For example, I would have felt bad about that pretty young lady—I suppose she's your daughter?"

"No, she's my stenographer."

"All the better. Now, please get out of the car, or let us pull you out, because the car is going to be destroyed."

"I prefer to be destroyed along with it."

"As you wish. By your leave, one more question! You're a prosecutor. I've never understood how a person can be a prosecutor. You make your living by bringing charges against other people, mostly poor devils, and having them sentenced to various punishments. Isn't that right?"

"That's right. I did my duty. It was my appointed office. Just as it is the office of the executioner to kill those I condemned. You yourself have assumed the same office, after all—you also kill."

"Correct. But we don't kill out of duty, but for pleasure, or rather: for displeasure, out of despair over the world. That's why we find killing fun, in a certain sense. Didn't you ever enjoy killing?"

"You're boring me. Be so kind as to finish your job. If you have no concept of duty . . ."

He fell silent and pursed his lips as if he wanted to spit. But all that came out was a little blood that clung to his chin.

"One moment please!" said Gustav politely. "It's true that I have no concept of duty, at least not anymore. It used to be quite an important part of my vocation, I was a professor of theology. I was also a soldier and fought in the war. Those things that seemed to be my duty, the particular orders I received from the authorities and from my superiors, were no good at all, I would have preferred

to do precisely the opposite in each case. But even if I no longer
believe in the concept of duty, I do believe in guilt—perhaps they
are one and the same. Simply because a mother gave birth to me,
I am guilty, I am condemned to live, I am obliged to belong to a
state, to be a soldier, to kill, to pay taxes for armaments. And now,
at this moment, the guilt of life requires me to kill again, just as I
once did in the war. And this time I have no qualms about killing,
I have surrendered to this guilt, it doesn't bother me if this stupid, overcrowded world goes to pieces, I'm happy to help, and I'm
happy to perish along with it."

The prosecutor made a great effort to force a smile, though his
lips were sticky with blood. It was not a rousing success, but his
good intentions were evident.

"Very good," he said. "So we are colleagues. Now please do your
duty, my esteemed colleague."

In the meantime, the pretty girl had sat down by the side of the
road and fainted.

Just at that moment, another car honked its horn and bar-
reled toward us at full speed. We pulled the girl a bit to the
side, pressed ourselves against the rock face, and watched as the
oncoming car headed straight toward the wreck from earlier. It
braked hard and reared up in the air, but managed to come to a
stop unscathed. We quickly took our rifles in hand and aimed at
the new arrivals.

"Out of the car!" Gustav ordered. "Hands up!"

Three men got out of the car and obediently put their hands in
the air.

"Any doctors here?" asked Gustav.

They said no.

"Then be so kind as to carefully help this gentleman out of his
seat, he's badly injured. And then take him with you in your car to
the nearest town. Get going, grab him!"

Soon the old gentleman was resting in the new car, Gustav gave the orders, and they took off.

In the meantime, our stenographer had regained consciousness, and she had been watching these events unfold. I was glad that we had captured this pretty booty.

"Young lady," Gustav said, "you've lost your employer. I hope the old gentleman wasn't dear to you in any other way. You work for me now, be a good ally! So, right now we're in a bit of a rush. Things are going to get dicey here pretty soon. Can you climb, young lady? Yes? Let's go then, we'll take you in between us and help you."

The three of us climbed up to our tree house as fast as we could. The young lady was feeling unwell when we arrived at the top, but we gave her a cognac, and soon she had recovered enough to appreciate the magnificent vista of the lake and the mountains, and to tell us that her name was Dora.

Just then another car passed by down below, carefully steering around the wrecked car without stopping, then immediately accelerating.

"Shirker!" laughed Gustav, then picked off the driver. The car weaved a bit, lurched toward the wall, plowed into it, and came to a stop, dangling off the edge of the precipice.

"Dora," I said, "can you handle a shotgun?"

She couldn't, but we taught her how to load a weapon. At first she was clumsy, and she sliced open a finger, started crying, and asked for a bandage. But Gustav explained to her that this was war and she needed to prove that she was a good, brave girl. That did the trick.

"But what will become of us?" she asked then.

"I don't know," said Gustav. "My friend Harry likes pretty women, he'll be your friend."

"But they'll come with police and soldiers and kill us."

"The police and those types aren't around anymore. We have a choice, Dora. Either we stay up here and keep quiet and shoot all the cars that try to pass by. Or we take a car ourselves, drive away, and let the others shoot at us. It doesn't make any difference which side we take. I say we stay here."

Another car approached below, its horn blaring loudly. It was soon dispatched, and came to rest with its wheels in the air.

"How strange," I said, "that shooting can be so much fun! To think that I used to be a pacifist!"

Gustav smiled. "Yes, there are just too many people in the world. It wasn't so obvious before. But now that people don't just want enough air to breathe, they also all insist on having cars, it's just gotten more conspicuous. Of course, what we're doing isn't reasonable, it's a childish prank, just as the war was one big childish prank. Later on, mankind will have to learn to keep its proliferation in check through reasonable means. For the time being, we're reacting to the intolerable conditions in a rather unreasonable way, but fundamentally we're doing the right thing: cutting back."

"Yes," I said, "what we're doing is probably insane, but still it's probably good and necessary. It's no good when mankind places too much pressure on the intellect, and tries to use reason to bring order to things that just aren't susceptible to reason yet. That's what gives rise to the kinds of ideals that the Americans or the Bolsheviks believe in; they're both extraordinarily reasonable, but because they simplify life so naïvely, they butcher it and bankrupt it terribly. The image of man, which was once a high ideal, is on the verge of becoming a cliché. We insane people may make it noble again."

Laughing, Gustav answered: "Well said, young man, it's a joy and a privilege to listen to this font of wisdom. And maybe you're even right about some of it. But be so good as to load your shotgun again now, you're a bit too much of a dreamer for me. At any moment a few little stags may come running our way again, and we can't shoot them dead with philosophy, ultimately there have to be rounds in the magazine."

A car came along and was immediately dispatched, blocking the road. A survivor, a stout redheaded man, stood beside the debris waving his hands wildly, peered up and down, discovered our hiding place, ran toward us, roaring, and fired his revolver up at us a number of times.

"Get out of here now or I'll shoot," Gustav shouted down. The man aimed at him and fired again. Then we laid him low with two shots.

Two more cars came, and we took them down. After that, the road was silent and empty, it seemed that word of its danger had spread. We had time to take in the beautiful view. Beyond the lake, in a valley, lay a small town, smoke was rising up above it, and soon we could see the fire leaping from rooftop to rooftop. We could also hear shooting. Dora cried a bit, I stroked her wet cheeks.

"Do we all have to die?" she asked. No one answered. Meanwhile, a pedestrian came along down below, saw the wrecked automobiles lying about, snooped around, leaned into one of them, pulled out a colorful parasol, a leather purse, and a bottle of wine, sat down peacefully on the wall, drank from the bottle, ate something wrapped in tin foil from the bag, drained the bottle down to the dregs, and walked on cheerfully, the parasol tucked under his arm. He went on his way peacefully, and I said to Gustav: "Would it be possible for you to shoot at this nice fellow and put a hole in his head? God knows I couldn't."

"No one's asking you to," my friend grumbled. But in his heart he felt uneasy about it, too. No sooner had we laid eyes on someone whose behavior was still harmless, peaceful, and childlike, a person who was still living in a state of innocence, than all our commendable and necessary actions suddenly seemed stupid and repugnant to us. The devil take it, all that blood! We were ashamed. But it's said that even generals have felt that way from time to time during the war.

"Let's not stay here any longer," Dora complained, "let's go down, surely we'll find something to eat in those cars. Aren't you hungry, you Bolsheviks?"

Down below, in the burning city, the bells were beginning to chime, sounding frantic and fearful. We began our descent. As I helped Dora over the edge, I kissed her knees. She laughed cheerfully. But then the structure gave way, and we both plunged into the void . . .

I FOUND MYSELF in the curving corridor again, still excited from my hunting adventure. And everywhere, on all the countless doors, the inscriptions beckoned:

> *Mutabor*
> *Be transformed into any animal or plant*

> *Kama Sutra*
> *Lessons in the Indian art of love*
> *Course for beginners: 42 different methods of making love*

> *Delightful Suicide!*
> *You'll die laughing*

> *Seeking Inspiration?*
> *Wisdom of the East*

> *O for a Thousand Tongues!*
> *Only for gentlemen*

> *Decline of the West*
> *Discount prices. Still unsurpassed*

> *The Epitome of Art*
> *The transformation of time into space through music*

> *The Laughing Tear*
> *Hall of humor*

> *Hermit Games*
> *A complete substitute for any social activity*

The series of inscriptions stretched on forever. One was called:

> *Guide to Constructing the Personality*
> *Success guaranteed*

That seemed worth investigating, so I stepped through the door.
I entered a dimly lit, quiet room, where a man was sitting on the floor without a chair, as they do in the Orient, with something resembling a large chessboard in front of him. At first glance, I thought it was my friend Pablo, at least the man was wearing a similar colorful silk jacket and had the same dark, sparkling eyes.

"Are you Pablo?" I asked.

"I'm nobody," he explained in a friendly tone. "We don't have names here, we're not people here. I'm a chess player. Are you interested in lessons in the construction of the personality?"

"Yes, please."

"Then kindly provide me with a few dozen of your pieces."

"My pieces . . . ?"

"The pieces of your so-called personality, which disintegrated before your eyes. I can't play without pieces."

He held up a mirror in front of me, once again I saw the unity of my self disintegrate into many selves, their number seemed to have grown even greater. But now the pieces were very small, about the size of standard chess pieces, and the player quietly, confidently took a few dozen of them in his fingers and placed them on the ground next to the chessboard. He spoke in a monotone, as if repeating a speech or a lesson that he had delivered many times:

"You are familiar with the erroneous and unfortunate conception that a human being is a permanent entity. You also know that man is made up of a multitude of souls, of very many selves. It is considered insane to divide up the apparently unified self into these many figures, science has given this the name of schizophrenia. Science is right, of course, insofar as it is impossible to control any multiplicity without leadership, without a certain order and organization. It is wrong, however, in that it believes that only a single, binding, lifelong order of the many subordinate selves is possible. This scientific fallacy has some unpleasant consequences; its only value lies in the fact that it simplifies matters for the teachers and educators who serve the state, it saves them the trouble of thinking and experimenting. As a result of this fallacy, many people who are incurably insane are considered 'normal,' even socially valuable, and conversely, some who are geniuses are considered insane. Hence, we augment this incomplete scientific theory of the soul with what we call the art of construction. When someone has experienced the disintegration of his ego, we show him that he can reassemble the pieces at any time in any order, and that he can thereby achieve infinite variety in the game of life. Just as the playwright creates a drama out of a handful of figures, so too we constantly construct new groups out of the pieces of our disintegrated ego, with new games and excitements, with ever new situations. Look!"

He grasped my pieces with his wise, quiet fingers—all the old men, young men, children, women, all the cheerful and sad, strong and delicate, nimble and clumsy pieces—and quickly arranged them on his board into a game, in which they swiftly formed groups, families, broke out in games and fights, made friends and enemies, constituted a world in miniature. Before my delighted eyes, he let the lively but orderly little world run its course for a while, as the pieces played and fought, formed alliances and pitched battles, wooed each other, married, multiplied; it was indeed a moving and exciting drama with a large cast of characters.

Then he blithely swept the board clean, gently knocking over all the pieces, pushing them into a pile, and then thoughtfully, with discriminating artistry, built a whole new game out of the same pieces, with completely different groupings, relationships, and interconnections. The second game was related to the first—it was the same world, built out of the same material—but it was played in a different key, at a different tempo, placing emphasis on different motifs, presenting the situations in a different way.

And so the clever builder built one game after another out of the same pieces, all those pieces of myself, and the games all resembled one another from a distance, they all recognizably belonged to the same world, shared a common origin, and yet each one was completely new.

"This is the art of life," he said in a didactic tone. "In the future, you may continue to shape and animate the game of your own life as you wish, to complicate it and enrich it; that is in your hands. Just as madness, in a higher sense, is the beginning of all wisdom, so schizophrenia is the beginning of all art, of all imagination. Even scholars have half recognized this, as one may read, for example, in *The Prince's Magic Horn*, that delightful book in which the laborious and diligent work of a scholar is ennobled by the brilliant collaboration of a number of insane and institutionalized artists.—Here, just take your figurines with you, this game will bring you a great deal of enjoyment. Any given piece may become an unbearable bogeyman and spoil your game one day, but you will reduce it to a harmless supporting character the next. A poor, dear little figurine may seem for a time to be condemned to bad luck and misfortune, but in the next game you will make a princess of her. I wish you great pleasure, dear sir."

I bowed deeply and gratefully to this gifted chess player, put the pieces in my pocket, and withdrew through the narrow door.

I had actually been planning to sit down on the floor of the corridor right away and play with the pieces for hours, for an eternity, but no sooner was I standing in the bright, curving corridor of the theater again than new currents, stronger than I, swept me away. A garish poster flashed before my eyes:

> *The Miracle of Steppenwolf Training*

These words aroused many feelings in me: all sorts of fears and worries from my past life, from the reality I had left behind, made my heart pound painfully. With a trembling hand I opened the door and stepped into a carnival booth, inside I saw iron bars separating me from the modest stage. But on the stage I saw an animal tamer, a somewhat ostentatious and pompous-looking gentleman who—despite his large mustache, his muscular upper arms, and his foppish circus attire—bore a rather sneering and unsavory resemblance to myself. This strong man led a large, beautiful, but terribly emaciated wolf on a leash like a dog, the wolf cast slavish, wary glances left and right—a pitiful sight! And it was as disgusting as it was exciting, as hideous as it was secretly pleasurable nonetheless, to see this brutal tamer lead the noble but shamefully obedient predator through a series of tricks and sensational stunts.

The man, my cursed fun-house-mirror twin, had certainly done a marvelous job of taming his wolf. It carefully obeyed his every command: responded like a dog to every call and crack of the whip, fell to its knees, played dead, sat up and begged, faithfully and obediently carried a loaf of bread, an egg, a piece of meat, and a little basket in its muzzle, indeed, it even had to pick up the whip that the tamer had dropped and carry it after him in its mouth, wagging its tail in an unbearably groveling manner all the while. The wolf was presented with a rabbit and then a white lamb, and although it bared its teeth and drooled, quivering with desire, it did not touch either of the animals, but sprang over them on command in an elegant leap as they crouched trembling on the ground, indeed, it lay down between the rabbit and the lamb and embraced them both with its front paws, creating a touching family scene. Then it ate a square of chocolate from the man's hand. It was agonizing to see how drastically this wolf had learned to deny its nature, it gave me goose bumps.

But the agitated spectator received compensation for this torment in the second part of the performance, as did the wolf himself. For after the elaborate training program had been completed and the tamer had bowed triumphantly over the little scene with the lamb and the wolf, smiling sweetly, the roles were reversed. The Harryesque animal tamer suddenly bent low, laid his whip at the wolf's feet, and began to tremble, to shrink, to appear just as miserable as the animal had before. The wolf, however, laughingly licked its jowls, its stiffness and duplicity fell away, its eyes lit up, its whole body grew taut and blossomed with renewed ferocity.

And now the wolf was giving the orders, and the man had to

obey. The man fell to his knees on command, he played the wolf, let his tongue hang out, ripped his clothes off his body with his lead-filled teeth. The man obeyed the human-trainer's orders: he walked on two legs or on all fours, sat up and begged, played dead, let the wolf ride on his back, carried the wolf's whip. With doglike servility and talent, he imaginatively embraced this humiliation and perversion. A beautiful girl came on stage, approached the trained man, stroked his chin, rubbed her cheek against his, but he remained on all fours like a beast, shook his head, and began to bare his teeth at the beautiful girl, until at last he grew so threatening and wolfish that she fled. Chocolate was set in front of him, but he scornfully sniffed at it and pushed it away. And finally the white lamb and the fat, spotted rabbit were brought in again, and the obedient man gave his all and played the wolf so well that it was a pleasure to behold. He grabbed the screaming little animals with his fingers and teeth, ripped out chunks of fur and flesh, chewed their living flesh with a grin, and drank their warm blood, closing his eyes and abandoning himself to his drunken pleasure.

Horrified, I fled through the door. This magic theater, I saw, was not a pure paradise at all, every imaginable hell was concealed beneath its pretty surface. Oh God, was there no salvation, even here?

I paced anxiously back and forth, my mouth tasting of blood and chocolate, one just as vile as the other, desperately wishing to escape from this dismal wave, furiously struggling to find more bearable, more benign images within myself. *"O Freunde, nicht diese Töne!"* sang the words within me—"O friends, not these tones!"—and I remembered with horror those hideous photographs from the front that had sometimes circulated during the war, those piles of intertwined corpses, their faces transformed by gas masks into satanic grins and grimaces. How stupid and childish I had been back then, when I was a humanitarian-minded pacifist, horrified by those images. Today I knew that whatever thoughts and images an animal tamer, a minister, a general, a madman might hatch within his brain, they could never be more hideous, wild and evil, raw and stupid, than those that I contained within myself.

Once I had caught my breath, I remembered the inscription that I had seen earlier, when this whole theater was just beginning, the inscription that the handsome youth had followed so impetuously:

> *All the Girls Are Yours*

and it seemed to me, all things considered, that nothing else could be so desirable. Relieved that I had managed to escape again from the cursed world of the wolf, I stepped inside.

How strange, it was the scent of my own youth that wafted toward me—a scent at once so fabled and yet so deeply familiar, it was the atmosphere of my boyhood and adolescence, and the blood of those days flowed in my heart. Everything that I had just been doing and thinking, everything that I myself had just been, receded behind me, and I was young again. Only an hour ago, only moments ago, I had thought that I knew quite well what love, desire, and longing were, but that had been the love and longing of an old man. Now I was young again, and what I felt inside me—this glowing, flowing fire, this tremendous tug of longing, this passion that melts the ice like a thawing March wind—was young, new, and authentic. Oh, how the forgotten fires flared up again, how dark and swollen those bygone tones sounded, how my blood blossomed, aquiver, how my soul cried out and sang! I was a boy, fifteen or sixteen years old, my head was full of Latin and Greek and beautiful lines of poetry, my thoughts full of striving and ambition, my fantasies full of an artist's dreams, but much deeper, stronger, and more terrible than all those blazing fires was the fire of love that burned and pulsed within me, the hunger of sex, the all-consuming anticipation of lust.

I was standing on one of the rocky outcroppings that over-looked my little hometown, I could smell the March wind and the first violets of spring, I could see the river and the windows of my father's house sparkling up from down below, and all of it looked, sounded, and smelled so breathtakingly rich, so fresh and intoxicated with creation, the colors glowed so brilliantly, and the spring breeze blew in such a supremely real, transcendent way, just as I had once seen the world in the fullest, most poetic hours of my first youth. I stood on the hill, the wind swept through my long hair; with a wandering hand, lost in my dreamy longing for love, I plucked a young, half-open leaf bud from the bushes that were just beginning to turn green, held it before my eyes, smelled it (and as I smelled it, all my memories of those times came glowing back to me), then playfully grasped the little green thing with my lips, which had yet to kiss a girl, and began to chew it. And at that sharp, fragrantly bitter taste, I suddenly knew exactly what I was experiencing, it was all there again. I was reliving an hour from the last year of my boyhood, a Sunday afternoon in early spring, the day I had set out on a solitary walk and met Rosa Kreisler, had greeted her shyly and fallen so stupefyingly in love with her.

Back then I had gazed with anxious anticipation at the beauti-ful girl, who was walking up the hill alone and lost in thought and hadn't seen me yet, I had seen her hair, which was done up in thick braids with loose strands falling down both of her cheeks, playing and flowing in the wind. I had seen, for the first time in my life, how beautiful this girl was, how beautifully and fantastically the wind played in her delicate hair, how beautifully and arousingly her thin blue dress cascaded down over her young limbs, and just as the bitter, pungent taste of the bud had filled me as I chewed it with all of the anxious, sweet desire and fear of spring, so at the sight of this girl I was filled with the whole deadly premonition of love, the premonition of woman, the devastating presentiment of immense possibilities and promises, nameless delights, unthinkable confusions, fears, and sufferings, the profoundest redemption and the deepest guilt. Oh, how the bitter taste of spring burned on my tongue! Oh, how the playful wind flowed through the loose hair that brushed her red cheeks! Then she had come close to me, had glanced up and recognized me, had faintly blushed for a moment and averted her eyes; then I greeted her, doffing my confirmation hat, and Rosa, instantly composed, returned my greeting with a slightly ladylike smile, her face upturned, and continued on her way slowly, confidently, and proudly, surrounded by the thousand wishes, demands, and tributes of love that I sent after her.

That's how it had been, one Sunday thirty-five years ago, and in this moment it all came rushing back to me: the hill and the town, the March wind and the smell of the bud, Rosa and her brown hair, my surging longing and my sweet, suffocating fear. It was all just the same as it had been back then, and it seemed to me that I had never loved again in my life the way I loved Rosa back then. But this time I was able to greet her differently than I had before. I saw the way she blushed as she recognized me, saw the way she struggled to conceal her blush, and knew at once that she liked me, that this encounter meant the same thing to her that it did to me. And instead of doffing my hat again and standing there solemnly with my hat off until she had passed, this time I did what my blood told me to do, despite my fear and trepidation, and I cried out: "Rosa! Thank God you've come, you beautiful, beautiful girl. I love you so much." That may not have been the most brilliant thing that I could have said at that moment, but this was no time for brilliance, it fully sufficed. Rosa didn't make a ladylike face and didn't continue on her way, Rosa stopped, looked at me, growing even redder than before, and said: "Good day, Harry, do you really like me?" Her brown eyes sparkled in her lively face, and I felt that in my previous life everything about the way I had lived and loved had been false and confused and filled with stupid unhappiness from the moment I had let Rosa get away that Sunday. But now the error had been rectified, and everything was different, everything was good.

We took each other's hands, and hand in hand we slowly walked on, unspeakably happy, very awkward, not knowing what to say or what to do, and in our awkwardness we began to walk faster, we trotted until we were out of breath and had to stop, but still we didn't let go of our hands. We were both children still, and we didn't really know what to do with each other, we didn't even get as far as a first kiss that Sunday, but we were immensely happy. We stood there catching our breath, we sat down in the grass, and I stroked her hand, and she cautiously ran her other hand through my hair, and then we stood up again and tried to see which of us was taller, and the truth is that I was taller by a finger's breadth, but I didn't admit it, instead I said that we were exactly the same height, and that the good Lord had made us for each other, and that later we'd get married. Then Rosa said she smelled violets, and we knelt down in the short spring grass to look for them, we found a few violets with short stems, and each of us gave our own violets to the other, and as it began to grow cooler and the light was falling on the rocks at an angle, Rosa said that she had to go home, and both of us were very sad, since I couldn't go with her, but now we shared a secret, and that was the most precious thing we possessed. I stayed up there among the rocks, sniffing Rosa's violets, I lay down on the ground, my face hanging over the edge of the precipice, and I looked down on the city and watched and waited until her sweet little figure appeared far below and hurried past the fountain and across the bridge. And now I knew she had arrived at her father's house, where she would be walking through the rooms while I lay up here far away from her, but there was a bond that ran from me to her, a current that flowed, a secret that drifted on the air.

We saw each other again here and there throughout the spring—up among the rocks, beside the garden fences—and just as the lilacs were beginning to bloom, we gave each other our first, anxious kiss. We children did not have much to offer one another, our kisses still lacked passion and intensity, and I dared only gently to stroke the loose curls of hair that fell around her ears, but whatever love and joy we were able to give each other belonged to us alone, and with every timid touch, with every premature word of love, with every anxious moment spent waiting for each other, we learned a new happiness, we climbed one small step higher on the ladder of love.

Thus, starting with Rosa and the violets, I lived my entire love life all over again, this time under happier stars. I lost Rosa, then Irmgard appeared, and the sun grew hotter, the stars more drunken, but neither Rosa nor Irmgard would be mine, I had to climb step by step, to experience a great deal, to learn a great deal, I had to lose Irmgard, too, and also Anna. I loved them again, each of the girls I had loved in my youth, but this time I also inspired love in each of them, I was able to give something to each of them, to receive something from each of them. Wishes, dreams, and possibilities that had once lived only in my imagination were now real, and I was living them out. Oh, all of you beautiful flowers, Ida and Lore, each one of you I once loved for a summer, for a month, for a day!

I realized that I was now the handsome, fiery little youth I had earlier seen running so eagerly toward the door of love, that I was now fulfilling and cultivating this piece of myself, this piece of my being and my life that had only fulfilled one-tenth, one-

thousandth of its potential, and I was doing this unburdened by
all the other figures of my ego, undisturbed by the thinker, unmo-
lested by the Steppenwolf, undiminished by the poet, the fanta-
sist, the moralist. No, now I was nothing but a lover, I breathed no
other happiness and no other suffering than that of love. Irmgard
had already taught me to dance, Ida to kiss, and the most beautiful
one of all, Emma, was the first to give me her bronzed breasts to
kiss, and to let me drink from the chalice of lust on that autumn
evening beneath the fluttering leaves of the elm.

I experienced many things in Pablo's little theater, and not even
one-thousandth of them can be put into words. All the girls I had
ever loved were now mine, each one gave me what she alone had to
give, and I gave each one what she alone knew how to take from
me. I tasted so much love, so much happiness, so much lust, so
much confusion, as well as suffering, all the unfulfilled loves of my
life blossomed magically in my garden in this enchanted hour—
chaste, delicate flowers, bright, blazing flowers, dark, quickly wilting flowers, fiery lust, intimate reverie, ardent melancholy, anxious
death, radiant rebirth. I found women who could only be taken
quickly, by storm, and others who could be wooed slowly and stu-
diously, to my great pleasure; each and every dimly lit corner of
my life reappeared in which once, if only for a minute, the voice
of sex had called out to me, a woman's gaze had kindled my flame,
the gleam of a girl's white skin had enticed me, and I made up for
all that I had missed. Each of them became mine, each in her own
way. The woman with the mysterious dark brown eyes beneath
her flaxen hair was there, I had once stood next to her for a quarter of an hour by the window in the aisle of an express train, and
she had later appeared to me several times in my dreams—she did
not speak a word, but she taught me unimaginable, frightening,
deadly arts of love. And the smooth, quiet, Chinese woman with
the glassy smile from the harbor in Marseille, with the straight,

jet-black hair and the watery eyes, she too knew unheard-of things. Each of them had her own secret, smelled of her own earth, kissed and laughed in her own way, had her own special combination of shame and shamelessness. They came and went, the stream carried them toward me, washed me toward them, away from them, such playful, childish swimming in the stream of sex, full of excitement, full of danger, full of surprise. And I marveled at how rich my life— my Steppenwolf life, which had seemed so poor and loveless—how rich that life had been in infatuations, in opportunities, in temptations. I had missed almost all of them, had fled, had stumbled over them, had forgotten them as quickly as I could—but now here they were, all of them, without exception, hundreds of them. And now I saw them, gave myself over to them, opened myself up to them, sank down into their rosy twilight underworld. The seduction that Pablo had once offered me returned, too, as well as other, earlier ones that I had not even understood at the time, fantastic games played in threes and fours, they whisked me along, smiling, in their circle dance. Many things happened, many games were played, that cannot be put into words.

When I broke the surface again, emerging out of that endless stream of temptations, of vices, of entanglements, I was calm, quiet, armed and ready, sated with knowledge, wise, deeply experienced, ripe for Hermine. And indeed, the final figure in my mythology of thousands, the final name in that infinite series, belonged to Hermine, and at just that moment my consciousness returned and put an end to that fairy tale of love, for I had no wish to encounter her here in the twilight of a magic mirror; not only that one figure in my chess game belonged to her, every bit of Harry belonged to her. Oh, now I would rearrange the pieces of my chess game so that it all related to her and led down the path to fulfillment.

The stream had washed me up onto dry land, once again I found myself standing in the silent corridor that led to the theater's box seats. What now? I reached for the little chess pieces in my pocket, but the urge had already subsided. This inexhaustible world of doors, inscriptions, magic mirrors surrounded me. Giving in, I read the next label and shuddered at what was written there:

How to Kill with Love

A memory returned to me, flashing up before me for a second: Hermine, seated at a table in a restaurant, suddenly distracted from her wine and food, engrossed in a momentous conversation, with that terribly serious look in her eyes as she told me that she was going to make me fall in love with her only so that she could be killed by my hand. A terrible wave of fear and darkness flooded my heart, suddenly it was all there before me again, suddenly I once again had that feeling of fatefulness and distress in my innermost being. I desperately plunged my hand into my pocket to pull out the chess pieces, to work a bit of magic and rearrange the order of my board. The pieces were gone. Instead of chess pieces, I drew a knife from my pocket. Scared to death, I dashed through the corridor, past the doors, suddenly found myself face-to-face with the enormous mirror, gazed into it. In the mirror I saw a huge, beautiful wolf, as tall as I was, standing still, its restless eyes sparkling warily. It blinked its glinting eyes at me, laughing softly, so that for just a moment the mouth opened slightly and the red tongue could be seen.

Where was Pablo? Where was Hermine? Where was the clever fellow who had chatted so nicely about the construction of the personality?

I glanced into the mirror again. I had been crazy. There was no wolf standing on the other side of that tall mirror, its tongue lolling in its mouth. The mirror showed no one but me, Harry, with my gray face, abandoned by all those games, exhausted by all those vices, hideously pale, and yet a human being, someone you could talk to.

"Harry," I said, "what are you doing?"

"Nothing," said the man in the mirror, "I'm just waiting. I'm waiting for death."

"And where is death?" I asked.

"He's coming," said the other. And I heard music emanating from the empty interior of the theater, beautiful and terrible music, the music from *Don Giovanni* that accompanies the entrance of the Stone Guest. Those icy strains echoed eerily through the haunted house, coming from the beyond, from the immortals.

"Mozart!" I thought, conjuring up the most beloved and exalted images of my inner life.

Then laughter rang out behind me, bright and icy laughter, it seemed to come from a place unknown to men, a place beyond suffering, it was the humor of the gods. I turned, chilled to the bone and transfixed by this laughter, only to see Mozart coming toward me, laughing; he passed me by, strolled casually toward one of the doors, opened it, and entered, and I eagerly followed him, the god of my youth, the object of my lifelong love and adoration. The music continued to play. Mozart stood at the railing of the theater box, nothing could be seen of the theater, the boundless space was filled with darkness.

"You see," said Mozart, "it works without the saxophone, too. Although I certainly wouldn't want to offend that fabulous instrument."

"Where are we?" I asked.

"We're in the final act of *Don Giovanni*, Leporello is already on his knees. An exquisite scene, and the music isn't half bad, either, you know. Even if it still has all sorts of very human elements in it, it does give you some sense of the beyond, that laughter—doesn't it?"

"It is the last great piece of music that was ever written," I said solemnly, like a schoolteacher. "To be sure, there was also Schubert, and Hugo Wolf, and I mustn't forget poor, glorious Chopin. You're frowning, maestro—oh yes, and Beethoven, he's wonderful, too. But all of that, as beautiful as it may be, is already starting to seem a bit fragmentary, as if it were beginning to break down; mankind has not produced a single work since *Don Giovanni* that is its equal in perfection."

"Don't try so hard," Mozart laughed in a frightfully mocking tone. "I suppose you're a musician, too, aren't you? Well, I've given up the trade myself, I've retired. I just keep an eye on the business from time to time for the fun of it."

He raised his hands as if he were conducting, and somewhere a moon or some other pale celestial body rose, I peered over the railing into the unfathomable depths of space, I could see fog and clouds drifting through it, mountains and seashores were fading into view, a barren plain or desert lay stretched out for miles below us. We saw a venerable-looking old gentleman with a long beard and a wistful face leading an enormous procession across this plain, some ten thousand men all dressed in black. He looked forlorn and hopeless, and Mozart said:

"Look down there, that's Brahms. He's seeking redemption, but he still has a long way to go."

I learned that the thousands of men in black were all the musicians who had played the parts and notes in his scores that God had judged to be superfluous.

"Too densely orchestrated, too much wasted material," Mozart nodded.

And the very next moment we saw Richard Wagner marching at the head of an equally large army and felt how those thousands of people weighed him down and sapped his strength; we saw him dragging himself along, too, with weary, long-suffering steps.

"When I was young," I remarked sadly, "those two musicians were thought to be the greatest opposites imaginable."

Mozart laughed.

"Yes, that's always the way. Seen from a certain distance, such opposites tend to resemble each other more and more closely. By the way, neither Wagner nor Brahms was personally to blame for that dense orchestration; it was a prejudice of their time."

"What? And now they have to pay for it so dearly?" I exclaimed in accusation.

"Of course. That's the official procedure. First they have to atone for the guilt of their time, and once they're done with that, it will become clear whether they bear enough personal guilt to justify any further reckoning."

"But they can't help it, neither one of them can!"

"Of course not. You also can't help it that Adam ate the apple, and yet you must atone for it."

"But that's terrible."

"Certainly, life is always terrible. We can't help it, and yet we're responsible. From the moment we're born, we're already guilty. You must have had a strange sort of religious upbringing if you didn't know that."

I was beginning to feel quite miserable. I saw myself, a pilgrim weary unto death, wandering through the desert of the hereafter, weighed down with the many useless books I had written, with all the essays, with all the newspaper columns, followed by the army of typesetters who had had to work on them, by the army of readers who had had to swallow it all. My God! And Adam and the apple and the whole story of original sin were all there, too. So all of that had to be atoned for, an endless purgatory, and only then would the question arise whether there was also something personal, something of my own beyond all that, or whether all of my actions and their consequences were just empty foam on the sea, just a senseless game played amid the flow of events!

When Mozart saw my long face, he began to laugh out loud. As he laughed, he turned somersaults in the air, his feet dancing in a lively trill. Then he shouted at me: "Hey, my boy, cat got your tongue, or maybe your lung? Thinking of your readers, those poor bottom-feeders, mouth breathers, and all your typesetters, bed wetters, aiders and abettors, saber whetters? That's a laugh, you giraffe, what a gaffe, makes me laugh till my pants split in half! Oh, your poor faithful heart, in love with the printer's dark art, how your soul comes apart, don't depart, let me give you a light, for a start. Snicker, snacker, paddywhacker, boast and bragger, old tail wagger, not a lazy lollygagger. Glory be to God, here's the devil with his rod, you'll be flogged and thrashed for writing for cash, what a clod, it's all just stolen and rehashed."

This, though, was all too much for me, my anger left me no time to indulge in melancholy. I grabbed Mozart by the braid and he went flying, his braid stretching longer and longer, like a comet's tail, and I clung to the end as it whirled me through this world. Damn, it was cold in this world! These immortals could tolerate terribly thin, icy air. But it was pleasurable, this icy air, that much was clear for the one brief moment before my senses failed me. I was filled with a bracingly bitter, steely, icy exhilaration, a desire to laugh just as Mozart had laughed, in that same bright, wild, alien way. But at just that moment, my breath and my consciousness gave out.

CONFUSED AND BATTERED, I came to my senses in the corridor, where the white light was reflected in the shiny floor. I was not among the immortals, not yet. I was still in this world of enigmas, of sorrows, of Steppenwolves, of agonizing entanglements. Not a good place, not a sustainable existence. It had to be brought to an end.

Harry was facing me in the large wall mirror. He didn't look well, he didn't look much different than he had that night when he had visited the professor and gone to the dance at the Black Eagle. But that was long ago, years, centuries; Harry had grown older, he had learned to dance, he had visited magic theaters, he had heard Mozart laugh, he no longer felt any fear of dances, of women, of knives. Even a moderately gifted person can reach maturity once he has raced through a few centuries. I gazed at Harry in the mirror for a long time: I still knew him well, he still looked just a little bit like the Harry of fifteen who had encountered Rosa among the rocks one Sunday in March and doffed his confirmation hat to her. And yet he had grown a few hundred little years older since then, he had practiced music and philosophy until he had his fill of them, had drunk Alsatian wine in the Steel Helmet Tavern and argued about Krishna with stuffy scholars, he had loved Erika and Maria, had become Hermine's friend, had shot up automobiles and slept with the smooth Chinese woman, had met Goethe and Mozart, and had torn various holes in the web of time and illusory reality in which he was still caught. Even if he had lost his pretty chess pieces, he still had a proper knife in his pocket. Onward, old Harry, you tired old fellow!

The devil take it, how bitter life tasted! I spat at the Harry in the mirror, I kicked him with my foot and he shattered and fell to pieces. I walked slowly along the echoing corridor, looking attentively at the doors that had promised such lovely things: all of the inscriptions were gone. I strode slowly past all the hundred doors of the magic theater. Hadn't I gone to a masquerade ball today? A hundred years had passed since then. Soon there will be no more years. There was still something to be done, Hermine was still waiting. It would be an unusual wedding. I swam toward it in a turbid wave, dragged dully along, a slave, a Steppenwolf. The devil take it!

I stopped at the last door. The turbid wave had dragged me there. O Rosa, O distant youth, O Goethe and Mozart!

I opened it. What I found behind the door was a simple and beautiful scene. I found two naked people lying on carpets on the floor, the beautiful Hermine and the beautiful Pablo, side by side, fast asleep, deeply exhausted from lovemaking, which seems so insatiable and yet so quickly satiates. Beautiful, beautiful people, magnificent images, wonderful bodies. Below Hermine's left breast was a fresh, round bruise with dark undertones, a love bite from Pablo's beautiful, gleaming teeth. At just that spot, I plunged my knife into her body, as deep as the blade would go. Blood ran over Hermine's delicate, white skin. If it had all been a little different, if it had all gone a little differently, I would have kissed that blood away. But now I didn't; I just watched the blood run and saw her eyes open for a brief moment, pained, deeply surprised. "Why is she surprised?" I thought. Then I thought that I ought to close her eyes. But they closed again of their own accord. It was finished. She just rolled a bit onto her side, I could see a fine, delicate shadow running from her armpit to her breast, it was trying to remind me of something. Forgotten! Then she lay still.

I looked at her for a long time. Finally I shuddered, as if just coming to my senses, and felt the urge to leave. Then I saw Pablo stretch, saw him open his eyes and stretch out his limbs, saw him bend over the dead woman and smile. This fellow will never be serious, I thought, everything makes him smile. Pablo carefully folded over a corner of the carpet to cover Hermine up to her chest, so that the wound could no longer be seen, and then he left the theater box without making a sound. Where was he going? Was everyone leaving me alone? I stayed there, alone with the half-covered dead woman whom I loved and envied. The boyish curl hung down over her pale forehead, her partly opened mouth radiated red from her completely pale face, her hair gave off a delicate fragrance and allowed her small, well-formed ear to peek through.

Now her wish had been granted. I had killed my beloved, even before she could become completely mine. I had done the unthinkable, and now I knelt and stared at her, not knowing what this deed meant, not even knowing whether it had been good and right or quite the opposite. What would the clever chess player say, what would Pablo say about it? I didn't know, I couldn't think. The painted mouth glowed redder and redder from the dying face. My whole life had been like that, my little bit of happiness and love had been like that rigid mouth: a bit of red, painted on a dead face.

And a shudder emanated from that dead face, from those dead, white shoulders, from those dead, white arms, slowly creeping, a wintry desolation and loneliness, a coldness that slowly, slowly grew, until my hands and lips began to freeze. Had I extinguished the sun? Had I killed the heart of all life? Was this the deathly cold of outer space, now rushing inside?

Shuddering, I stared at the stony forehead, at the stiff curl, at the pale, cool glow of the outer ear. The coldness that flowed from them was deadly, yet beautiful: it sounded, it resounded wonderfully, it was music!

Hadn't I felt that shudder once before, in an earlier time—that shudder that was simultaneously something like happiness? Hadn't I heard this music before? Yes, with Mozart, with the immortals.

I remembered some lines of poetry that I had found somewhere once upon a time:

We, though, have found a place we call our own
Amidst the starry ice of ether's cold,
The days, the hours remain to us unknown,
We are not man nor woman, young nor old . . .
Our being, cool and changeless, is forever,
Our laughter, cool and star-bright, knows no end . . .

THEN THE DOOR of the theater box opened, and in came Mozart, without his braid, without his knee breeches or buckled shoes, dressed in modern clothes, so that I only recognized him at second glance. He sat down close to me, I almost touched him and held him back so that he wouldn't soil himself with the blood that had spilled from Hermine's breast onto the floor. He sat down and busied himself with some of the small devices and instruments that were sitting around there, he took it very seriously, moving things around and tinkering with them, and I gazed with admiration at his dexterous, nimble fingers, which I would have loved to see play the piano one day. Lost in thought, I watched him work, or actually not lost in thought, but rather dreamily, and lost in the sight of his beautiful, intelligent hands, feeling warmed by his nearness, and also a little frightened. I paid no attention at all to what he was actually doing there, what he was screwing and tinkering with.

But the object that he had been working on was a radio set, he had gotten it going, and now he turned on the speaker and said: "You're listening to Munich, the *Concerto Grosso in F Major* by Handel."

And indeed, to my indescribable astonishment and horror, that diabolical tin funnel immediately spewed forth the mixture of bronchial phlegm and used chewing gum that gramophone owners and dues-paying radio listeners have agreed to call music—and through all that garbled squelching and squawking it really was just possible to make out the noble structure of that divine music—like a precious old picture seen through a thick crust of dirt—the regal structure, the cool, expansive breath, the rich, broad sound of the strings.

"My God," I cried in horror, "what are you doing, Mozart? Are you serious about inflicting this monstrosity upon yourself, and upon me? About subjecting us to this hideous contraption, this triumph of our time, the final, victorious weapon that our age deploys in its war of annihilation against art? Is that really necessary, Mozart?"

Oh, how that uncanny man laughed, how coldly and hauntingly he laughed, it was a silent laughter, and yet it shattered everything to pieces! He regarded my agonies with deep pleasure, he turned the cursed screws, adjusted the metal cone. Laughing, he continued to let the distorted, disfigured, and poisoned music seep into the room; laughing, he gave me my answer.

"No pathos, please, dear neighbor! By the way, did you notice the ritardando there? A stroke of genius, no? Ah yes, and now, you impatient man, let the spirit of that ritardando sink in—do you hear the basses? They stride along like gods—and let old Handel's stroke of genius penetrate and calm your restless heart! Listen without pathos and without mockery, my little man, and behind the veil of this ridiculous contraption—which really is hopelessly idiotic—you will hear the distant figure of that godly music passing by! Pay attention, you can learn something from it. Observe this absurd metal cone, it seems to be doing the stupidest, most useless, most forbidden thing in the world, just taking music that's being played in one place and indiscriminately blasting it into another place where it doesn't belong—stupidly, crudely, and miserably distorted, too—and nevertheless it can't destroy the original spirit of that music, all it can do is use that music to demonstrate the helplessness of its own technology, the mindlessness of its mechanical operations! Listen carefully, little man, it's important for you! Now, open your ears! There. And what you're hearing now is not just a Handel who's been abused by the radio—a Handel who nevertheless remains divine, even in this hideous incarnation—no, my worthy man, at the same time you are also hearing and seeing an excellent parable of life itself.

When you listen to the radio, you are hearing and seeing the fundamental struggle between idea and appearance, between eternity and time, between the divine and the human. My dear man, just as the radio indiscriminately blares the most glorious music in the world into the most impossible rooms for ten minutes at a time—into bourgeois salons and garrets, among chattering, feasting, yawning, and sleeping listeners—just as it robs this music of its sensual beauty, spoils it, scratches it, and muddies it, yet never quite manages to kill its spirit—in just the same way, life, or what we call reality, makes a jumble of all the glorious images that constitute our world, one minute it gives us Handel, and the next minute it gives us a lecture about how medium-sized industrial enterprises cook their balance sheets, it turns enchanting orchestral melodies into unappetizing musical mucus, and everywhere it interposes its technology, its industry, its desolate neediness and vanity between idea and reality, between the orchestra and the ear. That's just the way life is, my boy, and we have to let it be that way, and unless we're jackasses, we'll laugh at it, too. People like you have no right to criticize the radio or life. You ought to learn to listen first! Learn to take seriously what deserves to be taken seriously, and to laugh at the rest! Or could it be that you've done it better yourself—more nobly, more cleverly, more tastefully? Oh no, Monsieur Harry, that you have not. You have turned your life into a dreadful tale of affliction, your talent into misfortune. And I see that you've had no better use for such a pretty, charming young girl than to plunge a knife into her body and kill her! Do you think that's the right thing to do?"

"The right thing? Oh no!" I cried in despair. "My God, it's all so wrong, so infernally stupid and awful! I'm a beast, Mozart, a stupid, evil beast, sick and depraved, you're right a thousand times over.—But as for this girl: that's exactly what she wanted, I was only fulfilling her wish."

Mozart laughed silently, but at least now he was so kind as to turn the radio off.

My defense suddenly sounded quite foolish, even to me, though only moments ago I had truly believed it. All at once I remembered how when Hermine had spoken of time and eternity, I had immediately been disposed to regard her ideas as a reflection of my own thoughts. Yet I had taken it for granted that the thought of being killed by me was entirely her own idea and wish, and that in this matter Hermine had not been influenced by me in the slightest. But why was it that I had not only accepted and believed that terrible and disturbing thought at the time, but even anticipated it? Perhaps because it was my own thought after all? And why had I killed Hermine at the very moment when I found her naked in the arms of another man? Mozart's silent laughter sounded omniscient and full of mockery.

"Harry," he said, "you're a joker. Do you really suppose that this beautiful girl wanted nothing more from you than a knife between the ribs? Tell that to someone else! Well, at least you stabbed her well and good, the poor child is dead as a doornail. Maybe now it's time for you to consider the consequences of the gallantry you've shown this lady. Or were you hoping to avoid the consequences?"

"No," I shouted, "don't you understand anything? Avoid the consequences? I want nothing more than to atone, atone, atone, to lay my head under the blade and allow myself to be punished and annihilated."

Mozart looked at me with unbearable mockery.

"You're always so terribly melodramatic! But you'll get a sense of humor yet, Harry. Humor is always gallows humor, and you'll get it on the gallows if you have to. Are you ready? Yes? Very well, then go to the prosecutor's office and put yourself at the mercy of the whole humorless machinery of the legal system, until at last they coolly chop off your head early one morning in the prison yard. Are you ready for that?"

An inscription suddenly flashed up before me:

> *Harry's Execution*

and I nodded in affirmation. An empty courtyard surrounded by four walls with small, barred windows, a properly prepared guillotine, a dozen gentlemen in robes and frock coats, and I was standing in their midst, shivering in the gray early-morning air, my heart clenched in piteous anguish, yet I was ready to accept my fate. I stepped forward on command, I knelt down on command. The prosecutor doffed his cap and cleared his throat, all the other gentlemen cleared their throats as well. He unfolded a formal document, held it before him, and read aloud:

"Gentlemen, before you stands Mr. Haller, who has been accused and found guilty of wanton abuse of our magic theater. Not only has Haller committed blasphemy against high art by confusing our beautiful picture gallery with so-called reality and stabbing the mirror image of a girl to death with the mirror image of a knife, he has also demonstrated the intention to use our theater as a means of committing suicide, all without the slightest sense of humor. Therefore, we sentence Haller to the penalty of eternal life, and we suspend his entry privileges to our theater for twelve hours. Nor can the defendant be spared the punishment of being laughed out of court just this once. Gentlemen, raise your voices: One—two—three!"

And on three, all those in attendance flawlessly joined their voices in laughter, a laughter in high chorus, a terrible laughter from the great beyond that mere mortals can scarcely bear.

When I came to, Mozart was sitting next to me as he had been before, patting me on the shoulder and saying: "You have heard the verdict. So you will have to reconcile yourself to listening to the radio music of life. It will be good for you. You have unusually limited abilities, my dear, silly fellow, but by now you must have come to understand what is required of you. You must learn to laugh, that is what is required of you. You must grasp the humor of life, the gallows humor of this life. But of course you are prepared to do anything in the world, anything except what is required of you! You are prepared to stab girls to death, you are prepared to be executed with great ceremony, you would certainly be prepared to mortify and flagellate yourself for a hundred years. Wouldn't you?"

"Oh yes, from the bottom of my heart," I cried in my misery.

"Of course! You're open to every stupid and humorless undertaking, you magnanimous gentleman, you're open to everything that is melodramatic and thoroughly lacking in levity! Well, for my part, I can't be bothered with all that, I won't give you a penny for all your romantic penance. You actually want to be executed, you actually want to have your head chopped off, you berserker! You'd commit ten more murders if that would make your stupid ideal a reality. You want to die, you coward, but not to live. But damn it, you're supposed to be figuring out how to live! It would serve you right if you were sentenced to the most severe punishment."

"Oh, and what kind of punishment would that be?"

"Well, for one thing, we could bring the girl back to life and have you marry her."

"No, I wouldn't be willing to do that. It would be a catastrophe."

"As if what you've already done weren't catastrophic enough! But it's time to put an end to all this melodrama and manslaughter. Come to your senses at last! You shall live, and you shall learn to laugh. You shall learn to listen to the cursed radio music of life, you shall worship the spirit that animates it, you shall learn to laugh at all its stuff and nonsense. That's it, that's all that's required of you."

Softly, through clenched teeth, I asked: "And what if I refuse?

What if I deny you, Herr Mozart, this authority over the Steppen-wolf, and this right to intervene in his fate?"

"In that case," said Mozart peacefully, "I would suggest that you smoke another one of my lovely cigarettes." And even as he was saying this and conjuring up a cigarette for me from his waistcoat pocket, suddenly I saw that he was no longer Mozart, instead he was gazing at me warmly with his dark, exotic eyes, he was my friend Pablo, and he also looked as if he could be the twin brother of the man who had taught me the game of chess with the little figurines.

"Pablo!" I cried, startled. "Pablo, where are we?"

Pablo gave me the cigarette and a light.

"We are," he smiled, "in my magic theater, and if you want to learn the tango, or become a general, or converse with Alexander the Great, all those options will be available to you next time. But I must say, Harry, you've disappointed me a bit. You really lost con-trol of yourself there, you spoiled the humor of my little theater and made a mess of it, you stabbed someone with a knife and sul-lied our pretty world of images with stains of reality. That wasn't very nice of you. I hope at least you did it out of jealousy when you saw Hermine and me lying there. Unfortunately, you didn't know how to handle that piece—I thought you'd learned to play the game better than that. Well, we can fix that."

He took Hermine, who immediately shrank down and became a little figurine that he held in his fingers, and he put her in the same waistcoat pocket from which he had earlier extracted the cigarette.

The sweet, heavy smoke had a pleasant smell, and I felt hollowed out and ready to sleep for a year.

Oh, I understood everything, understood Pablo, understood Mozart, heard his terrible laughter somewhere behind me, I knew all the hundred thousand pieces of the game of life that I held in my pocket, and I tremblingly divined its meaning, I was willing to start the game all over again, to taste its torments once more, to shudder at its nonsense once more, to pass through my own inner hell once more, many more times.

One day I would play this game better. One day I would learn to laugh. Pablo was waiting for me. Mozart was waiting for me.

ALSO TRANSLATED BY
KURT BEALS

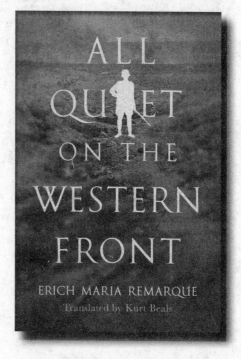

"Crisp, fresh, and very much more faithful to the German original version. . . . Beals's translation makes it clear why the book has sold millions of copies in almost every language."
—Michael Korda, author of *Muse of Fire:*
World War I as Seen Through the Lives of the Soldier Poets

"This fluent new translation captures the devastating experiences of ordinary soldiers with renewed urgency."
—Martin Puchner, author of *The Language of Thieves:*
My Family's Obsession with a Secret
Code the Nazis Tried to Eliminate